The

Cloud

Architect

by

Dugald Black

ISBN: 978-1-326-46249-9

PublishNation, London
www.publishnation.co.uk

For Kylie, Sebastian and Dean.

Thank you for your support and patience and belief in me.

You are, and shall always be, my Order of the Quill.

One

Things were never the same for Adam once his mum was diagnosed with Cancer. The door to the Consultant's waiting room gently brushed along the pale lino floor casually pushing the dust around the corners and legs of the chairs and tables.

Adam stared intently at the patterned lino floor as he feebly attempted to construct some rhythm or structure to its mesmerising twists and turns. He felt if he could at least find the crease where the pattern was cut and the next section laid then he would, in some way, be able to make sense of this endless sea of questions that were boiling inside of him. The solution that not everything is continuous and that at some stage the pattern is forced to stop in order to be restarted made him think that this lump resting in his throat and the disease attacking his mother were only part of a process that inevitably had to stop at some point.

His grandmother watched him from the doorway. Adam could smell her perfume as it was gently carried in on the breeze. Breathing in slowly he raised his head and looked directly at her. She was different; she was not the grandmother he knew. Growing up, Adam always saw his grandmother as the centre of any social occasion. Always wearing a black turtleneck top, pearl necklace, jeans and high heels, she never submitted to the stereotypes expected of grandmothers. During Adam's early pre-teen years she was the catalyst for much of the trouble he found himself in, otherwise known by his mother as his terror years. His mother grew in despair as she would often find them both covered in mud from making mud pies out of the vegetable patch or Cowboys & Indians in the living room. Unable to tame her own mother, Adam found himself bearing the full brunt of the post pie making/General Custer's last stand, and consistently had early nights after being scrubbed red in the bath with the nailbrush to remove ground in mud or her favourite red lipstick and eye liner. This time though, she was different. At eighty she was still a regular at the Conservative Club, her bouncy, blonde hair and confident red lipstick were still prominent but behind all this was the look of an old lady battling a multitude of emotions in order to remain strong for Adam. As they made eye contact she let out a slow quivering sigh. Her entire body deflated knowing that she could not lie to her only Grandson and he had seen straight through her facade. Adam's gaze returned to the floor and he continued to stare at its nonsensical patterns.

Crossing the room, she let the door glide back into its resting position, gently nudging against its partner door. Sitting down next to him, she stared with him at the floor hoping that it would inspire her with words to console. The hospital chair creaked as she leaned across to capture his hands in hers.

"Adam?"

She attempted to speak but the words stumbled out of her. Quivering and reluctant, they simply fell to the ground unnoticed. Resettling, she tried again, this time leaning in to impress her words upon him.

"Adam?"

He looked up slowly and as they established eye contact he knew that the fun loving grandmother that he had always known was not there anymore. The person who sat in front of him now was a scared mother clasping at straws of hope, smothered hope, lost hope, but still, hope. He rested his head in her lap as a single tear ran away from him and there they stayed.

■■

Adam awoke to the stark beep of the alarm coming from his phone. He reached out across his bedside table and fumbled for the off switch, knocking over the small pile of coins he had removed from his pocket before going to bed. The sun broke through the crack in the curtains and he lay there staring as the dust moved and danced in the stillness of the light. He let out a small groan and raised his head to begin the crawl from the security of his bed. His duvet was warm and the thought of leaving it made him feel immeasurably sad.

It was a Sunday and Adam was tired from staying up all night looking through pictures, memories of his past. Since his mother had passed Adam had moved in with his grandmother and he could hear her in the kitchen as she attempted to prepare his breakfast; she was never one for staying in and playing the dutiful stay at home mother. He expected a calamity to ensue from her cooking and knowing that he would be needed to rescue the house before she burnt it down, he placed himself on the edge of his bed trying to prepare for what the world was about to deliver. His hair cascaded over his eyes as he pulled on his jeans, fastened his belt and grabbed on old grey T-shirt from the floor.

His grandmother had affectionately started to call his floor *'Adam's Floor-drobe'* as most of his clothes found their way there whether they were clean or dirty. Adam gave himself one last look in the mirror before he made his way to the kitchen.

He had changed drastically in the six months since his mother's death. His thick black hair had grown beyond his eyebrows and Adam enjoyed knowing that it shielded his eyes from view. He had grown in height and was a statue over his grandmother. His eyes had become bluer and brighter as he grew in years and to those that were fortunate to see behind the mask of his pitch black hair, they commented on how they could pierce the soul of anyone who dared to gaze into them. As he bent to collect his black trainers, the only shoes he now wore, his hip bones protruded over the tops of his trousers and his spine stuck out from his skin like a disciplined mountain range. He wore a belt that had run out of holes to hold up the black jeans he wore daily. As he rose, he clutched the belt loops with his thumbs and hoisted them up, a routine that he would repeat as the day passed.

He opened the door to leave, taking in one last look; he saw his room for what it was. Surrounded by nostalgia, this room had become a shrine for his despair. Picture frames filled with smiling faces, a desk covered in random scribbling's and posters of well-known music bands.

Unable to move beyond the loss of both his parents as a boy, he had built this fortress of solitude within himself, within this room. The dust continued to float aimlessly in the sunlight, pausing and resting, only for a moment before finding the will to lift and drifting into the darkness beyond the starkness of the light. Pictures of his parents glimmered from behind their glass cages. He recalled a time when they would celebrate the weekend with a movie night. He would sit at their feet as they sat nestled on the sofa in the small living room of their tiny two bed flat. Movie night was a treat saved only for a Friday night and Adam relished each moment. Not for the movie, or the fact that it was the one day that he was allowed to devour his body weight in popcorn, despite his mother and Father putting down dips and carrots, but for the simple pleasure of seeing a moment shared by his parents. The love that they shared made Adam realise that he was always safe and that they would do whatever was in their power to protect him. Even as a young boy he knew the value of love and the strength it can offer. He watched the grains of dust as they caressed the dark wooden frame. Startled by the memory of them, Adam grabbed his hooded jumper and camera before wandering off towards the kitchen.

As he entered the kitchen he halted to watch his grandmother play conductor to an orchestra of chaos. There were days when the loss of her daughter showed more than she would want it to and today was one of those days. Adam saw black smoke rise from the toaster and jumped over to salvage whatever was left of the crumpets that she had placed in, with good intentions only moments before.

"Oh! Adam you made me jump!" she remarked, "I didn't hear you come in, sit down dear, I'm making our Sunday breakfast!" Her voice was rushed and excited as she placed a pan of freshly boiled eggs into the sink to cool.

Adam raised a smile from underneath his covered brow and turned the blackened crumpets that rested on the gold rimmed, ornate plate. He always thought it a travesty that such a delicate piece of craftsmanship should hold home to such a culinary disaster.

It was a Sunday and Sunday meant that both of them would take time out of their week to sit down and share a meal together. This always resulted in some catastrophe of sorts. Last week she managed to burn one of three vintage tea towels as she ventured into the world of French toast. Her only remark was to comment on how the towel must have been French as well, to give up the fight and burn so quickly. Adam wandered over to the fridge,

"Well I do enjoy some crumpet with my charcoal".

"Oh stop it!" she retorted.

She never took any offence from Adam, she knew as well as he did that her cooking was somewhat of a gamble than a guaranteed delight. Many a meal had made it to the bin rather than the dining table and the microwave became the friend in need for them both. Adam wondered how his mother ever got past five years old after having experienced her cooking thus far.

The kettle switch clunked down as it came to its boil,

"Get that for me dear, please?"

Adam picked up the kettle and poured it into the vintage tea pot. Sunday was for Sunday best after all. He placed on the lid and returned to the fridge.

"Where is the butter Granny?"

"It's in the butter dish next to the sugar, dear"

Adam looked over to where he had just stood and saw the cow shaped butter dish. Not all of the crockery in her house was as classy and historic as her vintage Sunday best. He closed the fridge and picked up the plate of crumpets. Taking a knife from the drawer he scraped the burned top layer into the bin before scooping the knife into the butter.

"Your eggs are done dear. Sit down."

Adam sat down at the breakfast bar placed near the entrance of the kitchen. He looked around as she served his boiled eggs on crumpets. The kitchen was a capsule in time. The metal handles that ran along the bottom and tops of yellow stained cupboards. The kitchen was filled with mismatched appliances of varying eras; vintage interspersed with modern. From a crank handle whisk to a luxury coffee maker, Adam's grandmother was raised in the generation of *'if it aint broke, don't fix it'*

As they both started eating, she poured the tea from the pot into two mismatching tea cups. "Adam?" she inquired, "I have a question."

Adam swallowed down his mouthful, "Yes?" he replied.

Her voice was soft and direct as she asked him "Where do you go?"

Adam looked up from this plate, placed down his knife and fork and looked at her. She was looking directly at him, "What? I don't understand. Go where?"

Instantly Adam felt uncomfortable, he wriggled on his stool thinking of what to say. His mind turned over and over, he was confused, but there was this small part of him that wondered if he knew of what she was asking. Did she know about the daydreams? The hours spent remembering his childhood? The nights spent up trawling through images of his mother and Father. Trying to work out where his Father had gone, why did he feel so alone and different to everyone else? Why was his mother taken so early? Did she know that these questions haunted him like some repetitive nightmare, living in his mind each second of the day?

"What do you mean Granny, I don't go anywhere."

Since leaving school, he wasn't lying; he stayed at home every day. Prior to leaving, Adam was a top student on his photography modules in Art class. His landscape photos had always won local competitions as a child and this was noticed by his lecturers. Encouraged by his parents on weekends away, he would spend his days taking photos of the mountains, hills, fields, flowers and clouds. Making up stories about heroes and legends, Knights and Dragons of the skies and how one day he would be a legend himself. A Knight sent to save the world from the darkness of an evil Lord. When his mother passed he stopped attending, slowly the letters from the school stopped coming to the house as Adam slipped into this world of solitude.

Adam noticed that his grandmother did not avert her gaze from him.

"This may be a new house Adam and the floorboards are new, but I heard you stop at the top of your stairs. Where did you go? What memory played through that head of yours?"

Knowing that he couldn't hide himself from her, he let out a defeated sigh.

"I thought about Mum and Dad. It was when we had movie nights at home. Mum always bought popcorn and Dad would order the pizza. I was around five." He looked down at his cup, a skin had formed over his tea and it was starting to go cold.

"Fresh cup?"

Adam nodded and drank down the lukewarm tea before offering his cup for it to be filled.

"It's ok you know. When I lost your grandpa I would spend days in the house alone. I very nearly went mad just staring at the walls. I think you need to get out of the house for a while. I want you to go to London, see other people. Just be around strangers. It might help. One step at a time"

From the moment the words left her mouth Adam knew she was right. Over the past few months his daydreams had got worse, the feeling of abandonment, the loss of purpose. Maybe being in a big city around people would help.

"I'll go today" he said.

"Great, Charlie says he'll meet you at the Station"

"What?" Adam was confused. Was this a pre-planned conversation? Had she already spoken to Charlie? Who was Charlie? Adam sat looking at her with a confused look fixed on his face.

"Oh don't give me that look!" she said, "Charlie is a very dear friend of mine, and we have known each other for years. I have spoken to him about you and he says you should meet."

Adam finished his eggs and crumpets and stood to put the empty plate in the sink.

"Have I got time to go and have a shower and get ready before I go?"

"Yes dear, I was hoping that you'd say that!"

Insulted, Adam made his way out of the kitchen and upstairs.

He looked around his room, scooped up the clothes he intended to wear for that day and walked to the bathroom. The shower was hot and Adam stood allowing the heat to relax every muscle in his body. He watched as the water ran down his arm and off the tips of his fingers. He always enjoyed watching this and imagining himself as some mutated superhero. As he played out each fight scene his mind raced from great battles with his arch nemesis, to bar fights as a misunderstood wanderer. He moved his arm up to shoot the water at the tiled wall, smiling to himself; it was always his favourite thing to do. His black hair was slicked back with the water and he made his way to the shelf at the end of bath for his shower gel. He picked up the bottle as the water continued to run off the tip of his fingers and onto the wall. He traced the water up his arm and to his left shoulder; he looked back at the shower which was still running at the other end of the bath. Adam stood in complete confusion as the water travelled through the air and wrapped itself around his shoulders like a blanket. He raised his hand to the water and watched as it smothered his hand. Adam grew fearful of what he could see and as soon as the thought entered his mind the water fell to the base of the bath and ran its natural course. Unnerved, he turned the taps off and stumbled out the bath, almost taking the blue polka-dot shower curtain with him. He stood staring as the curtain fell, resting against the side of the bath. Adam became aware of his panting and he ran his hand through his now dishevelled hair whilst the other held the towel around his waist. Unable to explain or understand what just happened, Adam left the bathroom half washed. He returned to his bedroom to dress himself. The now damp clothes that he had taken back into his bedroom from the bathroom sat in a pile on his chair. He chose not to wear those now and pulled out almost the exact same outfit that he had on that morning. Dressed and half washed, he made his way back downstairs.

"What were you doing up there?" she said, "I thought a gorilla had poured out of the shower head!"

"Nothing, well I slipped. Nearly took the curtain with me but its ok"

As the words left his mouth she struggled to contain a smile, breaking out into a full blown laugh.

"You must have really gone for it with the noise that came from upstairs! All I can imagine is a spider on roller-skates!" She placed one hand on her side and continued to laugh as she walked into the kitchen. Adam couldn't help but smile at how much amusement this brought her but he also thought about what happened in the shower and how very bizarre it was. He followed her into the kitchen only to be met by a mountain of dishes in the sink. Considering there were only a few plates for breakfast, Adam couldn't help but wonder how such a mess could be created.

"How, Granny?"

She looked over, "Oh Adam dear, you know how much of a culinary queen I am!"

"Well leave them out, I will do them when I get home, ok?"

"No dear, you head into London, I'll do these."

"Phew, dodged that bullet, thanks Granny"

She threw the tea towel at him as he ran from the kitchen sniggering.

"Right, I'm just going to grab my wallet and then I shall head off."

Adam ran up the stairs and into his bedroom, picked up his wallet from the cluttered desk, pulled open his curtains and closed the door behind him as he left.

At the bottom of the stairs waited his grandmother, she gave him a big hug and walked him to the door.

"Have a safe journey and send my regards to Charlie"

"Sure, of course I will"

As Adam left the house he pulled up the hood of his hooded jumper, placed in his earphones and started walking.

It had rained the night before and the sun was drying out the road. The incident in the shower ran through Adams mind as he played through each moment. How did it happen? Why did it happen? Should he tell his grandmother to call the plumber? The shortcut to the station travelled from the town and through a Farmer's meadow. As he walked to the station he couldn't help but feel a presence, almost like someone was watching him. He looked around and realised that he was indeed, very much alone. The sun was still high in the sky and beaming down. Adam stopped walking to take yet another look around. The feeling of not being alone grew stronger and stronger. He took out his earphones and listened but could hear nothing. The path stretched along the field, through a kissing gate and back onto the concrete path up to the entrance of the station. He noticed a figure sat beside the fence on the other side of the field. He strained to try to make out the shape but it was too far for Adam to make out. The figure was watching him walk along the field. He picked up his pace and walked briskly to the station. The train was pulling into the station and Adam could hear its brakes screech as it came to a halt. He ran the last road and jumped on as its doors closed and started to pull away.

Two

Adam watched as the fields passed by in a blur from the misty train window. Streams turned into rivers, path into roads, and fields into playgrounds. The carriages shuffled along the tracks onwards to London. Adam enjoyed the repetitive, gentle motion that trains offered; each with a purpose, they trudge along loyally, following in suit without care for consequences. In some regards he was jealous of their existence, never needing to worry about what choices they may make throughout the day.

Trying not to dwell on the curious figure too much, Adam cast his mind back to a time that he went on a train with his parents. They took the train on a Friday afternoon, when his Father was home from work. Adam barely remembers the destination or the time that they travelled. He can recall the dark wooden table that sat under the carriage window, the brightly coloured red seats with dark rubber armrests. The carriage smelled of lemon where it had been cleaned prior to the journey. Adam's mother had prepared a packed lunch for the train. Spread out across the table laid a variety of sandwiches and treats, juice, and cheeses of all kinds. He played a game of cards with his Father as his mother watched on, intervening and helping him when his Father started to get the upper hand. Adam always enjoyed playing games with his Father, knowing that he wouldn't win as he took no prisoners. It wasn't the winning or losing for Adam, it was the sharing of a game with his Father, watching him shuffle the cards as they floated from hand to hand, drifting as if he could command the air that carried them. To Adam, he was a magician, hero, and all-round strong man. Constantly up to tricks, Adam would find himself forever on the trail for treasure or hidden trinkets. The cards that they played with were unlike any that he had seen before, nor since. Like conventional cards, the pack was divided into suits, not Hearts, Spades, Diamonds and Clubs but compass points; North, South, East and West. The picture cards were not faces of Royalty but a Dove, a Bee and a Winged Serpent. The number cards were named after the seven Tectonic Plates; African, Antarctic, Eurasian, Indo-Australian, North American, Pacific, and South American. Adam struggled to recall how the game was played. All he could remember was his Father serving the winning blow and taking the final card from him as he beamed from ear to ear. He had learned more in those games about his Father than he had about the strategy of the game.

"Final stop son, you need to get off." Adam was sat in his seat at London Liverpool Street Station. He looked up and saw the ticket warden towering over him.

"Sorry?" Adam was confused; his daydream came to a sudden stop and reality crashed down around him.

"Oh, yes, sorry." He said as he grabbed his bag and departed the carriage onto the platform. The weather was warm in London and the breeze carried the smell of the food stalls in the main terminal. Adam was hungry and the daydreaming had taken its toll, so he made his way to the nearest stall to buy himself something to eat. He put his ticket into the machine and the gates opened on command, Adam felt like a magician and with his head held high and his chest puffed he gallantly strode through the entrance before they slammed shut behind him. The station was quiet as the few Sunday travellers made their way out into the broad daylight. The sun broke through the panelled glass roof and poured onto the grey stone floor. Adam wandered over to an empty bench, sitting to eat his sandwich he watched the world move on around him. Silhouettes of passing birds danced across the vacant canvas floor as business men walked with purpose whilst on their official business mobile phones. The stark female voice boomed across the station's public address system drawing a multitude of unknowing gazes to the departures board. As Adam finished his sandwich, he made his way out of the station through the East exit, up the escalator, past a coffee shop and out onto the street. He wasn't due to meet Charlie for another hour and so had plenty of time to kill. He remembered as a child visiting the Spitalfields market and decided to venture over there and see what was on offer. Unlike the station the streets were alive with activity; cars filled the roads and the pavements were teeming with tourists, Sunday afternoon revellers, and those who had no place else to go but the city. Seeing drivers waiting in their cars in London always brought a smile to Adam, his Father always referred to them as luxurious waiting rooms, driving on the road to stationary. As he navigated the thoroughfare and dodged the stragglers, it became abundantly apparent that he was not a city boy and despite his love for the architecture and the history which played to his photographic nature, he preferred the stillness and majesty of the countryside. As Adam entered the market he was met with a wall of noise and activity. The market was filled with all manner of people, stalls and books. Today was antique book day and buyers and sellers from all over the country had come to take part. Adam wandered aimlessly around the market, passing through the stalls and past the enthusiastic sellers. There were books of all colours and shapes, books with gilded pages, leather books, books covered with fabric, and books with no covers at all. As he paced the walkways between the stalls he heard conversations of price bartering and arguments over the authenticity of their wares. Every so often he would stop and peruse the selection that was laid out in front of him; the older the books, the more intrigue there was for Adam. It was the old battered leather and the embossed print that always drew his curiosity. As he wandered, he stumbled across a quiet tea shop and never being one to turn down the opportunity for a hot beverage, he made his way inside. The noise in the shop was loud and chaotic; cups clinked as the baristas grabbed and tossed them like juggling balls. Adam enjoyed ordering tea from a well-trained barista. The look of muffled disappointment from the server at the till as the expectation of a coffee order turns out to be a simple tea with milk always made him smile. With hot tea in hand, Adam made his way back to the market and the bustle of buyers. In the centre of the market Adam found an unassuming book stall complete with a long wooden table that was piled precariously high with an assortment of books. Behind the table stood an old lady who looked as old as the books she was selling. She was wearing grey knitted fingerless gloves and a blue shawl with her hair combed back into a bun and her hands clasped together across her chest. Dwarfed by the book stalls either side of her she stood frail yet bold with only her books and wooden stool to accompany her.

"Hello love, can I help you with anything today?"

Adam smiled

"No thank you, just looking."

"Well if you see anything, you just let me know."

The pile of books looked inviting as they lay heaped in disarray. As Adam leafed through the pile he took in some of the names and marvelled at the curious titles: *Dogget & Flinch Tame the molten Igneus, The Drabbled Fromoss, Kites and their Riders,* each title more bizarre than the next.

"Oh! That's a good one! It's a personal favourite of mine."

"The Tales of Samuel Baggedge?"

"Oh yes! A great book for children, pixies and trolls!" her voice beamed with excitement.

Adam looked up from the leather book held in his hand, his face filled with confusion. As he placed the book back on the pile it slipped off to reveal a dark brown leather book underneath. His eyes fixed on the book as he recognised the symbol burned into the leather cover. Picking it up, he recalled that it was the exact same symbol that was on the playing cards and of a pin badge that his mother and grandmother used to wear. The symbol was an emblem of a bird, a bee and a winged serpent. In the centre was the bird with its wings spread wide and its head turned to the right. On the birds chest was the bee, short and fat it had its wings on show. Finally there was the winged serpent. Its twists and turns circled around the bird and bee circling it like a laurel wreath. The gold writing on the cover had started to chip away and in places all that remained was the black leather where it had once been bright and bold. His thumb rubbed over the letters that read: *The Order of The Quill.*

"How much for this one?" he asked?

The old lady reached out for the book and held it in her fragile hands. The gold glistened in the light as she turned it over as if inspecting it.

"This one, you take it dear. I think you will have more use with it than I will."

She handed the book back to him and gave him a reassuring smile.

"Are you sure?"

"Of course!" she was insistent and somewhat dismissive with him. Knowing not to look a gift horse in the mouth, he placed his tea precariously on the edge of the table, took his bag off his back and placed the book in the main compartment.

"Thank you!"

"You're welcome Adam"

He smiled, nodded, picked up his tea and turned to walk on to the next stall. He was only a few steps away when he realised that she knew his name without him ever telling her. He stepped back and started to ask his question with a fixed look of confusion on his face.

"It's on your cup dear." She answered his question before he had the chance to ask it.

His frown turned into smile and his fears and confusion vanished.

"Ha! Yes it is." He turned and started to walk away glancing down at his cup but was unable to see his name. He lifted the cup and removed the protective sleeve that was there to stop it from burning his hand. His name was illegible and hidden under the sleeve. How did she see it? It was hidden the whole time. He turned to face the stall only to realise it was gone and the stalls that dwarfed it left and right were now in the space that she once was. Rushing over to the nearest stall, Adam placed down his tea on the table and checked his bag.

"Oi! Get that brew away from my books!" the voice was booming and aggressive. Startled, Adam looked in the direction of the voice. There stood a monster of a man scowling as he stared at the cup balancing on the books that made up the table.

"Sorry," he zipped up his bag and walked off with his tea.

Making his way to a seated area on the edge of the market, he sat and thought about the day's events; first the shower and now this. What is going on? As he looked in his bag, he felt the book lying at the bottom and knew that it wasn't some elaborate dream.

Adam returned to the streets to make his way to the meeting point with Charlie. His grandmother told him to be at the entrance of where Austin Friars Passage meets Great Winchester Street for 1pm. The passage was a covered walkway between two quiet roads measuring approximately one hundred metres in length. It was long

15

and dark and the sunlight at its end shone fierce and bright. He checked his watch and it was precisely 1pm when he heard a warm, friendly voice.

"Hello, you must be Adam?"

As if from nowhere there stood a middle aged man in a full length brown fur coat. He carried a black cane with a silver head in the shape of a dragon. His bowler hat was pitch black and somewhat accentuated by the curls in the ends of his moustache. As Adam went to greet him he couldn't help but notice how well turned out he was. The brogues he wore were highly polished and gleamed in the sun. Adam was positive the crease that ran down the front of his pinstriped suit trousers was sharp enough to cut through the air as he walked. Feeling somewhat underdressed in his hooded jumper, jeans and converse, Adam shook his hand.

"Hello,"

"I am Charlemagne Gravelio, please, call me Charlie. Thank you for taking the time to come and see me today, especially on a Sunday!"

"You're welcome." said Adam

"Granny told me that you said we should chat?"

"Indeed, now tell me, do you drink coffee? I know a great little place just round the corner."

Adam nodded as Charlie led the way down the passage, Adam followed behind trying to tuck in his t-shirt as they walked. He hoped that by having his t-shirt removed from view it would somehow make his appearance more acceptable.

The light was blinding as they exited the passage and Charlie led Adam to a small coffee shop near the passageway as they made idle chit chat.

"How was the journey down? Did you come by train? How is your grandmother? Is she keeping well? She sounded well in her letter."

"Granny is well thank you, still a disaster in the kitchen; she wouldn't mind me saying that. Yes, I got the train, it was ok as far as trains go, Thank you. I got in early so went across to the Spitalfields market…"

16

His mind drifted back to the curious book stall and how it vanished with nothing to show for it.

"Ah yes, she was never one to enjoy the delights that come from mashing the common potato. Oh! You visited the old Market. I haven't been there in years. I used to love going on a Thursday to the antiques market. There was a stall there once upon a time that used to sell antique maps. I'm a collector you see."

"Oh really, that's cool. You have a fair few at home then?" Adam asked without really caring for the response. Whether he did or did not have a few at home would not dictate Adam's reaction. He already had the raised eyebrow, intrigued look prepared for the answer.

"You asking to see them or just asking so as not to appear rude?"

Adam was shocked and unprepared for this response and his face showed it. Charlie roared with laughter and heavily placed his hand on Adam's shoulder.

"Relax Adam, I'm playing with you. Thank you for inquiring but I can tell small talk is not your preferred form of communication, coffee or tea?"

They were stood at the counter of possibly the most bizarre coffee shop that Adam had ever been in. In the centre of the shop there stood a large wood burner with a bench circling it for customers to sit on. Adam thought that in this weather there wouldn't be anyone in their right mind who would want to sit next to a roaring fire but to his surprise there were people enjoying the warmth of the heat. From the top of the burner fed a large round tube that ran down to the floor, around the room and through a tin bath filled with water, next to the counter, before leaving the building. Each seat in the room was different as Adam looked around and saw levers and handles hanging from the ceiling that lead to a complicated network of cogs and pulleys. He wondered if they were for show or actually served a purpose. The walls were exposed brick and there hung heavy framed pictures of hill walkers and mountaineers in a variety of places. The images ranged from two men standing amongst the clouds on what must have been a mountain top to three women standing in a field of brightly coloured flowers. Each image was different but they all shared one thing in common. At least one person in each image was

17

holding a Celtic cross in their hand. Adam put it down to the people in the pictures belonging to a group that carried the cross as part of a charity event that went on to set up a coffee shop. There was no other reasonable explanation in his mind.

"Uh, tea please." he said still feeling embarrassed for thinking about the boring maps. It was almost as if Charlie was in his head. Did he make his feelings on the subject so obvious?

"One tea and a double espresso please" Charlie said to the young barista.

"Of course, take a seat and we will bring it right over Mr Gravelio."

"Thank you, right come on Adam, let's find a seat and have a chat."

As they turned to find a seat Adam saw the young girl fill a small tea pot with steaming water from a tap at the side of the tin bath.

"Right Adam, I have asked you to meet with me today because I believe I have an opportunity for you."

Charlie sat back in his winged, leather armchair. He had removed his coat and hung it on a nearby deer antler acting as a coat hook.

The barista brought the drinks over to the table and gave Adam his tea. The pot was silver with a tiny trigger in the handle that led to an intricate pulley system to lift the lid of the pot. Adam marvelled at its workings and pulled the trigger so as to stir the tea inside. Charlie dropped a brown sugar cube in his drink, stirred it and then resumed his place in the chair.

"Thank you dear. Could you put this on my tab please?"

She nodded, smiled and returned to the bar.

Adam had foolishly picked a short stool to sit on and was now trying to awkwardly find where to place his feet. Charlie smiled and looked around the room.

"Take the chair from over there Adam." He pointed to a wooden framed chair. Adam stood and carried it from across the room, by now he was certain that Charlie could read his mind.

"An opportunity; doing what?"

"Things are not always as they seem Adam. There are many changes afoot and I will need your assistance should things turn sour. I need you to travel to Dover for twelve o'clock tomorrow to meet a

18

man by the name of Durward Scriniarii. He will deliver you further instructions. I have spoken with your grandmother and she is content for me to ask you this."

Adam had absolutely no idea what he was talking about. Go where, with whom, what changes, tomorrow? He poured the tea from the pot into his tea cup, added his milk and sugar and took a sip. It was sweet and tasted unlike the normal English breakfast he expected. Charlie changed the subject and they spoke for a, what felt like an eternity to Adam, about the bar they were in, the weather and the delights of Adams grandmother's cooking.

"I must dash now Adam, I have an important meeting to get to. I apologise for leaving you so soon and not really offering you much detail but all shall become clear soon." Charlie drank the last of his espresso and stood to leave. He placed two gold coins on the saucer of his espresso before walking to retrieve his coat. Adam stood to depart with him but Charlie signalled him to remain seated.

"You finish your tea Adam, relax. The bill has been sorted so just leave when you wish." Charlie went to depart and paused.

"Oh! Before I forget, you will need to take this with you." Charlie reached into his coat pocket and pulled a red cloth. Adam took it and felt a hard object concealed inside. He thanked Charlie and returned to his seat. Charlie nodded to the Baristas and left through the heavy wooden door. As Adam unravelled the cloth he saw that carefully wrapped inside was an intricately carved wooden Celtic cross, the very same that appeared in the pictures around the walls.

Three

It was dark when Adam found himself on the porch to his grandmother's house. His journey home from London had been filled with questions and confusion. Was the incident in the shower, the figure in the field, and the book all linked? Did Charlie know more than he let on? Adam's head felt heavy as he put the key in to open the front door. As the door fell open he found that all the lights were off meaning his grandmother was either in bed already, or would return home later that evening from the Conservative Club. She would be sporting her signature red teeth and tongue, a direct result from the bottles of red wine she would have consumed. He headed straight up to his room and collapsed on his bed.

He woke the next day with the same questions running wild inside his head. The sun was no longer beaming through his curtains like the day before, and like Adam, it was grey and overcast. He felt more lost today than he had done in previous days, as though he was on the edge of a huge turning point in his life but someone else was in the driving seat. He stood from his bed and realised he was still in the same clothes that he was in the day before and so dragged his body to the bathroom to wake himself up. Showered and dressed he made his way downstairs to the kitchen where he expected to smell warm coffee boiling in its pot. As he entered the room he saw that it was dark, empty and untouched. Opening the fridge his eyes stung as the bright light shone out at him. He poured himself a glass of apple juice and pulled out a stool from the breakfast bar before reaching for a banana. Sat in front of the fruit bowl was an envelope with his name handwritten on the front. It was his grandmother's handwriting.

My dearest Adam,

Sorry I am not here to talk to you about your trip to London to meet Charlie. A very dear friend of mine has had an emergency that means they require my assistance. I will be gone for a few days so I won't be there to see you depart for Dover. Take the book that Cella gave you and read it on the train, I hope it will be enlightening for you. You are different from others Adam and I know that things have been tough of late but fresh opportunities are on the horizon. Remember; have faith, be bold and crest the horizon.

Love always

Granny
X

Bewildered, he sat for a moment in the dull grey of the lifeless kitchen. Who was Cella? Did she mean the vanishing book seller? How could she possibly know about that? Adam grew frustrated as his head became inundated with more questions. What on earth was happening to him and why did everyone else know but him! He finished his apple juice and checked the kitchen clock. Ten thirty! He was running late and would need to hurry if he wanted to make the train to Dover in time. He ran up the stairs into his bedroom, grabbed his rucksack and threw some items in it; socks, pants, his music player, headphones, and camera were some of the items that made the cut to the bag. He looked around for a coat and spotted his hooded jumper; he bundled it up off the floor and felt the Celtic Cross Charlie had given him. Placing it in his rucksack, he zipped it up and left his room. As he ran down the stairs towards the front door he darted into the kitchen and grabbed the letter with its envelope from off the breakfast bar. Locking the front door he ran towards the train station.

Adam sat on the train platform waiting for the train, panting. He had run the whole way to the station and was now paying the price. The taste of copper ran strong in his mouth and he regretted eating a Banana before physical exercise. He placed his bag between his legs and pulled the hooded jumper from his rucksack. As he put it on he felt the cross bump him in the head and so when sorted he took it out of the pouch in his hooded jumper. Unravelling it, he was once again

21

drawn to the intricate carvings along the edges. The cross was no bigger than the length of his hand and made from several sections of carefully crafted wood. The circle on the cross was pinned through the centre and ran through purpose cut grooves in the cross. It spun on the pin revealing the supporting arms, to look more like a wheel than a circle. Adam held the longest part of the cross that was smoothed into a rectangular handle and noticed that one part of the wheel was weighted. As he moved the handle left and right the wheel always remained in the same spot with the weight pulling to the floor. At the top end of the cross was a hole drilled straight through the wood with detailed lines carved around it. Adam started to see how the circle always remained in one state much like a spirit level as the cross moved. There were numbers inscribed on the wheel and Adam inspected it further when he found a second hole halfway down the handle where the circle met the cross and he saw the numbers through the handle. He was stunned by the craftsmanship of such a little item and in that moment placed more value in the cross than he had done previously. As he spun the wheel he thought about the pictures in the coffee shop. Why did they all have one in each picture? What were they using it for? Maybe it was some form of advanced compass that only the most elite of walkers/adventurers use. Was this the plan for Adam? Was he off on some expedition? As he sat there on the platform his mind ran wild with the possibilities of what met him in Dover.

The train pulled into the station and Adam boarded it to start his journey to Dover. He found himself a table and sat down, placing his bag on the seat next to him and the cross on the table. He reached into his pocket and pulled out the letter from his grandmother. He placed the envelope on the counter and heard a tap as it hit the hard table surface. Adam frowned and picked it up feeling the weight inside slide down to the corner. He was sure that this was not in the envelope when he first picked it up whilst sat in the house. Maybe he was more tired than he first thought. As he opened it he knew immediately what it was inside. He held the pin badge in his hand and recognised it as his mother's pin badge. She had always worn it as Adam was growing up. He recalled toying and pulling at it when she carried him around the house. Like every child, Adam tried putting it in his mouth but only did that once as the pointy edges poked at his lips and tongue. He remembered feeling most upset about the whole affair and very confused as to why his mother would wear something so close to his mouth, and yet it be unpleasant to suck on. In that moment he remembered the book he got from Cella and in a flurry he opened his bag. Reaching to the bottom he pulled out the beaten leather book. He placed the pin in one hand and the book in the other, comparing them both as he realised that they were exactly the same. The train jolted as it entered a station on its scheduled stop. Adam clutched the pin as it was almost thrown from his hand. He looked out of the window and watched as the people went about their daily business. The platform was small and Adam didn't recognise the station as he inspected the the bizarre items that littered it. He realised that this was no ordinary train station. There were three Conductors on the platform; marching about wearing forage caps with shiny peaks, blue ties on white shirts and dark blue three piece suits. They looked like well-disciplined soldiers who ran a very tight ship. Each one had a pocket watch resting in their waistcoats as they checked it almost every few seconds. Adam observed the Conductor with the bushiest beard marching over to a hanging chain at the front end of the station. Standing tall he bellowed to the remaining passengers on the platform;

"Train is now departing, all aboard!" He pulled the chain that was now starting to sway from the wind created by his voice. A filter slid up from a hidden sleeve into a lantern changing the light from a red to green. He promptly pulled a whistle from his pocket and gave it three large blows. The Train started to pull from the station. As it gained speed Adams eye was drawn to a black dog sat on the platform. The dog sat proud and was staring directly at Adam. He knew then that this was the same figure that was watching him from across the field when he caught the train to London yesterday morning. Adam likened the beast to the size of a Border collie as it sat motionless, staring at him. As Adams seat passed the dog's position on the platform it stood and started to follow the carriage. The platform ended and Adam was now straining to see what would happen to the dog as it ran out of space to run. As the station disappeared out of view Adam pressed his face against the window in a final attempt to see what would happen. The train curved away from the station and in the last moment he saw two large black wings appear from its front shoulders and lift from the concrete into flight. He sat back in his seat, eyebrows raised and a smile appeared. He mumbled to himself;

"That's weird!"

"What's weird?" Adam heard an unfamiliar voice.

He looked up to see a young girl sat across the table from him. She had long dark red hair that fell over her shoulders and deep green eyes. Her gaze was wide and she stared directly at him waiting for his answer. Unsettled by the sudden appearance of her, Adam stuttered and struggled to form the words he needed.

"Uh, I...um, nothing"

She smiled and settled back into her chair. Adam was blown away by this girl. She wore a pink cable knit jumper, blue jeans, brightly laced trainers and a bow in her hair.

"Nothing is weird? That's cool!" She had an air of innocence about her and was completely comfortable to make conversation with Adam.

"Sorry," Adam apologised,

"I just thought I saw a dog take flight." As soon as the words left his lips Adam felt a twinge of regret. Why did he say that? He now sounded completely ridiculous and she probably won't talk to him again!

"Oh, you mean Chester? Yes, he's flying ahead to meet us on the Ferry before we make port in Reddington. Allow me to introduce myself; my name is Etty, Etty Gravelio"

She reached out and offered him her hand to shake. Adam sat forward in his seat and took her hand, they were soft and Adams stomach began to fill with butterflies. She knew about the flying dog! How did she know its name? How did she know who he was? Who was this mysterious girl?

"Gravelio, do you know Charlie Gravelio?"

"Yes, he's my Father. He told me all about you and that I should come to keep you company. He said you would have a lot of questions. You have a beautiful marchosiar, when did you get him?"

"Get who?" Adam had no idea of whom or what she was talking about.

"Chester, he is yours isn't he? He told me that he looks forward to finally meeting you."

"I have never seen him before in my life until today. How did he tell you? Did it say on his collar? We are off to Dover, not Reddington to meet a chap name Durward Scriniarii."

Etty giggled,

"Father was right, you really don't know much. Marchosiars are one of many protectors. When with an Architect they are keepers and herders of the grippilos, the cloud builders. Chester has been yours since your birth, you two are destined to keep the skies; a pairing of man and beast. We are all destined to be with our protector, I won't meet mine until I turn sixteen. That's the rules."

Adam was now convinced that he was not the crazy one out of the two of them. He nervously sat in his chair and tried to make sense of all that Etty had said.

"I'm an Architect? I don't understand. Cloud builders?" Adam was now trying to add everything together, the dog, the shower, the Cross. It was all starting to make his head hurt. He ran his hands through his long black hair.

"Oh, you have the Order of the Quill?" She reached out and whipped the leather book from the table. I hear that you only get this when you are selected. They are held by the Quartermaster and she is as cunning as a cratcher." She was thumbing through the thin pages, loitering on one for only a moment and then moving onto the next. Adam noticed that the writing on each page was intricately hand written. The leather cover was flexible and Etty was bending it back, much to Adam's frustrations.

"You mean as a fox." Adam corrected her.

"No, definitely a cratcher, they are cunning beasts, part of the herfacious family. I am learning you see. I am going to be a Watcher."

Adam looked confused, Watchers, Architects, what was she going on about.

"I'm sorry; I am a little behind, what is a Watcher?"

As Etty shuffled in her chair, Adam saw a light shine from underneath where her hair covered her jumper. He looked and saw that she was wearing the same pin badge as his mothers, the very same one that he had been holding when the train stopped at the bizarre station.

"Where did you get that?" He pointed to the pin badge

"This is given to those in the Order or those selected to join the Order when they turn of age. It must be given to them by the Flight, the Bee, or the Ophy."

These were more words that confused Adam. Who were these people and what was the Order?

"The Order?" he questioned.

Etty handed back the book to Adam,

"You should take a read of this. It may explain more than I can."

Adam looked down at the book that was now in his hands.

The train pulled into the Station at Dover and they both stood to depart the carriage. Adam collected his things from off the table and shoved them into his bag. Etty picked up her satchel and placed the straps on her shoulders. She turned to Adam before running off down the aisle.

"This way!"

Adam smiled as she vanished onto the platform. She was full to the brim on life and wasn't going to allow anyone to stamp it out. He threw on his rucksack and made his way off the train.

Etty was waiting for Adam on the platform. When he got to her she was frozen where she stood and staring into the hordes of passengers.

"Come on then he said, we should try to look for this Durward fellow"

As he started to walk towards the exit Etty placed her hand on his arm,

"No" she said,

"We can't. We need to go, it's not safe here."

Confused, Adam allowed himself to be taken by the hand as she led him to a nearby alcove.

"What's up? Why can't we go that way?"

Etty took off her satchel and placed it on the floor. She opened it and from the bag pulled out a creature no bigger than her hands. The creature blinked and looked up at her with large green eyes. It wore only a tiny light brown loin cloth and had long pointy ears with white wisps of hair at the tips. Adam noted how the skin of the creature was wrinkly and its feet were long and wide. It had thin fingers that moved gently as it sat up in her hands. Etty brought the creature close to her face and spoke softly to it. She finished speaking, looked at it and gave the little fellow time to adjust. It stood up, nodded and fluttered a set of wings on his back. As it flew off into the station it vanished from view and Adam was left standing with his mouth wide open.

"What was that!" he asked Etty.

"That was Mr Crumbleton. I rescued him from the Trill. They were going to kill him you see. Mr Crumbleton is a pixie. He looks after the flora."

"Who are the Trill?" Adam asked. At this point, after the flying dog and the talk of cratchers, grippilos and marchosiars he was no longer surprised.

Etty looked up at him and spoke softly,

"There are three that make up the Order of the Quill; Architects, Watchers and Guardians. The Architects decide the balance of light and shadow, water and drought. They keep the earth bright and replenished. The Watchers keep the earth green; using what the Architects deliver from the skies. The Watchers build the green earth we live in; forging rivers from rock and sowing fields of forests. Finally there are the Guardians. They are the protectors of the Order, keeping us safe and warding off any threats, natural and malicious. My Father is a Guardian, I will be a Watcher and you have been selected to be an Architect. Together they maintain the balance of life, but with balance comes imbalance. The Trill is a corrupt cell of the Guardians. Not content in serving the Architects and Watchers they want to create disorder and chaos. My Father is The Ophy, the head of the Guardians. The Trill want to remove him from power and so will not stop at anything until they do. They are after me. By having me they can hold my Father to ransom."

27

"Ok and they are here?"

"Yes, so Mr Crumbleton has kindly gone to see if Mr Durward Scriniarii is here for us."

In that moment they heard a softly spoken voice.

"Etty?"

Adam looked over to see a thin, frail looking man. His hair was long and slicked back and he wore a long brown leather coat. Etty stood and gave him a huge hug.

"You must be Adam? The Flight told me about you. I expected you to be taller." He smiled and offered his hand to Adam.

"I've not got my Cuban heels on today, sorry" Adam retorted

Durward Scriniarii's smile grew across his face to reveal several poorly kept teeth.

"Fantastic" he said. He turned to Mr Crumbleton and thanked him for his service before bowing and fluttering back to Etty. She kissed his bald head and placed him back into her bag.

"We need to move fast, The Trill knows that we are here and so have come in large numbers. Adam, do you have your Cheltiagh?"

Adam looked confused and his frown showed it. Durward Scriniarii realised his audience and reposed his question.

"The cross?"

Adam checked the pouch of his hooded jumper and pulled it out to show him.

"Great! Keep it close. Right stick to me and move fast!"

They marched quickly and swiftly out of the station and onto the street outside.

■■■

The Order of the Quill

In the beginning...

Before man could walk, there was flight and in that flight were the council of three; this council was known as the Order of Quill. An Order forged to maintain and protect the balance of life on the green earth.

28

The first of the Quill was the Flight. Honest and true, the Flight was the Commander of the skies. Charged with the power of the water and the air, the Flight ensured that life would always find a way.

Second came the Bee. Strong and loyal, the Bee was the keeper of the earth and all that lived on it. Proud protector of evolution and its fragile change, the Bee was the warden to all things living and good.

Third came the Ophy Amphipteroto. Fierce and cunning, the Ophy was the guardian and protector of the balance. Charged with protecting the Order, the Ophy was the defender of the Balance against all who wished to do it harm.

Thus formed the trinity of the Order and this was how it was meant to be and all was good and well.

Four

Adam was hot and sweaty as they chose a seat on the ferry. The journey to get to there had been fraught with close calls and near misses. Etty sat down, placed her satchel on her lap and tended to Mr Crumbleton from inside her bag; who was a bit shaken up after the running, as Durward went off to find some water for them all. Throughout the entire ordeal Adam had not seen a single Trill but Durward had taken them through some very bizarre routes and snuck them onto the Ferry without being seen and so Adam considered himself lucky. It had been a few years since Adam had been on a ferry. As he sat in the chair panting, his mind started to wander. He recalled how his parents had taken him on a ferry to go to France. Adam found it curious how a boat could carry such heavy cars, and so many of them. He would stare at the lights as they shone orange and lit the path up into the bright white parking queues aboard the ferry. His parents would park and start to get ready to leave the car as Adam would grab his pre-packed rucksack filled with all manner of ridiculous items that he *had* to have for the two hour journey. When they got to the passenger area his parents would insist on sitting down and grabbing a coffee for the journey but to Adam this ship was a labyrinth of mystery and wonder. Wanting to run the length of the ship thrice over he would sit patiently until his parents reluctantly agreed to go for a walk with him. They would always start at one end of the ship and walk from front to back or back to front depending on where they were sat closest to where they began. Adam's favourite part was standing on the deck at the back of the ship watching the waves crest with a white froth before rippling out into the wide ocean. He would stare at it for as long as he was permitted before being dragged back inside continuing the walk around the ship to find another seated area. Adam never felt unsafe on the deck of the ship. His Father's hands were large and rough and always held him tight, his mother's however, were soft and gentle and although they weren't as tight as his Father's, he could feel the strength behind her fingers as she clamped down should he wish to launch out to see something.

Durward returned with three bottles of water and four clear plastic cups.

"Here we are." He groaned as he sat down heavily into the chair.

Etty looked up and smiled,

"Look Mr Crumbleton, water!" From her satchel Mr Crumbleton poked his head up, smiled and fluttered his wings over to the table. Etty poured a little water into the bottom of the cup and offered it to him. He was as tall as the cup and placed both arms around to lift it to his tiny pursed lips. Leaning back the pixie poured the cool liquid down his throat and placed the cup back on the table before stumbling back and releasing a little burp. Etty chuckled, scooped him up and placed him back into his bag.

"Wow! He's strong for a little chap! I thought he was going to wear the cup at one point" remarked Adam.

"Careful Adam, Pixies are very proud creatures and don't like people to think that they aren't capable. They are after all, caretakers to all Flora." Durward was now looking at Adam before looking down to Etty's satchel where Adam saw a pair of bright green eyes scowling at him from under the flap.

"My sincerest apologies Mr Crumbleton, I meant no malice or jest. I was merely impressed by your strength."

The eyes softened from the darkness of the satchel and Adam could see the skin on his cheeks starting to turn pink as he blushed. Etty placed her hand into the satchel and stroked his bald head. His eyes started to drift off to sleep and close gently as his face disappeared from view into the darkness of the bag.

They sat there with the low hum of the ferry to keep them company. Adam looked at Durward despite his unsavoury appearance; he was a kind and gentle man who clearly cared greatly for Etty and doted on her. Adam slowly felt himself coming to terms with this new chapter in his life and was growing more curious about what was planned for him. What was an Architect? He's never built anything in his life well, except a sandwich! Where was Chester and how could Etty speak to him? His eyes had now drifted to the floor as he ran through the million questions running through his mind.

"Adam?" said the soft voice from Durward

He looked up to see them both looking at him. Shuffling uncomfortably in his chair Adam felt as though they had been looking for a while as he pensively stared at the hideous ferry carpet.

"You ok there son? You look a million miles away" Durward was now sitting forward in his seat with his hands clasped together. Adam noticed that he wore a very distinct ring on the little finger of his right hand. The ring was small and had a crest engraved onto the top. Adam struggled to make it out but from what he could see it looked like a winged Deer. The sun was now setting as the boat ploughed on into the horizon.

"No, I was just wondering where we are going when we get to France."

Durward sat back in his seat as a smile grew across his face.

"Well son, we won't be making port in France. We have to change ships before then."

Adam looked between Etty and Durward baffled by the idea of changing ferries before France. Was the ferry really that old that we had to change halfway?

"Change ships? Where are we making port to do that, Jersey?"

Durward stood from his chair, drank the last of the water in his cup and looked down at Adam with a broad grin. The sun was now a warm orange as it glowed through the ship causing the stubble on Durward's chin to glisten, making him look villainous.

"This way Sir and you shall find out."

Adam stood with Etty and they followed the tall thin man as his coat billowed out behind him.

She was looking tired now and she had spent the last five minutes looking into her satchel at Mr Crumbleton as he slept. They walked down the corridor of the ferry towards the stairs that led to the car deck as Durward made his way to a service door. He removed a peculiar looking object from his inside coat pocket. It was a flat metal rod the same length as a credit card and at one end was a round tip the same size as a coin that had the Order's symbol engraved onto it. He inserted it into the key hole as far as it would go and held the remaining part of the rod with one hand and the flat surface with the other. There was a loud click as the flat surface turned in his fingers. He stood up, held the door handle and looked back at Adam.

"We change ships here!" he winked and at that moment turned the handle of the door to reveal a room bustling with people.

Durward held the ferry door open to allow Adam and Etty through into a room that was unlike any Adam had ever seen before. The floor was made from wide planks of dark wood that were polished to a high mirror shine. From the ceiling hung several intricate glass chandeliers, each with white candles placed in the centre causing the flame to reflect in through the carefully crafted pieces of glass. Round metal poles were placed strategically throughout the room running from the floor to the ceiling and were painted a deep maroon. The passengers looked like extras from a period drama as they waltzed through the open space. The ladies wore tight corsets with bustles that dragged on the floor behind them and tiny detailed hats atop complicated braids and chignons. The men wore dark top hats, white ruffled shirts with bow ties and long coat tails matched with long tight riding trousers and glimmering Chelsea boots. As Adam walked through the vast room a member of the Captains crew marched past him. Adam noticed that this man wore the same outfit as the train station conductor that he saw on the platform that morning, but this suit was a deep green and not the dark blue from before. Durward came up to Adam and placed his hand on his shoulder.

"Things aren't quite what they seem" muttered Adam. A quote he remembered from the coffee shop with Charlie.

"Indeed so! This Paddle Steamer won't board in France. We are on the way to Reddington." "Paddle Steamer?" Adam turned to look at him now.

"Yes, look."

Adam followed his raised arm to see a large wheel turning slowly on the outside of the boat as water dripped off the sides. In between the side of the windows looking out onto the ocean and the turning wheel was a veranda running around the outside of the boat. The railings were white with a wooden beam running along the top. The wheel was a bright red and stood next to it was Etty staring out to the horizon. The Sun was almost gone now and the sky was clear and filled with a mystical blue. The stars were starting to poke through the blanket of blue as he made his way out to meet her.

"Is everything alright Etty?" he asked her,

"Me? Of course! I am not very good on the water you see. Watchers are earth creatures. This is more your area. Architects decide which part of the oceans to use to build clouds that provide the rain for the earth, me."

"Decide? How?" Adam asked knowing that he probably wouldn't get the full answer as things never seemed to work out that way of late. Etty smiled and looked at him,

"You'll see." She said with a wry smile.

From the door of the cabin Adam heard Durward's voice call to them.

"We should get you down to your rooms. Get you settled for the evening and Adam, you need to change."

Adam looked himself up and down realising that amongst the other passengers he looked like the homeless man who had struck lucky, but changed, into what? All he had was the bag on his back and the clothes in there were the same as what he had on.

Durward led the way down an intricate set of wrought iron spiral stairs and carpeted corridors that were elaborate and soft underfoot. Adam felt bad for even treading on such luxury and in some vain attempt to preserve it he tip toed behind Durward. Etty started to watch him and as his walk became more and more ridiculous she couldn't help but to giggle. Durward halted and turned to face Adam, his face was confused as Adam stopped mid step.

"It's the carpet....it's just.....soft, you know....I didn't want to...." His voice mumbled off into a quiet noise as Durward maintained his stern look of bewilderment.

"I'm making the most of it Adam! It's the first time I've ever been let down this part of the Paddle Steamer." His face relaxed and he gave him a reassuring smile. Dark panels of wood lined the walls of the corridor and oil fuelled wicks sat burning on intricate iron stands with frosted hurricane lamp shades. Each door had a Paddle

Steamer boat embossed onto round brass door handles and the number was engraved onto an oval brass plate which was pinned to the centre of the door, both highly polished.

"This is you" he said stopping at a door with the number eleven engraved on the brass plate. Durward handed Etty a key and turned to Adam.

"You are next door at number nine, here you go." He handed Adam a small brass key with a rectangular block of wood attached. On one side of the wood was the Paddle Steamer burned on the surface and the other had a brass number nine.

"Cella has assured me that all your belongings will be there. If you have any problems then head downstairs to room twenty-one and knock for me. If I am not there then I shall be in the Drawing Room, you remember where that is?"

Adam assumed that Durward was talking to Etty as she nodded to his question. Adam knew that he had all his belongings in his rucksack and gripped the strap tightly as he thought of its bizarre and precious contents

"Goodnight. Sleep well, breakfast is at eight. Adam? I shall see you at the bar in an hour and remember, get changed!" He called back to Adam before departing through a door at the end of the corridor. Adam placed the key into the lock and before turning he glanced over to Etty. She was looking at him with her bright eyes; the tiredness was now clear and visible in her face.

"Are you ok?" Adam enquired.

"Yes, she responded. You are exactly as my Father described. The grippilos are super excited to meet you. They have been waiting a long time for you." She turned the key in its lock and entered her room leaving Adam alone in the corridor, alone with his thoughts.

The key turned with a heavy click and Adam twisted the doorknob to enter the brightly lit room. It was the same as the corridor with the dark wood panels lining the walls. The oil lamps were brighter and the light was overwhelming. The room was a perfect square with a brass rimmed porthole to the ocean opposite the door. Immediately on the right was a thin wardrobe door facing Adam. Beyond that lay a pull down bed with brass chains leading from the walls to the foot and head of the bed. The sheets were a brilliant white and looked plump and inviting. On the left of the room nearest the door was a small bureau with a leather table top and letter headed 'Paddle Steamer' paper accompanied by a blue feathered quill and glass ink pot to the side. In the corner of the room stood a white basin complete with bright gold taps and a fluffy white towel that was hanging over the bar attached to the legs supporting the sink. Adam quickly took it all in before he was knocked off his feet and pinned to the floor. Startled Adam lay there as two great big paws dug into his chest. It was the dog from the train platform that morning. Adam looked at the dog who was now panting in excitement, as hot dribble from its tongue landed on his forehead. He struggled on the floor and managed to remove himself from the dog's heavy weight to stand. As he looked at the beast, its wings were spread wide and stretched across the room. The wings ran from the dog's shoulders and were covered in thick black feathers that turned grey at the tips. The dog's fur was black with a pink tongue, white teeth and bright blue eyes. As Adam inspected the beast, it slowed its panting, folded away its wings to lie along the side of its body, and sat staring at him. Where did he come from? How did he get here? Suddenly there was a knock at the door. Adam rushed over to the door and opened it gently to reveal a slit. As he peeked out, he saw Etty holding Mr Crumbleton who was hanging limp, with both hands like a doll.

"Hello Etty, Is everything ok? Is there a problem with your room?" Adam spoke through the crack in the door.

"Is Chester in there? I swear I heard him!" She was more animated than before and seemed very excited.

"Sure, come in!" Adam opened the door to allow Etty in. The moment Chester saw her, his wings spread wide once more and his tail wagged furiously. Etty ran in and fell to her knees as Mr Crumbleton took flight and perched on Adam's shoulder, they greeted each other as old friends and Chester was clearly happy to see her. Adam stood nervously as Mr Crumbleton stood holding onto his ear for support. Etty started stroking Chester's head as his excitement subdued and he sat in-front of her.

"Chester is very pleased to meet you. He has been waiting a long time and was very excited. He apologises if he hurt you when he knocked you...Mr Crumbleton!" She shrieked. She stood from her knees and placed her hands on her hips.

"You should know better than to stand on people." Adam heard Mr Crumbleton's wings flutter as he let go of his ear and flew over to Etty.

How did she know all that stuff about Chester? Adam would never admit it but he quite liked the idea of having a Pixie on his shoulder. Etty now had Mr Crumbleton in both hands held to her chest like before as Chester sat next to Adam.

"Chester is your marchosiar. Each member of the Order has a protector."

"Yes, I remember you telling me on the train. You won't meet your marchosiar until you are sixteen. Which is when?"

"In under a month's time and each of us are different, our beasts choose us. Chester is the protector of the Royal Architects. I don't know what my protector will be but I am very excited. You were sixteen last week weren't you?" she asked.

"Yes, how did you know?"

"Father, he has been talking about you for weeks now. They were wondering how to tell you about the Order."

Adam went to ask a further question when Mr Crumbleton came to life and wriggled from her grasp. His wings flapped into action and he drifted up to Etty's ear. As he whispered her face dropped and mouth opened.

"Mr Crumbleton you are right! Adam, you need to get ready or you will be late for Durward."

She rushed to the door and grabbed the handle, as she pulled it open she turned back into the room.

"I realise that you don't always understand as this is all new to you so I shall do my best to explain stuff to you. Pixies look after all the fauna so work on the sun and moon's rotation. They're the most accurate timekeepers in the world. I have invited Chester to sit with me until you are ready. You can take him with you when you leave. Is that ok?"

37

"Sure, I'll knock on my way past." Adam realised that time was against him and so turned to investigate what was in the room to wear that was smarter than a hooded jumper and jeans. Just before the door closed Adam called to Etty. Her head popped back into the room from the corridor.

"Yes?" she asked.

"Thank you, for everything." She smiled, nodded and left the room with Chester following behind as the door closed with a click.

Adam searched the room to find two leather trunks resting under his bed. He dragged them out and opened them up. The first chest had a brown tag tied to the handle labelled *'general clothes'*. It was empty, so he returned it under the bed and pulled out the second. This chest had the same style of tag but was labelled *'Architects uniform and Tools'*. With not enough time to open and investigate, Adam pushed the case under the bed next to the first. He walked over to the thin wardrobe and opened its fragile door, inside hung several items of clothing. Adam pulled out a collarless white shirt, a dark blue Montrose jacket and thin black trousers all hung on a single hanger. The jacket had a dove embossed on each button and a tiny pin badge of a dove on the left breast. A shiny set of dress Wellington boots shimmered at the foot of the wardrobe. Adam methodically placed the clothes on, ensuring that he touched the fabric gently and only with the tips of his fingers so as not to crease the pressed garment. The shirt was tight around his neck and Adam couldn't recall a time when he felt more uncomfortable. He looked in the full length mirror that he found on the inside of the wardrobe door, combed his hair back and made his way into the corridor. Locking his door behind him he knocked on number eleven for Chester. Etty opened the door and out trotted Chester looking proud, he ruffled his wings and then looked up at Adam.

"We chatted and then he had a snooze. He's been flying a lot today. Oh my! You look very smart." exclaimed Etty.

"Thank you, I suppose I best head up." said Adam.

"Goodnight Architect" said Etty joyfully as he turned and walked down the corridor with Chester joining him on his right side.

"Goodnight." He replied.

Sat in the Drawing room of the Paddle Steamer was Durward. He was wearing the same style jacket as Adam but his was a dark brown and instead of trousers, he had on a black kilt with Green, Blue and Maroon colours running through it. Sat next to him in deep conversation, was a gentleman of similar age in the same colour jacket as Adam. He was a short, round man who sat slouched in the comfortable armchairs of the Drawing Room. His hair was wild and unkempt and to his side lay a small creature curled in a ball. As Adam came closer to the pair, Durward looked up and stood to greet Adam.

"Ah, welcome, and my, don't you look smart." Durward looked him up and down as Adam felt the collar rub on his neck.

"Adam, I'd like you to meet Wilbur Whisspe."

"Hello Adam very pleased to meet ye'. I can see ye' enjoy wearing this high collared outfit as much as I do then" he said with a smile. He shook Adam's hand as Durward continued on.

"Wilbur is an Architect as well; he is on his way to the Order to speak to the Flight."

"Indeed I am, and knowing ye' have things te' discuss, I shall retire. Dolly!" his accent was Scottish and thick and as he stood Adam noticed the gold trim around the cuffs and base of his jacket.

The small creature sleeping by his side woke and looked up at him. Chester ventured forward now the creature was awake to touch noses. The creature looked like a ferret, but much like all things Adam had encountered, this also had wings tucked away down its sides and a pair of horns growing out from its head.

"Gentlemen, I bid you a pleasant evening." As Wilbur walked away, Dolly bowed to Adam and spread out her wings to follow Wilbur, leaving Durward with Adam.

"Please sit, can I get you a drink?" He offered as he sat down, Adam declined and saw that Durward wore the pin of a winged Stag on his jacket. It was the same as the ring on his finger that he spotted earlier that day. The same animal was also on each button of his jacket.

"Adam, I am the Warden, the keeper of keys and papers for the Order. I have been asked by The Ophy, Charlemagne Gravelio, to escort you to the Order for duties. Ordinarily this would be done by a selected mentor to brief and advise you but you are special Adam, for reasons I can't yet tell you. Right now I guess I should start at the beginning, it's about your Father."

Five

Adam's mind raced, Father? What did Durward know about his Father? Adam shuffled in his chair as Durward continued on.

"Do you know what your Father and mother did for work when you were growing up?" Durward leaned forward to engage with Adam as he became more removed from the conversation with growing thoughts about his parents.

"Your mother and Father were of the Order, your Father a Guardian and your mother a Watcher. There's a war going on, a war raging for many years now. There was a Guardian named Trillian who grew tired of the balance and how the Architects and Watchers created whilst they, the Guardians, stood by as Protectors of the balance. Trillian believed that the Guardians should be Lords of the Balance and the Architects and Watchers serve them, so he forged a secret Council to undermine the Order and bring it down from the inside. There are those who stood to fight the Trill and won but there have been many losses. The Trill seeks to unsettle the balance causing it to shift and create devastation. Think about Hurricanes, Floods, and Earthquakes to name but a few. All natural disasters caused by a shift in the balance. Those occasions are where the Trill has been successful in overwhelming a member of the Order. I am telling you this because your Father stood against the Trill when you were very young and was captured. They took him to a secret location and he hasn't been heard of since. You are the son of the bravest Guardian to serve in the Order of the Quill."

Adam's eyes were bright and wide. This would explain about his Father's vanishing from his life when he was very young. His mother's tears and why they had to move so often. The questions raced around in his mind, why didn't they tell him? Why all the secrecy? What happened to his mother? Durward sat back in his chair and took a long drink from the crystal cut glass placed on a small stool next to his chair.

"Tomorrow we make Port in Reddington before moving North towards Yeolight where you will meet your Mentor and start your training."

Adam was now more nervous than he was before. Mentor? But he knew nothing of Cloud Architecture, Reddington, Yeolight, where were these places?

"Sure, Reddington and then Yeolight." Adam repeated the destinations like he was trying to remember a shopping list.

The day was starting to take its toll on Adam and as he sat there in the grandiose drawing room of a Paddle Steamer boat headed to Reddington, Chester curled up next to his feet and slept.

"I think that may be enough for today. You need to sleep. I have requested that some food be taken to your room."

Relieved, Adam stood, thanked Durward for his time and wandered off to bed with Chester following on by his side.

When he arrived at his room, Durward was correct. On the bureau was a tray piled high with a variety of sandwiches, cakes, scones complete with whipped cream and jam, a steaming silver pot of tea, a silver jug of milk and a pot of sugar cubes. On the floor were two blue dog bowls, the lighter one contained water and the darker, dog food. Chester wasted no time and got stuck straight in. Adam was fuelled with questions, nerves and worry. He sat on his chair walking through what Durward had mentioned in the drawing room. So his Father may well be alive? The shrill of excitement filled his stomach, maybe he could find him, rescue him. At that moment Adam heard a knock at the door.

"Adam?" He heard a whisper from the corridor. It was Etty and she wanted to know what Durward had said.

As she walked into the room Adam noticed she was wearing dark green pyjamas and her hair was hanging loose and pulled over one shoulder. She was without Mr Crumbleton now and held her hair together with both hands revealing her pale neck line on one side. The pyjamas had a fat Bee embroidered on the top left pocket of the pyjama shirt and the ends of her trousers fell over her feet and dragged on the floor. Her green eyes now seemed brighter against the green of her pyjamas and the red of her hair. She sat cross-legged on the end of Adam's bed and enquired into his meeting. As Adam sat in the chair by the bureau, Chester made his way over to her hands that now lay clasped on her lap and poked his cold nose at them until she stroked his head and scratched behind his ears.

"Where is Mr Crumbleton?" He asked. She smiled and cradled Chester's head in her hands as he turned it sideways for more scratching behind his ears.

"He is tucked into bed. The little pumpkin devoured three cakes and then passed out on the sandwiches with a full belly, so I thought best to not disturb him. So how did it go?"

"It went ok." He said,

"He mentioned some guy called Trillian and my dad." He said as he loosened a few buttons on his tight jacket and shirt. Her eyes grew wide in wonder.

"He told you about Blake Dempsey? Did he tell you how he fought off seven of the Order's strongest Guardians whilst protecting an Architect that was trying to deconstruct a Nimbostratus cloud, a storm cloud?"

"No, he didn't mention that." Said Adam, astonished,

"He just said he was captured and has not been seen since." Etty's eyes dropped to the floor,

"Yes, sad isn't it" she said quietly.

"Not really, what if he's alive? I can find him and save him!" Adam was now getting animated and sat forward in his chair.

"You need to train first." Adam was shocked that Etty could settle his mind instantly from one comment, the reality of the task ahead and the possible challenges to overcome.

"Yes, you are right. Tomorrow we make port in Reddington."

"Well this is all very exciting!" exclaimed Etty as she bounced on his bed. Her mature approach to life was gone in a heartbeat and her zest for life and adventure was back. She stood off the bed and gave Adam a hug before skipping off to her room next door.

"Goodnight Architect!" as her door came to a close Adam stood from the chair and closed the door. He stripped from his tight outfit and placed it back on the hanger it came from. He found a pair of light blue pyjamas in a drawer at the bottom of the Wardrobe and held them out to inspect. They were the exact same as Etty's except blue, and where she had an embroidered bumblebee, he had a dove.

As he slid into bed, Chester jumped up, walked to his head and licked his cheek before walking to the foot of the bed, turning three times on the spot and then settling down to sleep. He looked up at the oil burner above his head. Hanging from it were two chains with metal weights at the ends. Adam pulled the shorter chain and the flame shrunk causing the room to darken. As he rested his head on the pillow he thought about that morning and the letter from his grandmother.

Adam was woken abruptly by a loud knocking on his door followed by Etty bursting into his room.

"We're nearly here! Look!" She pointed to the porthole. Her voice was filled with excitement as she pressed her face up against the glass. Mr Crumbleton entered the room, his wings fluttering and his long fingers rubbing his eyes as he was clearly still waking up. Chester raised his head, blinking his eyes as he looked at Etty and ruffled his wings before resting his head back on the bed. Adam sat up and looked out the window.

"Where?"

"Reddington of course!" Etty sat next to Adam as he let out a large yawn and ran his hands through his hair. He could smell the perfume on her as she sat close to him. Adam felt nervous and his stomach started fluttering.

"Well we had better get up then!" he stated as he drew in his knees to get out of bed. Etty went over to the wardrobe and started pulling clothes out inspecting them and placing them back.

"I wouldn't wear the formal clothes that you wore last night. Here, wear these." She threw some trousers on the bed with a white collared t-shirt and a blue wool knit jumper. The clothes landed on Mr Crumbleton who was now snuggled into Chester's fur and had fallen back to sleep.

"Hmm, and these." She pulled out a pair of brown walking boots with Red laces.

"I'll look ridiculous!"

"It's what all the Architects wear, silly! Right, I am off to get ready." Etty ran out the room as Mr Crumbleton crawled out from under the clothes and flew off after her. He turned at the door, placed both hands on the door handle, grabbed it tightly and pulled with all his might. His wings fluttered faster and his face started to turn red when Etty returned to the door.

"I shall get that Mr Crumbleton; you get started on with your breakfast." Mr Crumbleton released the door handle and flew off for his breakfast. Etty looked into the room and whispered to Adam,

"Too proud!" She gave him a smile and closed the door.

Smiling, Adam crawled out of bed and stood to look out of the window. The sun was bright and the sea blue with white clouds scattered across the sky like fluffy candy floss. Adam could see smoke rising from the horizon as land came into view. As he opened his rucksack and pulled out his toothbrush, he saw the leather book from the market with the emblem of the Order printed on the front. He felt inside a pocket of the bag and reached for his mother's pin badge. He was reminded of the conversation yesterday with Durward and how his parents had both been members of the Order. He brushed his teeth, soaked his thick black hair in the warm water from the sink and turned to put his clothes on. As he dressed he realised that in the seams of all the clothes was sewn in a thin copper wire. The jumper was thick and again on the left breast of the jumper was a cloth patch of a dove sewn on. He inspected himself in the mirror and looked at his outfit. Poking out of his pocket was his Cheltiagh, since the train station he always had it close by. He felt like a modern day hill walker, not an outfit he was uncomfortable wearing but certainly not something he had worn in a while. He placed all his belongings in his rucksack and made his way into the corridor. Before he left, he turned to Chester,

"Are you coming?" Chester sprung off the bed, spread his wings wide and gave them one large flap. Adam felt the wind bash his face and smiled as he thought to himself that he has a dog with wings!

Adam knocked on Etty's door and a voice shouted from the inside.

"One minute Architect!" He smiled and responded in kind.

"Hurry up Watcher!" He had a surge of happiness and struggled to recall a time when he had a friend like Etty. As she opened the door Adam saw that she had placed her hair in a loose bun and she wore leather Wellington boots with dark chinos, a white shirt, and a dark green tank top. She straightened herself up and walked out into the corridor. She now wore a green canvas satchel and had a light green Macintosh raincoat hanging over the top.

"Ok, let's do this! Breakfast is served in the Dining room." She said as she marched off down the corridor with Mr Crumbleton in tow. Adam looked down at Chester as he looked up at him and shook his head in disbelief as Adam reached over to close her door.

Adam and Etty entered the Anteroom of the Paddle Steamer and met Durward who looked like he had been up for hours.

"How did you know to meet us here at this time?" Adam asked.

"I'm the Warden Adam, I know everything." He said as a huge smile ran across his face. He was wearing the same brown coat that he was wearing the day prior.

They walked into the dining room to be met with a sea of round tables, each dressed with all kinds of intricately made crockery and cutlery. Durward stopped them at the door,

"Protectors are to be left at the door. There are some that don't like Protectors in the dining room and we must respect that."

Adam looked down at Chester who knew immediately that he would not be allowed entrance and so sat by the door. Etty opened her bag and ushered Mr Crumbleton to sit and relax. Before they entered Adam saw Dolly, Wilbur's Protector sitting on a table with newspapers scattered across it. She was alert and attentive and watched them both enter the room of tables. Durward led the pair to a table near the window and suggested where they should sit. Etty sat first with Adam and Durward standing behind their chairs. Adam was always interested by etiquette and his Father constantly drilled him on the correct way to greet a fellow Gentleman, and to walk on the outside of the pavement when escorting a Lady down the road. As they sat, it was moments before a young man was stood at their table in a white tunic. He carried a large tray filled with breads, hams, cheeses, and spreads. There was a silver pot of hot coffee steaming on the table next to a smaller, fatter silver pot filled with tea. Adam noted how both had the same trigger that was on the tea pot in the coffee shop he had been in with Charlie. He started to wonder if he was even in London at all when he exited Austin Friars Passage. As they started to eat Durward started to discuss the day's activities.

"Adam, when we port in Reddington, we will make our way to the Order. I shall give you your tickets and you will get the ship from the Air Station to Yeolight. Benedict Baudier will accompany you on your journey to ensure that you get there safely. He will brief you further." He took a sip of his coffee and turned to Etty.

"Etty dear, you and I shall head west to the farmlands of Torringsdour where you will meet your Father." He now turned to address them both.

"Your belongings will meet you at your destination."

Adam felt a worry drift through him as he thought about the Air Station. He thought about what Durward said about his belongings and remembered the chest with the tag labelled '*Architects uniform and Tools*'. He nodded to Durward and carried on eating the sweet bread he had on his plate in front of him. They sat in silence eating their breakfast when Adam felt a prod at his thigh from under the table. He looked down to see Chester had snuck into the dining room. Adam reached across the table to take a rasher of the crisp bacon that was piled high next to a mound of sausages. Thinking no one was watching he slipped the bacon to Chester who chomped it down before licking his lips with glee.

"He'll follow ye forever if ya make that a habit!" He heard across the room. Adam looked in the direction the voice was coming from and saw Wilbur walking across the room towards him as Dolly perched on his shoulder. Durward looked at Wilbur confused; he then lifted the table cloth to reveal Chester looking very sheepish under the table. Durward looked at Adam with a frown before smiling.

"Boys and their protectors!" Wilbur said as he arrived at the table.

Wilbur's hair was still as wild as the night before and his outfit more relaxed. He wore a blue shirt with the sleeves rolled up and the top two buttons undone to reveal a leather band hanging around his neck with a silver charm of a thistle dangling off it, sandy coloured chinos and the same walking boots that Adam had on. Although the

47

boots looked older, Adam noted that they were immaculate and didn't look like they had ever had a single drop of mud on them in the time that he had worn them.

"Like naughty siblings!" returned Durward. They both smiled as Durward continued.

"You of all people should know that protectors are not allowed in the Dining room on the Paddle Steamer. It may be acceptable at the Order, but there are rules amongst the Aecor!"

Wilbur gave a frown and shook his head with disappointment.

"The Aecor have more rules than fun Durward, you know that! Anyhow, Dolly came to tell me news. There are reports of the Trill in Reemingham and the Trolls are nervous. I am telling you Durward, the Trill are growing and are on the move!" He said as he sat down at the table with an audible groan. Dolly jumped off his shoulder and onto the floor where she ran rings round Chester's paws. Adam looked to Etty who was breaking cheese and passing it into her bag. Her concentration was broken by Adam's stare as he looked at her.

"Trolls?" he whispered as he leaned over to be sure he wasn't disturbing Durward and Wilbur's conversation, which were now in the throes of a full blown discussion.

"Trolls maintain the rivers and streams to allow all the flora and fauna to grow and prosper. They are very grumpy and can become very possessive over anything near rivers; bridges, overhanging trees, large boulders." She whispered back, winked at him and smiled as she picked up an entire croissant and placed it her bag to Mr Crumbleton, who had snuck in with Chester.

"Shall we go outside and take a look at Reddington?" she asked.

"Yes, that would be cool."

They made their excuses and wandered over to the door that led out to the veranda.

The morning sea breeze was warm on his face as Adam stepped out onto the varnished wooden boards. On the horizon Adam could see smoke rising from large cylindrical tubes that punctured the skyline. Reddington looked like a large fishing town that had been forced unwillingly to take on larger business. The buildings were crooked and weathered with no more than three stories in height. As they drew closer Adam could make out buildings with exposed beams and bricked chimneys thrusting up into the sky. The sea surrounding Reddington was filled with various other Paddle Steamers as they disappeared onto the horizon leaving a trail of smoke from their dual exhaust pipes or arrived in style announcing their presence with large fog horns breaking the morning peace. Seagulls squawked overhead and circled the steamers as they ploughed through the water and into the harbour. Adam looked to Etty who was now admiring the seagulls as they swooped in and down to the water. She let out a gasp as a family of Dolphins led the steamer in taking it in turns to crest the water and display their fins before disappearing into the water. The morning sun made her face glow and the ocean wind took the wisps of her red hair and danced with them causing her to hook them behind her ears. She caught Adam looking and smiled before collecting in some more stragglers and hooking them behind her ear, leaving her hand on her neck as she coyly looked at the ocean. Adam looked away and in that moment knew that he would desperately miss her. Suddenly Adam felt a gust from behind him and he fell forward towards Etty, holding onto the wooden topped barrier he managed to steady himself before looking around and seeing Chester flapping his great wings and jumping on his hind legs as he watched the seagulls floating up above them. Etty let out a chuckle and placed her hand on his, Adam felt a surge of butterflies in his stomach as she looked on at Chester.

"He wants to play with them." She said through her smile.

"Right you two!" they heard a shout from the door. It was Durward who was now looking very flustered.

"You ok Durward?" asked Etty as they stepped back inside the Dining room. He looked at them both and said with urgency.

"Word has it that the Trill are on the move and are currently on their way here to intercept you Etty before we get to the Order. I need you to listen very carefully. When we get off this Steamer you need to stay close and move fast. We won't have much time. Understand?"

"Understand" they both repeated in unison.

"Good, grab your bags. We are leaving as soon as we make Port."

49

Durward marched off with purpose towards the Anteroom where Wilbur was now sat with Dolly perched on his lap performing tricks for him for treats.

The Paddle Steamer arrived in Reddington and was secured to the harbour as Adam and Etty made their way back to their table to collect their bags before going to meet Durward in the Anteroom. Adam threw his rucksack on his shoulder when suddenly there came a deafening noise which shook the whole boat and threw them both to the floor. Durward ran into the room and kneeled next to Etty. He looked over to Adam who was now starting to collect himself to stand as Chester nudged him with concern.

"Are you both alright?" he asked. Etty nodded and reached into her bag to check on Mr Crumbleton.

"Right, we need to go right now! The Trill are here and there's been an explosion on the Steamer. Follow me!" Durward spoke with urgency and after he had helped Etty to her feet ran off to the front of the boat towards the kitchens.

Six

"We'll go through the crew's entrance, quick now. We can't waste time."

Adam followed behind Etty who was now running to keep up with Durward as they left the prestige of the Dining room and entered the kitchens. Durward suddenly stopped as he came face to face with a tall, heavily set figure. The man was bald with wide shoulders and thin legs. A scar ran across his left eye and down into his shirt, away from view. He wore a red tunic with bright gold buttons and blue trousers which made him look bigger than he actually was. A winged serpent was pinned to the left breast of his tunic which was stood upright with its wings spread wide and its head looking down.

"Trying to escape using the common man's exit? How very regal of you Warden" His voice was heavy and laced with malice.

"Lafayette Ogblett, strange we should meet here. We were just on our way to make a sandwich."

Lafayette lunged and grabbed Durward by the throat pinning him against the wall.

"Too many lies Librarian, you know why I am here!" his voice grew shallow and he grimaced to show a pair of sharp fangs. Chester now started to growl at him.

Etty looked to Adam as he stared onto Durward, she gently touched his arm to attract his attention. As he turned to her she held out her hand and whispered for him to hand her his Cheltiagh. Confused but with complete trust in her, he pulled it from his pocket and handed it over. She unravelled it from the cloth and cradled it in her hands. Harried, she undid the buckles on her bag, steadied her feet, lifted the Cheltiagh and cleared her throat.

"Put him down you hideous brute!"

Lafayette turned his head to her and roared with laughter all the while Durward kicked and thrashed his feet in an attempt to wriggle from his grasp.

"Silly girl! You are a long way from land! There's nothing over water that can help you, Watcher!" He gave a villainous grin and returned his gaze to Durward. Etty took a deep breath and placed the Cheltiagh in one hand with her thumb running up the centre of the stem. She closed her eyes and exhaled a long deep breath as the intricate carvings on the Cheltiagh started to glow green. In that moment Mr Crumbleton erupted from her bag, his skin had turned a dark green and his eyes were black. Looking around the room, he turned his palms up to the sky before waving them around. Suddenly sprouts of grass and flowers appeared from around Lafayette's feet. The grass was green and lush and at first there were bright white daisies with golden centres but they were soon overtaken by rose vines that twisted and turned up his legs. As Lafayette stood gloating over his capture, Durward remained perfectly still. Mr Crumbleton now darted down to where the rose vines were growing and with some simple movements of his hands signalled them to grow up his legs and wrap tight. The vines tightened and buds appeared to produce roses of magnificent colours. Adam's jaw dropped as he watched, red, white, yellow and blue roses burst from the vines into full bloomed flowers. Lafayette looked down to see Mr Crumbleton flying rings around his legs as the vines chased him growing faster and faster. He lashed out to swipe him away only to have the rose vine snatch his wrist and entwine itself around his fingers. Thorns grew sharp and fierce on the vines and Lafayette screamed out in agony releasing Durward from his grasp. Collapsing on the floor coughing, Adam ran to help him, looking back to see Etty standing like a statue with her thumb remaining on the stem of the Cheltiagh. He could see that the intricate carvings on the stem were still burning green as she stood there with her closed eyes and her stance firm. Adam helped Durward up as Lafayette struggled against the rose vines, fighting their snake like grip. With one arm over his shoulder, they made their way past Lafayette and towards the exit. Chester rubbed his head against Etty's leg as she opened her eyes and removed her thumb from the stem of the Cheltiagh. In that moment Mr Crumbleton blinked and looked around the room. His eyes returned to their deep green colour and his skin returned pink. He looked over at Etty and floated to her bag.

"Thank you Chester and well done Mr Crumbleton, you were fantastic." She opened her bag as Mr Crumbleton fluttered his wings one last time before lying down and drifting off to sleep. Lafayette was now entangled in a web of brightly flowered twines, with inch long thorns protecting the buds. Each move he made caused the thorns to prick his skin, thereby being stuck to the floor of the Paddle Steamer's kitchen.

Adam helped Durward down the metal stairs from the crew exit onto the Harbour deck as Chester and Etty followed. The hubbub of daily life resumed as black smoke from the explosion filled the air. Passengers from the Paddle Steamer flocked to the harbours market square to be met by members of the public who offered them blankets and water. The chaos that was beginning to ensue provided adequate cover for them to get away as they moved behind a stack of wooden crates to be removed from view

"Thank you Etty, that was very brave! I promise not to tell the order that you commanded a pixie under the age of control. We must go now! There may be more of the Trill here, let us not loiter and be found."

"It was all I could think of at the time, here Adam, thank you." She handed the Cheltiagh back to him, wrapped up in the red cloth. In that moment it all made sense to Adam. The balance, Architects, Watchers, how they keep the balance and allow life to grow and prosper, but as one question was answered, several more replaced it. Why and how was he selected? How would he be able to do what Etty just did? What if he wasn't the one they were looking for? Durward stood on his own and patted Adam on the shoulder thanking him for his assistance. As they turned to leave the harbour with haste they were met by a fox. It flapped its bright red wings at them before bowing and lowering its head. Chester stepped in front of them and returned the bow.

"His name is Henrik, he is the protector to…"

"Benedict Baudier." Durward finished her sentence.

"He is your Guardian, Adam."

Durward looked to Etty and Adam. As he glanced back at the Paddle Steamer smoking from the explosion he turned to Adam.

"I fear that this is where we must part; You and Chester must go with Henrik, and Etty and I shall head to Torringsdour. They will expect us to head to the Order and seek to cut us off on the way. Adam, when you arrive at Yeolight, Benedict will introduce you to a Ruairi Candidus, Chief Architect at Yeolight and Harry Flint who is to be your mentor, listen and learn and I hope to see you soon. Come Etty let's go!"

Adam turned to Etty and after a moment, offered his hand to her.

"Nice to meet you Etty, see you again soon?"

"Oh shush" she said as she bashed his hand out the way and threw herself into his arms wrapping her arms around him. Adam caught a trace of her perfume and enclosed her in his embrace. The sinking feeling of never seeing her again grew stronger and he grew sad inside.

"Goodbye Architect" she whispered and then turned to Durward as they walked off, using the stacked wooden boxes littered around the harbour for cover.

Henrik led the way through the town as they ran from back street to alleyway. The town was stacked with wooden beamed houses and narrow streets that were decorated with intricate cobbled designs as they followed signs for the Air Station which was at the top of the Town. The street names grew more and more bizarre as they navigated themselves towards the red and orange balloon that Adam could see poking out from the slatted rooftops. They passed over Fooley Street and onto Leftern Lane when Adam realised he was chasing two four legged animals and that his fitness was not what it once was when at school. As they skirted past the town's main market square Adam stopped near a pile of old fruit crates to catch his breath. Sitting down Chester stopped running and turned to look at him. He walked over and nudged his hands to have Adam stroke his head before running off into the square. He sat up and watched as Chester blended in to the mass of people in the town only to return moments later with a leather pouch filled with water. The market square was bustling with people and stalls selling all manner of items from fruit and vegetables to clothes & curious looking hats, ocular devices mounted on leather straps & top hats to clockwork animals scuttling around wooden tables. Adam could hear music resonating around the market and as he strained his neck to see if he could identify its source he felt a paw brush his leg. He looked down and saw Chester sat proud looking at him with his bright blue eyes. Adam uncapped the leather pouch and took a large mouthful of water. He turned to Chester and Henrik and offered them the water but they both looked down and turned their backs to him with their noses pointed in the direction that they needed to move towards. Adam took one last look at the town square and as they stepped off he yearned for the opportunity to wander the aisles, investigate the stalls and seek out the unusual. He remembered the book stall in Spitalfields and the curious names of the books Cella was selling. If there were wondrous things on that one book stall in London then what could there be in that market in Reddington? As they turned the corner and headed down Avalone Alley Adam saw an Owl soar into the sky from the Market. It was made entirely out of brass cogs and silver springs, and for each time it beat it wings it rose higher and higher before swooping down and flying around the chimney tops and stall flags and then returning to the swarms of people and disappearing, from view. Adam felt a tug at the cuff of his jumper as Chester pulled it to regain his concentration.

"Sorry, but did you see that?" Adam was astonished at what he saw, surely a metal bird made from cogs and springs would be too heavy to fly? Chester shook his head and returned to Henrik who was now stood at the corner of the alley before it poured out into the main street. Henrik was using the shelter of the shadow offered by the alleyway as he glanced around the corner. Adam approached the shadow and copied Chester as he stuck close to the wall behind Henrik. He could hear a loud noise approaching from the main street. A chaos of sound filled the air and as it drew closer Adam could distinguish the sound of music, shouting and thumping. His stomach sunk as he pinned himself to the cool bricks, trying to remove himself from the bright sunlight in the main street. Fearing for what may present itself Adam looked at the animals to his feet; both had raised hackles on their backs and steadied themselves for the approaching thumps. An Elephant trunk was the first thing that Adam saw marching past the Alleyway. His jaw dropped as the huge pachyderm slowly plodded past whilst being led by a man in a tight leather waistcoat, top hat, complete with peacock feather, and a billowing white shirt. His trousers were a dark black and he wore high leather boots. The Sam Browne that he wore over his waistcoat had various straps and buckles dangling off it. In his right hand he held the strap that was connected to the harness around the elephants head and in his left a perfectly coiled whip. The elephant walked steadily and as it passed the entrance of the alleyway Adam could see that it had two sets of tusks where normally there would be only one. The quadruple tusked elephant was marked with intricate patterns and waves down its body which led down to its colossal feet. On its back lay a single red rug with a girl on top performing various acrobatics and tricks with fire. She was young with bright blonde hair and wearing a gold leotard. The elephant moved beyond Adams sight as a camel drawn carriage slowly moved past. The man sat on top with the reins wore a similar outfit to that of the man with the elephant but this one had a black beard which separated into two intricate curls. In the open carriage was a large music box, fuelled by fire and steam, this black machine had every instrument Adam could think of, attached in some peculiar manner. There were cymbals hanging from wire stands with trumpets and various other wind instruments protruding from the side. As the wheels turned on the carriage, a pair of drumsticks battered away on a steel pan and snare drum. Adam realised that this was a very well put together piece of equipment and he was impressed by the intricacies of the box. Swarms of people from the town, each in their own yet similar outfits to the two men, now started to follow the carriage as it headed down towards the town square. Once the noise and people had dispersed and moved on, Henrik left the safety of the alleyway. Looking back at them both he signalled with his head for them to follow. They ran up the main street towards the balloon as it grew the closer they got. At the end of the street was a large open courtyard lined with a variety of wooden houses. Adam stopped to admire the bright balloon of the Air Ship. A rope net covered the top of a red and orange segmented balloon as several long ropes fed down onto the body of a wooden ship that floated just off the ground. The ship was grounded by mooring lines that were tied to cast iron bollards drilled into the cobbled courtyard. As Adam looked around the empty courtyard he saw two figures near a set of steel stairs that led up to the deck of the ship.

Henrik ran over to the figures and spread his wings with glee as one of them knelt down to welcome him. Adam and Chester walked over cautiously towards the ship; the two figures were very different in size and stature. The man closest to the stairs was still standing as the other now rolled on the floor with Henrik. He was an elderly man with a slight and frail frame and white hair escaping from underneath his black bowler hat. He had a long grey moustache that curled at its ends and around his neck hung a pair of round lensed welding goggles containing dark blue lenses. Adam admired his large black shirt and dark blue waistcoat that was intricately detailed with light blue stitching, instead of buttons were buckles holding the waistcoat closed. His hat had a second pair of round goggles sat on the rim which had a luggage tag hanging off them labelled '*spare*'. Holstered on his leg rested a brass monocular that had the letters '*AHC*' engraved onto the eyepiece.

"Sorry, I should really introduce myself." Said the man that Adam assumed must be Benedict, who was now dragging himself up off the floor. Adam's eyes grew wide as he noticed the red tunic with bright gold buttons, and blue trousers that was the same outfit as Lafayette Ogblett. He stepped back in fear and could feel the adrenaline surge through his body readying himself to flee.

"My name is Benedict Baudier." Smiling, he offered out his hand. Adam hesitated and tried to work out why Durward would send him to the Trill. Had he been betrayed?

"So you met the Trill then? And Lafayette no less, I was right to send Henrik to collect you." His smile was reassuring but as he looked at Adam it changed to intrigue.

"Etty commanded a pixie underage? Well I shall keep that a secret! She could get in lots of trouble using a Cheltiagh under the age of sixteen" Adam stood still, how did he know about Lafayette and Etty? The rose vines that Etty created with Mr Crumbleton and the Cheltiagh? As his mind raced and he thought of possible ways to escape, Benedict stepped forward and spoke calmly to him.

57

"Lafayette wore a pin of a serpent about here, correct?" he tapped his pin which was in the same place where Lafayette wore his. Both pins were of the same creature but where Lafayette's serpent was standing upright looking down, Benedict's was curled on its side looking up. All Benedict's was missing was the bird and the bee and it would be the exact same as his mothers and the cover of the book.

"It's different right? The upright Serpent is the sign of the Trill and symbolises how the Guardians are superior and consider themselves Lords of the Order. My Serpent is in its rightful place, protecting the Architects and the Watchers and ensuring the balance is maintained. Listen, I can explain all when we set sail but for now, time is of the essence and we must depart. I urge you to trust me"

Adam considered his options; he had nowhere else to go and no one to explain where he was. He trusted Durward and if Durward trusted Benedict then maybe he should too. He shook Benedict by the hand and looked to the man in the bowler hat.

"Arfigerous Harold Clutcherbald, Sir! Welcome aboard the Nebula!" Arfigerous bent at his waist, placing one hand in front of him and the other up, guiding Adam to the stairs and up to the ship.

Adam looked down to Chester who was now looking more reassured and had lost the look of concern that had plagued his face. He held onto the thin banister and made his climb up into the ship. Once aboard, Arfigerous signalled down to Benedict to release the mooring lines. Adam felt the ship rise a little as each rope was released. The ship was a large solid vessel that held a staged area to the bow and stern with stairs leading up to both. The railings off the Port and Starboard sides were intricately carved and clearly very well maintained. As the last rope was released Benedict held onto it tightly and was dragged into the air. He started to climb the rope and hauled himself aboard. Arfigerous smiled as he stood at the helm behind a large wood and brass wheel.

"Hold on tight!" He bellowed as he grabbed hold of a metal lever and pushed it forward causing the large engine sat at the end of the stern to grow with noise and spit bright orange flames from two huge exhausts. Pulling a second lever, two huge wings, the entire length of the ship groaned out of their resting places and started to drift up and down. The ship lifted quicker now as Reddington grew smaller and smaller. Adam looked at the houses with their crooked tiled roofs and abstract chimneys. He could see the bustling market and the clockwork animals that ran rings around the market goers and under the ladies skirts. Hagglers trying to reduce the item they wanted to a ridiculous amount and the market sellers trying to convince them of its high quality, the large grey buildings that lined the square complete with their pillared fronts and grand steps. Adam took one final look back down to the courtyard as it grew smaller and smaller as he spotted a large man in a red tunic looking up at the ship, it was Lafayette.

Seven

The sun was high in the sky as the ship cut through the clouds on its way to Yeolight. The roar of the engine was now reduced to a low hum as they cruised at a steady speed. Adam stood with Chester at the bow of the ship watching the fields and rivers passing by below. The green of the fields reminded him of Etty and the deep green of her eyes. He missed her dreadfully and was creating ways in which they would meet again. He worried that that may have been the last time he would see her. Do those from the Quill get to see the others? Adam heard footsteps approaching and to his left appeared Benedict. He spoke softly as he looked out to the horizon.

"I know you have lots of questions and I will do my best to answer all of them, well..." he paused,

"...as many as I can." He smiled and caught Adam's gaze. Adam felt more at ease and had taken the time to reflect on what Benedict had said about the pin. He also thought how the Trill are after Etty so what sense would it make to take Adam when Etty is the target and she was far away with Durward now. Benedict looked back at the horizon before starting to speak.

"We can read minds you know, that's the gift of the Guardian. I can hear your thoughts when they are most urgent in your mind." Adam felt alarmed as he tried to recall what he had been thinking in the presence of him. Benedict let out a chuckle.

"Do not worry Architect. We do not invade your thoughts. We can predict thought patterns and hear questions but that is the extent of our gift."

Adam cast his mind back to the bizarre coffee shop with Charlie. That's how he knew about the maps! Adam's mind raced to recall what else they spoke of, did he think of anything rude and malicious towards Charlie. Benedict now had a broad smile that displayed his bright white teeth.

"The Ophy is a wise man and would not have taken any offence by your thoughts. As Guardians we maintain the balance and in that balance is the knowledge that a person's mind is their own and what we hear is to be learned from, not to take offence. Relax Adam, your mind is your own and I can teach you methods that will evade the Guardians from your thoughts. That's what Etty managed to do that prevented Lafayette from knowing she would command the Pixie"

"Mr Crumbleton" Adam jumped in.

Benedict's confused look was soon replaced with his infectious smile.

"Pixies don't carry names; they are of the earth and tend to the flora, they have no need for them, how curious that he should be named Mr Crumbleton."

Adam thought about Etty and Mr Crumbleton and how she must have given him that name. He smiled as he was reminded of her quirkiness and how she could see the good in all things but still, she had a side to her, a side that forced her act out against Lafayette. This led Adam to think of his Cheltiagh and how before the Lafayette incident all he believed it to be was a simple cross or even some form of spirit level. He recalled how the carvings glowed when she closed her eyes and Mr Crumbleton changed colour. How would it work with Adam? Would he need it to be an Architect?

"It works differently depending on the user." Said Benedict as he pulled his Cheltiagh out of his pocket and placed the handle in the palm of his hand. Adam looked on as Benedict held his Cheltiagh.

"Watchers place their thumb on the stem, the longest part, the earth. Only if a watcher places their thumb on the stem will the engravings glow green. Were you or I to place our thumbs there then it would reveal nothing. No colour, no pixies, nothing. I know your next question will be about how does the Cheltiagh know who is who? It's your birth right to be an Architect as it is mine to be a Guardian. You are born for the role; there are forces beyond our understanding Adam, forces to which we can only try to understand. You have always been an Architect but you must be sixteen before you can wield the power that a Cheltiagh can offer. Hence the reason Etty could be in trouble. She could have endangered herself and those around her."

Adam fished his Cheltiagh from his pocket and curiously placed his thumb on the stem. As predicted, nothing happened. Benedict looked over and watched Adam for a moment.

"Thought you'd try it anyway? I don't blame you. I did the same when I heard about it."

"So what about you? I mean Guardians, what about Guardians?"

Benedict looked at him before placing his thumb on the side of the Cheltiagh.

"The edge is the protection, the skin, if you will." The engravings on the side started to glow red with the touch of his thumb, and like before, Adam copied with nothing to show for it. Benedict released his thumb and then wrapped it over his fingers so to clamp down on the handle.

"Architects are different. With water buds life, the Architects keep the balance with water. They manage it, move it, gather and collect it like a wheel, constantly moving. They are the providers. To ignite your Cheltiagh you simply place your hand like mine and spin the wheel."

Adam ran his fingers over the wheel that was embedded into the Cross.

"I would strongly advise you to not try it now. Without training who knows what you could muster!" Adam released the wheel from his fingers and allowed the weighted section to fall, swinging as gravity took its course.

"Thank you Benedict, I just thought it was just an ornament." Adam smiled at him and placed his Cheltiagh in his pocket.

"You are very welcome. I hope that gives you a bit more of a steer as to what awaits you in Yeolight."

Adam nodded and returned his gaze to the horizon.

"I must speak with Arfigerous, excuse me." Benedict placed his hand on Adam's shoulder before walking away towards the helm.

The sun was starting to fade now and the sky was filled with a bright orange. Adam looked at the deep red clouds as they resonated in the sky, capturing the last of the sun before it vanished. Adam turned and sat with his back against the wooden bulwark as Chester approached him and lay down in his lap. As the sun set, Adam pondered over the Cheltiagh, what Harry would be like, would his grandmother know about his journey, and did she know who Charlie really was, but most of all he thought about Etty. He hoped she made it from Reddington ok, he hoped she wasn't going to get into trouble for using the Cheltiagh, he hoped he would see her again. For the first time in a long time, Adam began to hope.

"Here, drink this. It'll keep you warm." Benedict handed him a large brown mug filled with a steaming liquid before taking a seat next to him. The drink smelled unlike anything that Adam had encountered before. As Adam looked around, taking in his surroundings he noticed the sky was now black and littered with stars.

"What is it? How long have I been daydreaming?" he enquired.

"That is a good question." replied Benedict.

"It's a pixies recipe. Nobody knows what is in it but the Pixies call it Hunchers Brew and its blooming delicious! You've been sat here for an hour now. Chester has been with you the whole time. He hasn't moved from off your lap"

"Sorry, I was..." before he could finish Benedict chirped in.

"She's fine. She made it out of Reddington and is now on her way with Durward to Torringsdour, Sorry, I didn't mean to intrude but your thoughts were so strong, I was unable to keep them out of my head. I asked Henrik to check on them. He has just returned and is now flat out on my bag below deck."

"Thank you." Adam responded as he raised the mug to his lips and took a sip of the smooth hot drink. As it ran down his throat and into his stomach, Adam felt the heat running through his veins and into the tips of his fingers. His eyes grew wide and he turned to Benedict with a huge smile.

"This is fantastic!" His voice rose in glee and Chester raised his head from Adam's lap to look at them both before returning to sleep.

"It is indeed! Chester really loves you! He won't leave your side! Wait 'til he flies, then you'll see him in his full splendour."

"He flies? Is that how Henrik checked on Etty?" Adam said with disbelief!

"Well why do you think he has wings? Chester is your Protector; he joins you in the skies of course."

Adam reached out and stroked Chester on the head causing him to let out a groan of delight, before taking another sip of his Hunchers Brew.

"Can you tell me more? If Guardians can hear thoughts, what can Watchers do? And Architects?"

"Well that is an easy question to answer." He said with a smile. "I suppose you have guessed what Watchers can do?"

"They can talk to animals"

"Yes, that is correct. They can hear an animal's thoughts and wants. It's akin to their innocence. Watchers are innocent creatures that see the beauty and light in everything. To see a watcher sad is like seeing the darkness of a dying flower or hearing the cry of a mourning mother."

Adam thought about Etty and what she said about Chester on the train, how she knew about Chester on the Paddle Steamer, and how she burst into his room that morning to show him the view of Reddington. She was so innocent and fragile, Adam saw her as something that he needed to protect, something that he wanted to do, something he could do.

"...and Architects?" he finally asked.

"Well, that's a good one." Benedict smirked.

"They can walk on clouds."

Adam's heart raced with fear and excitement.

"Clouds?" his voice was filled with disbelief.

Benedict took the last swig of his drink before placing it on the deck.

"Yes, you control the clouds and their volume. You command the grippilos, the cloud builders."

Adam looked down at Chester before closing his eyes and struggled to understand the concept of standing on a cloud. As the fear and excitement rose in his stomach he opened his eyes to stare at the stars that hovered above him. The Milky Way sparkled and cascaded out into the millions of stars that covered the black canvas of space moments before a streak of green shot across the sky. Adam watched as the green danced and skipped on amongst the stars as it turned to a vibrant red. Amazed, Adam stood to watch the majestic display of nature.

"We're nearly there." Benedict was close to Adam, watching with him as the sky became a dancefloor of colour and movement.

"Nearly where?" he queried.

"Yeolight. Prepare your stuff. Arfigerous hasn't got the best reputation for landings." He caught Adams eye, winked and walked off towards the helm where Arfigerous was grasping the wheel.

Adam looked off the boat for any sign of Yeolight but instead of fields and smartly kept lines of hedges hiding in the dark, he saw snow topped daggers piercing the night sky with treacherous ravines carved and hacked into the rock. Chester jumped up and placed his paws next to Adams hands as they both watched the Nebula gracefully navigate through the mountains. It was then that Adam saw a light at the end of a lake filled ravine. They turned and were now heading directly for it. As the light drew closer Adam could see a large tower with a blue flame burning fiercely at its pinnacle. Beneath the tower lay snow covered buildings each with windows that radiated with a warm orange glow. The Nebula was dropping now and as Adam leaned over the ship he could see its reflection in the crystal clear lake. He held on tightly as the ship circled the village and started to prepare itself to land. Adam looked down the valley and could see the ridgelines either side of the lake leading away from the village. The ship dropped down below the houses to lower itself as it landed in a cobbled courtyard. The oil burning lanterns lining the courtyard spread light across the cobbles and the glimmering snow that filled the crevices between the cobbles. Adam spotted two men waiting in the courtyard for the lowering ship both in the same outfit as Adam but with dark blue coachman capes over the top. As they got closer he saw one was older than other. The older of the two Adam guessed had to be in his late fourties. Adam noticed how his coachman's cape had gold trim on the cuffs and around the cape, the same as Wilbur's jacket that night on the Paddle Streamer. The cape was open to reveal his clothes underneath. His hair was short and brown with grey patches on the side. He wore thin square glasses and carried his hands behind his back. The other man was around twenty years of age and stood on the right of the first man. He had short curly hair and stood with his hands in his pocket. As they slowed down to land the entire ship shook and was followed by a loud bang knocking Adam off his feet. Adam looked over to the helm and saw Arfigerous bashfully pulling at levers in a frantic state before standing proud and announcing to the ship,

"Another successful landing for the Nebula!"

Benedict rose from his feet and let out a loud roar of laughter!

"Aren't they always my friend!" he said as he clapped his hand down onto Arfigerous' shoulder causing him to wince.

"Adam! Let's go!" Benedict called to him as he made his way to a set of wooden stairs.

Adam thanked Arfigerous for the journey and his superb landing before clambering off the ship. Chester jumped the bulwark and followed Adam down the stairs to where the two men were now waiting.

"Adam Dempsey! Welcome to Yeolight!" said the elder of the two men as he extended his hand to Adam.

"I am Ruairi Candidus, Chief Architect here at Yeolight. And this young man to my right is Harry Flint, your mentor whilst you are here."

Adam shook both their hands as Harry spoke.

"Hello Adam, it's great to finally meet you!" he said

"Ruairi!" A voice bellowed from the top of the stairs. Ruairi looked up and beamed a smile at Benedict.

"Last one off I see?" replied Ruairi.

"Had to get Henrik, lazy boy was still asleep on my kit below deck even through that landing!" He said now at the bottom of the stairs.

"Ahem!" came a voice from the side of the boat. Benedict looked up and spotted Arfigerous leaning over the side. His moustache now dishevelled due to the wind and the luggage tag flapping like a loose flag.

"...that textbook landing!" Benedict shouted up before returning his gaze to Adam and winking. Arfigerous shook his head and rolled his eyes before disappearing back onto the ship. Adam swore he heard him tut 'Blooming Guardians' before returning to his post landing duties.

He embraced Ruairi before releasing him and shaking Harry by the hand. Henrik followed behind shivering and looking thoroughly vexed from being woken up in such a snowy cold place.

"Blue flame?" Benedict asked pointing to the top of the tower.

Ruairi looked up at the tower and then back at Benedict.

"Yes, for Adam." Adam looked up at the blue tower and back to them as they stood by the huge floating vessel. A blue flame for him? Why? And what colour was it normally?

"Come, let's retire to the warmth." Ruairi led them towards a large wooden door at the gable end of a rectangular building attached to the tower. Adam could hear the great wings of the nebula return to their resting place as they walked away from the ship towards what looked like a village church. The building was high and made of stone and looked out of place against the wooden buildings that were littered around the village. Ruairi grabbed and turned the black iron handle before leaning on it with his entire body weight. The door creaked and groaned as the light contained inside spilled out onto the snow filled floor.

"Front door, we must have been good!" said Benedict.

Inside Adam was met by flagstone floor that fed into high stone walls. The ceiling was arched and made from detailed wooden beams from which hung iron chains attached to round chandeliers filled with burning candles. Adam wondered whose job it is to light all those candles, and how did they get up there to do it. Scattered around the room were large round wooden tables with heavy wooden chairs spaced evenly around them. On the right side of the room was a large stone fireplace complete with roaring fire burning bright on a bed of heavy logs. Above the fireplace on each corner of the stone mantelpiece were two Doves looking into the flames. Two animals lay on the floor in front of the fire. One was a full grown grey wolf and the other a badger; both with a set of wings wrapped along the side of their bodies. Henrik wandered over to them and gave them each a sniff before lying down in the heat of the fire.

"Impressive, right?" said Ruairi as he wandered over to Adam.

"Except for those lazy beasts!" he pointed to the now three animals lying on the stone floor. Adam looked down and saw Chester stood by his right side.

"The Flight has requested to meet you when you arrive. I shall take you." He said now looking at Adam.

"You stay here." He called to Benedict.

"Sure!" replied Benedict from the other side of the room as he chose a table to sit at with Harry.

They walked towards the end of the room, underneath the spiral stonework leading to the top of the Tower and through a smaller wooden door.

"Dietrich!" he shouted to the fireplace as the wolf raised its head. It stood and opened its grey wings, giving them a shake before tucking them in and trotting over to him. Ruairi muttered under his breath with disdain,

"That beast!"

As Ruairi closed the door behind them Adam found himself in a long carpeted corridor with oil burning lanterns lining the walls. The corridor was tall and had a large stain glass window of the Quill emblem at the far end.

"What does the Flight want with me? Has there been a mistake?"

Ruairi smiled and walked with Adam down the corridor.

"No Adam, there has been no mistake."

"Who is the Flight?"

"The Flight is the Blue Dove, The Head of the Order and the one who guides and leads us. With The Bee and The Ophy, who I believe you have met, they are the key to the balance. The Flight normally remains in Reddington and rarely comes up to Yeolight to greet new Architects of the Order. This is the reason for the blue flame. The beacon on the tower signifies that the Flight is here. It burns for lost Architects to find their way home, but only ever blue for when the Flight is here."

They passed several dark doors before Ruairi slowed and eventually stopped outside one in particular. It was dark and there were no markings that made it any different from any other door that they had passed. He stood by the door and guided his hand to the handle, signalling for Adam to go in.

"I will be outside. Don't worry, the Flight is kind. Listen and learn. She is very wise and has led us through some troubled times."

Adam nodded, let out a long breath and knocked on the door. From inside the room he heard a female voice,

"Come in."

Adam turned the handle, entered the room and closed the door behind him.

At the end of the room sat a heavy wooden table in front of a large glass window. Adam could see the green and red lights dancing amidst the stars outside. On the left, the wall was lined with a bookcase filled with all manner of leather bound books. A ladder rested against the top shelf at the far end of the room nearest the window. Adam wondered if the bookcase held any of the magically titled books that he found in the market in Spitalfields. A large circular rug rested in the middle of the room on top of the varnished wooden floorboards. The same circular iron chandeliers hung from the ceiling with multiple candles lighting up the room. On the right was a fireplace holding home to another roaring fire. This one was different to the one in the hall; it had a wooden mantelpiece with a rounded mantel clock sat in the middle. Above the fireplace hung a wall rug of the valley that they had just flown over in the Nebula to get there. The tower was in the middle and the fire on the top was burning bright, the sky was black and the stars were delicately placed around it. The lights spread across the sky and were reflected in the lake below. Two red leather wing back chairs sat either side of the fireplace protecting a small stool that was hosting a pristine doily. Stood next to the fireplace was a lady in a light blue full length dress and silver high heels. She had a dark blue cape hanging off her shoulders that was held together by a clasp in the shape of Order of the Quill in the centre of her chest. She had bouncy blonde hair and bright red lipstick. She smiled at him as tears filled up her eyes. He looked at her confused as his heart began beating so fast he thought it would explode from his chest.

"Granny?"

Eight

"Hello dear," She had an audible lump in her throat as she opened her arms to welcome him. Adam ran across the room into her embrace.

"Welcome to the Order of the Quill."

Adam looked at her and smiled before returning to her embrace.

"How? Why? What?" his mind raced over and over. He couldn't understand what was going on. How was his grandmother, the Flight? How did she get there?

"Sit dear, you must have plenty of questions. Firstly, Hunchers Brew? I try to drink as much as I can when here. I mean, don't get me wrong dear, you make a fabulous tea but it's certainly no Hunchers Brew."

Adam smiled and sat back in the leather chair as Chester took his place by his right side. His grandmother leaned forward and Chester ran over to meet her. She placed her hands on his head and scratched his ears. Adam recognised Chester's reaction and remembered that the last time that he reacted like that to someone's touch it was Etty.

"So? Where do I start? You've met your protector I see, and he clearly thinks highly of you. So you know you are an Architect and that Harry is to be your Mentor. You've learnt about your Father and...Oh my, you've met Lafayette."

She stopped and looked at Adam with an astonished look on her face.

"I shall keep your secret about Etty and your Cheltiagh." She smiled causing a shocked Adam to lunge forward in his seat.

"But how? You weren't... you?" His confusion clouded his mind and restricted him from being able to finish his sentences. His stomach sank as he grew fearful that Etty would be in trouble for commanding a Pixie underage.

"Only a man can be an Architect Adam, Guardians can be either but only Women can be Watchers. It's the rules. I'm a Watcher; I have been since I turned sixteen. Your grandfather was an Architect, your Father a Guardian and your mother was also a Watcher. I am

70

merely a placeholder for the male heir to take the place of the Flight. That's you Adam."

Adam jerked out of his seat and ran his hands through his hair. He paced around the room before walking to the window. He stood staring out into the stars struggling to place the pieces together. His photos, his obsession with the clouds, the peculiar card games with his Father, the waves on the ferry. Were these all signs or just coincidences? Durward had already told him about his parents, but his grandmother, the Flight? Chester placed his head in Adam's right hand causing Adam to kneel down and hold him close. His grandmother joined him at the window. "What you have just been told I know is a lot to undertake, but I need you to understand that I am not asking you to be the Flight tomorrow. I will undertake the role until such a time that you are ready. You have many years ahead of you Adam; enjoy your time with Chester and the Order."

Adam took a deep breath and rose to his feet. He looked at her with confusion in his eyes.

"But mum? What happened?"

His grandmother took a step forward and took his hands in hers.

"Your mother was one of the best Watchers in the Order. Her Father, your grandfather, was the Flight and without a Son she was to assume the role until an heir was produced. Then something magical happened, you were born, an heir! She loved you so much but when the Trill found out they sought her out to have her and you killed when you were at your most vulnerable. Thus leaving the Order without an heir and presenting an opportunity to seize control and have the power they finally felt they deserved. An Architect you see is the most powerful of the Order. Having command of the skies and sun you have the power to determine the balance and ensure it is maintained. When she died I took the place as the Flight and hid you from the Trill. With the help of the Ophy we hid you away until you were of age, and here you are."

Adam frowned in confusion and looked at her. His mind was a mess as he tried to piece the puzzle together; his grandfather, the Flight, and now his grandmother, an Heir?

"I think you need some rest. From what Chester has told me you have had a busy couple of days. I shall be departing for Reddington in the morning to meet with Charlemagne. You'll be safe here. Learn and enjoy." She walked Adam to the door, gave him a hug and opened the door back out to the corridor where Ruairi and Dietrich were waiting. His grandmother looked at Ruairi and thanked him for bringing him to her. Ruairi nodded and both he and Dietrich bowed before escorting Adam and Chester back into the hall. As they entered the hall he saw Benedict and Harry supping away on large brown mugs filled with a steaming liquid. Ruairi placed his arm around Adam and made his way over to them "Hunchers Brew before bed?" Adam nodded and smiled. Benedict stood and welcomed them to the table as they approached.

"Welcome back, your Highness, and Adam!" He roared with laughter and took a low bow as Ruairi slapped him across the back of the head.

"Guardians! Be careful before I summon a bolt of Lightning to your backside!" Ruairi was now smiling as they sat around the table. Adam took the seat across from Harry with Benedict to his right and Ruairi to his left. A man in a sky blue tunic arrived at the table as they sat down. His hair was slicked back and he carried a white towel over his left arm.

"Four Hunchers!" exclaimed Benedict. The man nodded and walked off towards a smaller side door.

"So what did she tell you?" Benedict leaned in to Adam.

"Leave the boy Benedict, and no mind reading either! What were you two discussing whilst we were away. Tell me, what news of Frackingshulme?"

Benedict leaned back in his chair and clasped his hands together. His mood and tone changed as he addressed the question. He looked to Ruairi and spoke with a deliberate tone.

"The Trill remain in Reemingham and the Quill continue to maintain the Balance. The Ophy is seeking to deploy more Guardians to Haverpalm in order to delay their advance into Reddington."

As he spoke four steaming mugs returned, brimming with Hunchers Brew. Harry leaned forward and collected his first before looking at Adam and smiling.

"Take one mate! Or Benedict here will drink the lot!"

"Oi! I'll have you know I am on a weight loss regime at the moment." Again he roared with laughter before slamming his hand down on the table and looked to Adam.

"A lie of course, the only thing that I am taking a diet from is that blooming Nebula! How many years has he been crashing that balloon!"

"I am right here!" they looked to the voice that came from a table near the fire as Arfigerous leaned out of his chair to look over to them.

"Ruairi said it!" shouted Benedict before a handkerchief came flying across the table towards him.

The table erupted with laughter and Adam collected his Brew from the table.

"So no news from the Ophy?" asked Ruairi, in another attempt to settle the conversation.

"No, he returns from Torringsdour on the morrow after delivering his daughter, Etty." Adam marvelled at how Benedict could switch himself from humour to business in a flicker. He sat forward to hear more news about Etty but none came.

"Adam, tell me of London! I hear you met Durward!"

"Umm, well London is still there, I suppose, still grey and full of commuters." Adam felt lost with such a general question.

"Come on Harry! Ask better questions than that tosh!" Benedict threw the handkerchief that Ruairi had thrown at him at Harry.

"What he really wants to know is, are Durward's teeth still hideous?"

Adam smiled as he recalled Durward's poorly kept set of teeth that he noticed on the day he met him. Ruairi turned to Benedict,

"He's a Parytronious. They all have bad teeth, it's the antlers. You know that Benedict!"

Benedict chuckled to himself as Adam looked at Ruairi,

"Parytronious?"

"They are not of this plane. They are selected from their world, much like you were from yours to be an Architect. Parytronious' cast the shape of a man but the shadow of a Stag."

Adam thought about the Stag ring and pin badge that Durward wore when on the Paddle Steamer.

"Did you see it? His shadow?" enquired Harry.

"No, I didn't. Sorry. I didn't know to look. Sorry Ruairi, this plane? I don't understand"

"I think that is a conversation best kept for another night. I am retiring to bed and I suggest you all do the same." As Ruairi stood they all stood with him. He nodded to them all at the table before departing. As he left the room he gestured goodnight to Arfigerous before departing the hall with Dietrich following closely behind.

"Come on Harold, the old man was right!" Benedict looked at Harry and smirked!

"Sometimes Benedict, you can be a real jerk!" They both chuckled before Harry turned to Adam.

"Come on bud, I'll show you to your quarters." They left the room the same way as Ruairi, gesturing their goodnights to Arfigerous as they left. The corridor they were now in was wider and taller than the carpeted one that led to the room where his grandmother was. The floor was made from stone slabs that bowed in the middle from the years of feet that walked on them. Large portraits of men in long dark cloaks with pin badges of the Order and a winged beast at their feet, lined the walls. Smaller iron chandeliers hung from the ceiling with candles burning bright. They approached a crossroads in the corridor and stopped before Benedict turned to them both.

"This is me; I shall meet you in the hall for breakfast?"

"Yes, we shall be having breakfast around eight? We don't want to be too late; we need to catch the end of the morning cloud before it heads south." Benedict looked affronted.

"Eight? You mean nine, right? Are there two eights in one day?" His shocked face turned to a smile before he looked at Adam, winked, turned and walked away from them. Henrik was already waiting at Benedict's room door at the end of the corridor.

"Alright, I'm coming Henrik!" He shouted exasperated before calling back to them. "Until tomorrow Adam, sleep well! Harold? Brush your teeth; you're starting to look like Durward!" He turned to look at Harry and chuckled before jogging the last few feet to his room. Harry turned to Adam, who was now wearing a full teeth bearing smile.

74

"Come on; let's find you your room." He said with a sigh. They turned right at a crossroads and walked to the end of the corridor.

"Who are these people, Harry?" Adam was looking at the portraits as they walked. They were all similar; each had a man in a long blue coachman's cape with the same gold trim that both Ruairi and Wilbur wore. The winged animals ranged from huge bears to small rabbits all at the feet of their Architects. The background to each painting was different and ranged from a blue sky filled with clouds to the tower burning bright on a bright sky.

"They are all former Chief Architects of the Order. You have to serve a minimum time and master all the skills required of an Architect before you are entitled to wear the gold trim."

Adam slowed his pace to see more of the portraits,

"So my grandfather is up there?"

"No, your grandfather's portrait hangs in Reddington. All Flights, Bee's and Ophy have their portraits in the Great Hall of the Order. Yeolight only have Architects. It's our home."

In a flash Adam blurted out.

"Where is the home of the Wardens?"

Harry gave a knowing smirk and looked at Adam as he raised one eyebrow before asking.

"Keen to learn about Watchers?" Adam started to blush and he looked at the floor. Chester was as always, on his right, looking up at him, his eyes still piercing blue as he stood proud.

"No, I mean...my mother was a Watcher." Adam could feel Harry's gaze burning into him as he maintained his stare at the floor.

"The Watcher's reside in Torringsdour and the Guardians in Frackingshulme. Each is welcomed at the others but they are only permitted to hang their colours and display their historic artefacts in their own society's houses."

Adam felt an immediate urge to visit Torringsdour to see Etty. His heart raced and mind wandered thinking about her hair as it was plucked from her ear that morning on the Paddle Steamer.

"Here we are" Harry was stood next to a short door with a key hanging from the keyhole. "I am just across the corridor should you need me. I'll give you a knock at quarter to eight for breakfast?"

"Sure, thank you Harry."

No worries mate, sleep well and catch you in the hall in the morning." Harry walked over to his door and pulled his key from his trouser pocket before entering with the Badger that was sat in front of the fire that evening. Adam turned the key in the lock and entered the room. He was met by a wooden panelled wall that ran away from him on the right hand side. A leather topped desk and wardrobe lined the wall leaving enough room for the door to swing wide and let him in. He looked into the room and admired the wooden furniture that was presented to him. On the far side of the room on the wall closest to the corridor was a door with a bright brass handle. A four poster bed jutted out into the middle of the room with blue curtains gathered at the posts and a bedside table sat in-between the bed and the wall which housed a large window. Adam walked over to the window and pressed his face to the glass. He struggled to see anything in the darkness, except that the snow had now come in and outside blew a blizzard. Adam turned to look at the room. He felt like he had stepped into a period drama. The lights were oil burners and produced a low flickering flame. He walked to the door next to the bed and opened it to be met by a bright light. Inside was a white tiled bathroom with gold fixtures and fittings. On a shelf above the sink was a toothbrush and toothpaste placed on a folded flannel. Adam looked at the dove carefully hand stitched on the corners of all the towels. He heard a large gust from the bedroom and then a groan. Adam found it strangely comforting how he had come to hear Chester and consider it to be completely normal. He couldn't imagine a life now without the magnificent beast. He was always at his side wherever he went and Adam couldn't help feeling that Chester knew when he was scared or sad as he was always there to comfort him. He left the bathroom to find Chester curled up on the bed with his eyes closed. Feeling like this room had more to offer, Adam ventured over to the wardrobe to see what was hiding inside. When he opened it he saw the same clothes that were hanging in the wardrobe on the Paddle Steamer. At the bottom of the wardrobe sat a canvas rucksack with a metal frame on the inside keeping its shape. Sat next to the rucksack were the shiny Wellington boots he wore when he learned about his Father and the Order from Durward. Everything in the room was from when he was on the Paddle Boat.

He looked under the bed and found the two heavy chests dumped there. The labels were still hanging off them and the writing the same. How did they get here so fast? Who delivered them? Perplexed, he sat down on the end of the bed and felt something prod him in the hip. He pulled the Cheltiagh from his pocket and ran his fingers over the carvings. He thought about the green glow that came from it when Etty commanded the pixie and then when Benedict made his glow red with his touch. His mind wandered off thinking about the journey to Yeolight and the conversation with his grandmother. He came out of his daydream as the wooden edge of the bed was poking into his bum and was starting to hurt. He stood and searched the room for his pyjamas, hobbling as his bum grew numb. He found a pair of blue pyjamas folded in the bedside table cabinet. He picked them up and made his way to the bathroom to get ready for bed. Once changed, he picked up the toothbrush and toothpaste and turned the tap on. As he watched the water trickle down the sink into the plughole, he thought about the shower at his grandmothers and the water wrapping around his shoulders like a blanket. How did that happen? Was that part of being an Architect? He stood looking in the mirror thinking about the shower and the Order and what Benedict said about being able to stand on clouds. His gaze fell to the dove on his left breast pocket and he stood inspecting the intricate stitching around each feather as he thought about the wings on Chester and wondered, how many types of protectors were there? Standing there his mind rested on what Harry said about catching the end of the morning cloud. What did he mean? The realisation of being up early in the morning suddenly caught up with Adam and he looked down at the sink to rinse out his toothbrush. As he looked into the sink he saw that the water had started to pour from the tap, towards him and was circling up his toothbrush and around his wrist before spiralling back down and trickling down the plughole. The delicate movement of the water as it flowed up to his wrist caused Adam to freeze and stare. After a few moments he crouched slowly, trying not to disturb his wrist to get a closer look at the rope of water flowing up and around. He realised that the liquid did not touch any of the toothbrush, nor his skin, but merely glided over it by a few millimetres. Adam turned his arm to inspect the other side of his wrist to see where the water returned back to its spiral, when suddenly the rope like water fell limp and returned to the tap as it was before. Adam rinsed his toothbrush and splashed some water on his face before finding a towel. He walked towards the door that lead back into the bedroom and turned to take one last look at the sink before switching off the light. His hand rested on the lever connected to a series of cogs and pulleys that fed into the oil burners causing them to dim and he stared at the sink. How did that just happen? Why? He took his hand off the lever and walked back to the sink turning on the tap. The water poured furiously from the gold tap as Adam knelt so as to be at eye level with the water. Hooking his arms over the sink, he placed his hands into the water a few millimetres apart with the palms facing each other. He closed his eyes and took in a deep breath before pursing his lips and blowing slowly. He thought about the book in Spitalfields, the adventure he was on, his mother, his childhood, and his Granny and how they were inseparable. He thought about how he and his mother would hang out at home before his Father came home from work. They would craft things from paper and make elaborate paintings of sea creatures and flying reindeer. She was always a trusty aid to have in a gun battle from an onslaught of zombies, or his evil Deputy Head at school, his sidekick, his wingman. Adam lost himself in his thoughts before opening his eyes and seeing the water tumbling out of the tap into the sink before running up through the centre of his hands like a sheet of paper. As it reached the top it separated and crashed over his hands and back into the sink, down the plughole. He stood with a smile that stretched from ear to ear across his face and turned off the sink tap. Not content however, he turned sharply and blocked the plughole in the bath before turning on both taps. He stripped down to his boxers and jumped straight in. The water was filling fast and before he knew it was over his knees. When it reached his belly button he leaned forward and turned off the taps. He laid back into the bath and allowed it to wash over him. Again he closed his eyes and took a deep breath before releasing it and allowing his mind to wander. He thought about his mum again, about how she would play dress up with him and listen to his wild stories. He thought about his grandmother and how she would fuel him with sugar before returning him back to his mother, and how she would sneak him in food when it was bed time despite his mother and Father distinctly telling her not to but above all, he thought about Etty. His heart raced as he thought about her red hair cascading over her neck, her sweet perfume and the way she embraced him, the secret wink she shared with him at the breakfast table and how the sun made her face glow as she collected her hair from the wind. The way she touched his hand and looked at him like she saw the magic in him. He opened his eyes and saw the water stirring around his fingers. He sat forward and raised his hands from the water. It stuck to his hands like large woollen mittens, rolling and flowing between his fingers. Placing his palms towards each other, the water left his hands and formed a large ball of water. Hovering in his hands the water turned like a planet on its axis as it twisted and spun between his palms. Adam smiled and lost his concentration allowing the water to splash back into the bath rising up over the edges and onto the floor. He lay back and chuckled before heaving himself out of the bath and grabbing the nearest towel resting in the towel rack. He walked carefully from the bathroom to the bedroom, trying not to slip on the tiled floor, grabbing his pyjamas off the toilet on the way. He dried himself down and got back into his pyjamas. Looking over to his bed he saw Chester who was now no longer curled up in a ball but spread out and flat on his back. His tongue was hanging out of his mouth as he snored himself awake and rolled onto his side. Adam hung his towel over the chair at the desk and climbed into bed. As his head hit the pillow he felt a prick on his ear. Raising his head he looked at his pillow and saw a pin badge of a winged serpent stood upright looking down.

Nine

Adam woke to Chester licking his face, the sun was beaming through the window and Adam could see the snow topped mountains sat against the clear blue sky outside. He dragged himself out from underneath the excitable beast and threw himself from the bed to walk over to the window. From there he could see that the room was part of a building that was built on a solid stone pier that jutted out from the mountain. He pressed his face to the glass to see if he could see down for any roofs underneath his window. The glass was cold and immediately his face felt numb before he decided to get himself ready for breakfast. A mantle clock sat on the top of the desk ticked slowly as it displayed a time of quarter-past seven. Adam walked through to the bathroom and turned on the taps in the bath before pulling a plunger releasing cold water from the gold shower head directly above him, catching his hair as he lunged out of the way. The floor was still wet from the night before and he walked carefully so as not to fall. Showered and dressed he placed the pin that belonged to his mother onto the white collared t-shirt underneath his blue jumper. He returned to the bedside table where he had left his room key for the night and found the pin badge of the serpent. Chester had now jumped off the bed and walked up to Adam as he held the pin in his fingers. Chester sniffed it and raised his lips, bearing his teeth before growling and then seeking refuge behind Adam's legs. Adam opened the drawer to the bedside table and folded the pin in amongst a pair of socks. He took one last look around the room and patted down his pockets to check he had everything before leaving with Chester and making his way back down the corridor towards the hall. The corridor was filled with the smell of hot breads and Hunchers Brew as Adam wandered towards it. He could hear the noise level rising as he got closer, and as he entered the hall he saw it filled with people in all manner of attire. He glanced around the room trying to find a familiar face amongst the sea of noise, before he saw a single hand shoot into the air as quickly as a bullet from the crowd, shortly followed by a broad shouldered chap in the same jumper as Adam but in red.

"Adam!" The arm was now waving as he stood tall shouting across the room, it was Benedict. "Adam!" came from across the room again. Adam nodded and waved back before navigating the tables towards him. Sat next to him was Harry who was sat with his head hung in embarrassment.

As Adam got closer to the table Harry stood to shake his hand.

"Good morning, sleep well?"

"Yes thank you, you?" He asked Harry before looking towards Benedict who was now smiling and walking around the table. When he got to Adam he wrapped his arms around him and squeezed him tight. Adam felt the sheer power of Benedict as he felt the air rapidly escape from his lungs in the embrace of him.

"Good Morning Adam!" he said as he slowly released Adam and placed his hands on his shoulders.

"Sit! Eat!" he demanded. "Flight!"

"Hush! Quiet you fool" hissed Harry as he hit Benedict with his napkin before sitting down at the table.

"They need to stop using napkins here you know, I'm always getting hit with them." He looked at Adam and winked before smiling and picking up his mug.

"Henrik and Primrose are in the kitchens stealing food from the chefs. Chester is more than welcome to join them, if you will it." said Harry.

"If I will it? Sorry, who is Primrose?" Asked Adam as Harry chuckled,

"Primrose is my Protector; you may have seen her last night, the Badger?" Adam gave a knowing nod, "Chester moves to your will. He is your protector and your herder of the grippilos. You simply have to tell him. Try it, but without words."

Adam looked down at Chester and stared into his bright blue eyes. As soon as the thought entered his mind of how to tell him to visit the kitchens, Chester was gone.

"He is connected to you. When you are scared, he is scared. When you are happy, he is happy…"

81

"When you are sleepy, they are grumpy and will sleep anywhere!" Benedict added as he cut off Harry.

"I tell you, Henrik is always sleeping! I don't even always feel that tired, but, he is a good Protector."

Adam looked around the room and watched Chester depart towards the kitchen. He marvelled at the people gathered there. He spotted men with monocles and curly moustaches and women in riding trousers and aviator hats with goggles perched on their foreheads, each with some leather Sam Brown or cog and wheel operated device in a leather holster. He grew curious about who they were and what purpose they had in Yeolight, the home of the Architects. What truly caught his eye was the scattering of blue, red and green jumpers sat around tables. Adam returned his gaze to the table and plucked a floured pastry from a silver tray that sat in the centre like a monument to all baked goods!

"Who are they all?" Adam asked before taking a bite from the sweet bread. Harry looked around the room before looking at Adam.

"These people are the Sphera; they are pilots, travellers and explorers of the skies. You must have met the Aecor on your journey here. They would have been the people on the Paddle Steamer; they are the explorers of the seas and strange new worlds, new planes, and the others in red, blue and green are of the Order. They are seeking board here before moving on to keep the balance where required. This place welcomes anyone from the Order and also any travellers." Adam finished his pastry and looked around the table for what he could devour next. Each item on the table looked delicious and he wanted to take them and stuff them into his rucksack.

"Eat up Adam, we need to head down to collect your Sciaths that Cella has dropped off this morning and then head up to the clouds."

"Sciaths?" Adam asked. Harry smiled and sipped from his drink before replying,

"You'll see soon enough, but before then you'll need to return to your room and collect these things. Cella has assured me that they are there." He slipped a folded piece of paper across the table and carried on eating. Adam picked up the paper and quickly inspected its parchment like qualities before stuffing it into his pocket.

"What are you up to today Benedict? Are you coming with us?" asked Adam.

"No, I have business to complete here. I have a meeting with Ruairi and the Flight before she departs to Reddington and besides, I can't walk on clouds. I'm not an Architect. Remember, rufty tufty Guardian?" Adam smiled and realised that he knew that answer already.

"Benedict? What do Guardians do? I mean, you can read minds, but what else? What happens when you use the Cheltiagh?"

Benedict placed down his food and looked Adam clear in the eye. He could tell that Benedict was not about to reel out some cheesy quip or try to make a joke at Harry's expense.

"We are Guardians; we keep the balance and protect the Architects and Watchers at all costs. No fire can run too fierce or ice too sharp to stop our resolve. With the Cheltiagh in our hand we can summon walls of stone and creatures from the darkness so terrifying that you would wish for your nightmares to come. Not all of this world is light and in the darkness lays the tools to protect it or destroy it. Pixies, Trolls and grippilos are mere fantasies and child's play to the things that loiter and fester in the mind of those who wish to unbalance the fulcrum. We guard the gates and hold the keys." He sat back in the chair and smiled, "but these are things you need not worry about Architect. You keep the skies and I shall keep you in them." A napkin flew across the table into Benedict's face.

"Easy there Guardian! You'll scare the lad and it's only his first day."

Benedict smiled and tossed the napkin back to Harry before standing and looking at them both.

"Gentlemen, I must depart and I believe you have a cloud to climb." Benedict's voice was plum as he bowed and waved his napkin in the air.

"See you for dinner?" Adam asked as he returned from his bow.

"Dinner? Of course! Food here is the best in the district!"

They stood as he left and then returned to their seats. Adam looked over to Harry who was now drinking the last of his drink. Harry leaned back in his chair and looked at Adam.

"You all set bud?" Adam set down the pastry he was eating and nodded to Harry.

"Don't worry if you are still hungry, I've asked the kitchen to pack us a lunch for today and they always make too much." Harry smiled and stood causing Adam to stand as well.

"Right, you go off and get your kit and I shall book out and collect the lunches. Meet back here shortly."

"Sure." Adam replied and made his way towards his room. As he approached the door he thought about Chester and where he might be. As he turned to walk over to the kitchens he saw the door open and Chester trot out licking his lips. Adam smiled to see him as he heard a voice call from across the hall.

"Connected!" Adam looked over and saw Harry with Primrose running around his feet.

"Mine however, has come back covered in beans! How?" He shouted before releasing a huge smile, waving and walking off under the large tower. When Adam got to his room he unlocked the door and fished the list from his pocket reading the items off and searching the room for them. He found the rucksack in the wardrobe where he had seen it before and the Mackintosh coat was there also. Other items found were a compass that was in the style of a pocket watch complete with a thin chain dangling off the top, fingerless leather gloves, a wooden pocket telescope, dark lensed goggles, long woollen socks, a whistle, a metal drinking bottle with a dove engraved on the front, and long blue scarf. Adam stuffed all these into the rucksack before making his way with Chester back to the hall. Sat in the emptying room was Harry and Primrose with two large sticks. Adam walked over to them and saw that Primrose was now wet and sat on Harry's lap. Harry saw them wandering over and stood, placing Primrose on the ground.

"Great, this is yours now, look after it. And here is your lunch." Harry handed Adam a brown paper bag and one of the sticks. The stick that Harry gave Adam was to shoulder height and had complex and elaborate carvings along it.

"Thank you. How did she get wet?" Adam looked down at Primrose and then back up at Harry as Primrose touched noses with Chester before Chester sat behind Adam's legs. He took off his rucksack and placed it on the table putting the brown bag inside and doing up the leather buckles. "I put the hose on her. She'd managed to get jam on her as well. I have no idea how!" Harry leaned over to ruffle her fur before offering his hand to Chester who sniffed it and turned his head away. Harry stood quickly and turned to Adam,

"Right, let's do this." They collected their things and walked off towards an entrance under the tower before turning right and towards a door that led outside. Outside the weather was warm and the sun was bright as it hung on the stark blue back ground.

"There's not a single cloud in the sky." remarked Adam.

"Yet." As Harry threw on a black metal box and then his heavy pack and adjusted the straps. "Here, these are your Sciaths. I'll show you how to use them later but for now hook the straps over your shoulders and clip around your chest like mine and then it sits in-between your back and the rucksack." Adam threw the black metal box onto his back and clipped the straps around his chest before putting on his rucksack and picking up his stick. The box didn't feel uncomfortable and Adam felt the straps rest on his shoulders. He expected the slow dull pain to soak into his shoulders, but it never came.

"Be careful of the release pulley on the chest strap."

Adam looked down and saw a brass T-shaped handle tucked in under a brown leather strap held closed by a brass popper.

"Ready? Then follow me!" Harry walked off with Primrose shortly behind him away from the tower and the village towards a path that lead up the mountain. Adam followed with Chester loyally following behind, up the path that was wide and made of a light brown mud. As they walked, the valley opened up and the spectacular view grew more and more magnificent. Adam could see multiple lakes collecting in various valleys, and birds migrating overhead as the wind gently carried them along. Adam estimated that they had been walking along the track for nearly twenty minutes and in no direction other than up before Harry turned and perched on the edge of the track looking down towards the valley.

"We have to go high as this is where the clouds touch the Earth, rubbish isn't it?" Harry was pink in the cheeks and a little out of breath. Primrose was sat at his feet looking off into the valley and then back at him.

"It's not always this tough but we need to climb on a cloud fully made. New clouds are too risky for your first time. You'll meet the grippilos there."

Adam perched next to Harry as Chester sat at his feet, leaning on his legs, panting. The path was now a dark black from the rocks and dropped steeply away from them as they had now started to follow it along the side of the mountain. He looked into the distance and saw the mountains ripple off into the horizon before merging with the sky. The snow covering the tops fed into the mystery as to what was in the next valley, patches of light cloud floated past, caressing the tops of the rocks before drifting off unchanged by the encounter. Adam gazed around him and felt a pang of regret for not bringing his camera.

"How long have you been an Architect?" Adam asked.

"Five years now. Wow, I never really thought about it until now" His eyebrows raised as the realisation of time hit him. "It's the best job in the world."

"What did you do before this?" Adam was curious about Harry. He wanted to know how he came to be here with him. Was he selected? How did he get told? Did he always know he was going to be an Architect?

"I was told by my Father when I was a boy, I forget what age I was now but he brought me here to Yeolight and took me on my first cloud. On this very path, you know?" He poked his stick into the soft mud before looking to Adam.

"That's cool!" said Adam. Harry let out a sigh and a knowing smile as he nodded and looked at Adam,

"Yeah, but you want to see something really cool?" Adam nodded as Harry looked at Primrose. In that moment she ran and jumped off the path before stretching wide her wings and floating off down the valley, being carried on the wind. Adam sat there amazed as she beat her huge wings and rose up climbing and dropping as gracefully as a bird.

"Does Chester want a go?" Adam looked at Harry shocked and the thought entered his mind of how amazing it would be to see

Chester's grey tipped wings fully spread out in the bright sun; to see him gliding down the valley and beat the huge expanse of his wings majestically, like an eagle. He felt the weight on his legs from Chester disappear as Chester stood and ran towards the edge, jumping clear from the path and unfolding his black wings. He fell before the wind caught his brilliant feathers and lifted him high above Adam and Harry. He watched in awe as Chester circled above them and swooped down as he hovered next to them both, beating his wings as he floated on the spot before dropping and landing softly on the path.

"Impressive marchosiar you have there. You can see why they are only for Royalty."

Adam smiled and knelt on the path to welcome Chester back from his brief journey. Chester was clearly happy with being able to spread his wings and as Adam opened his arms, he rested his head under Adam's neck and rested his body against his chest.

"Shall we carry on?" Harry asked.

"What about Primrose?" Adam was concerned over Primrose being lost in the Valley and not being able to find him.

"Connected." Harry said as he tapped his head with his fingers, "She'll find us." He was now standing up and looking up the path

"Round this bend and we should be there." Adam was now stood with Chester by his side as they walked off up the hill. They carried on for a further twenty minutes before Adam could see the mist of the cloud resting on the path up ahead. The more they walked the less of the mountain range Adam could see. From the clouds, Adam could hear the movement of a creature as it approached and through the mist appeared Primrose as she hovered over a spot before beating her wings faster to steady herself for landing. Once back on the ground, she folded away her wings and trotted up the path towards Harry. As they reached the top of the mountain, the black path carved its way through the snow and spread out into a large circular area. The snow was deep and perfectly white as Adam struggled to determine where the edge of the mountain was. They stood at the centre of the top of the mountain as the mist filled the space around them. Adam wondered what the mountain range now looked like from there as Harry glanced around the edge before walking up to him.

"Are you ready to climb on?" he asked.

Adam grew nervous and afraid as he looked around into the mist unable to see anything but thin cloud.

"Right, lesson number one, take out your Cheltiagh and follow me to the edge." Adam pulled his Cheltiagh from his pocket and followed Harry towards the edge of the mountain.

"Hold it in your hand and take a deep breath." Adam held the handle of the Cheltiagh in his hand and placed the thumb over his fingers before taking a deep breath.

"Take the wheel, give it a good spin and breathe out." Harry was stood next to him speaking softly. Adam hooked his stick under his arm, took the wheel between his fingers and gave it a sharp spin. The inscriptions on the wheel glowed blue as the mist turned into a thick milky white. Harry took a step towards Adam and was now standing directly behind him as Adam heard Chester starting to growl causing Primrose to come between him and Adam.

"I'm sorry for doing this" he spoke softly and with both hands gave Adam a swift push off the edge of the mountain. Before he could realise what was happening, his leg instinctively stepped out to protect him and stop his fall knowing full well that there was nothing beyond the ledge. He opened his mouth to scream but before he had chance to, his foot found firm ground. He looked down to see the white mist drifting over his foot as he was standing on the cloud. Amazed, he turned to Harry who was now smiling as Primrose touched noses with Chester before bowing and returning to Harry.

"I'm sorry Adam but it has to be done that way. If I had asked you to step off the ledge then you would have never had believed me." Harry stepped out onto the cloud and walked beyond him taking him by his arm and helping him off the mountain and onto the cloud.

"But why didn't you go first? I would have followed you." Adam asked with curiosity in his voice.

"Because you had doubt and therefore would have always had doubt. This way you stamped on the cloud, used some force and created immediate trust in your ability, a leap of faith. Now you can put your Cheltiagh away."

"But what about..." Adam looked down at his feet. He was scared that without the wheel of the Cheltiagh spinning and the carvings glowing blue he would fall straight through the white cottony cloud.

"Come, you'll see. Step up like imaginary stairs. Place your feet into the cloud and walk up" Harry walked off into the mist stepping up as he went. Adam followed but as he stepped up in the mist he saw a dark outline in the clouds. He looked around for Chester and from the mist he saw his wings beating as he flew from the Mountain top to be with Adam.

"There you are, come on mate." Adam said to Chester before turning to see Harry but he was gone into the mist. Stepping up he looked back to where the dark outline was but this time he saw the silhouette of two figures in the mist. His heart raced as he started to climb, trying not to panic. He looked again and the dark shapes were now moving through the cloud towards him.

89

Ten

Adam saw a hand poke through the cloud above him, it was Harry and he was reaching out for him. Adam grabbed his hand and felt it pull as he was hoisted up out of the cloud and into the clear light of the sun. Adam was on his knees as he looked up at Harry to realise that he has not stood alone. Blinded by the sun he rose to his feet to see who was stood next to him as Chester clambered up the cloud to be with him. His eyes adjusted and he saw that the figure beside Harry was not human. Standing at what Adam guessed to be eight, or maybe even nine foot, was a beast that he could only akin to a human stick insect. He looked at the beast, as it stood towering over him, its hands connected to long skinny arms, hanging down by its side. Adam stared at the thin pointy twigs that were spread evenly at the ends of the arms. He looked up and was astonished as where there should have been a face he saw two black dots the size of buttons placed evenly apart on a head that resembled an egg. The cream coloured beast tilted its head as it stared at Adam through the black of its lifeless eyes. Harry smiled at Adam and placed his hand on his shoulder walking round to be next to him.

"Welcome Architect. I'd like you to meet the grippilos." With one arm around Adam, Harry raised the other, gesturing towards the beasts. They lowered their heads and slowly bent down onto one knee. Adam watched as more and more of them appeared from within the clouds, taking their lead off the other and slowly moving down to one knee.

"They have been looking forward to meeting the next Flight."

"But how do they talk? Where do they come from?" A confused look filled his face.

"They don't, in time you will know all but for now let's get to the top." Harry looked to the top of the billowing cloud and collected his stick from where he had left it stabbed, standing upright. He moved onto a flat section that was thinning. Adam stood next to him and could see the ground below moving. Rivers glistened as the sun bounced of the top of their crinkled glass surface. In the black rock valleys, Adam could see white frothy streams cascading over the boulders and rocks, making its way towards the river, and then the sea. The cloud was moving and Adam grew curious as to what they would do at the top. He turned to follow Harry as they both made their way over white fluffy hills and smooth soft boulders. The Cloud filled the sky and soared towards the sun. It curled and spiralled up producing great peaks and precarious ledges. Adam remembered as a child he would spend his days staring at the clouds as they stood like enormous mountains in the sky; the rounded edges and casual wisps that would drift away from the mother cloud before being pulled back in by the wind. He imagined Victorian mountaineers with their trousers tucked into their knee high socks and long spikey crampons, venturing into the unknown. He thought about how they would have had tufts of cloud trapped in their long bushy beards, and round circular goggles to stop the sun from blinding them. Adam would create stories in his head of how they would be in competition to reach the top before another team and that they would use rocks to lasso clumps of cloud so that they could cross treacherous ravines over the moving ground below. He smiled as he climbed thinking that he is now the mountaineer and that all his fantasies of scaling the enormous cloud in the sky were now coming to life. Chester walked on behind him, as the wind blew back the black fur from his face revealing his panting pink tongue and strong white teeth.

"How are you finding it? Are you ok?" Harry called to Adam.

"This is amazing!" Adam called back as he continued to climb up, using his stick to help with his balance. They walked together for hours, jumping shallow white ditches and topping feathery crests. Adam liked to stop to glance around and observe the ground below as the mountain ridges became smaller and started to resemble that of a crumpled shirt. His mind started to drift and he began to think about his grandmother's house. The clothes that were left on his bedroom floor, her vintage mismatching kitchen, the secret life she was leading and the burden of keeping Adam hidden for all those years. Why couldn't she tell him? What happened to his Father? His mind now wandered to memories of him, the Guardian. The moments when Adam would call in the night as the darkness woke him and he would arrive, still with sleep in his eyes. How did he know? How did he get there so fast? He remembered how he would carry him around and swing him up over his head. His strength knew no limits; he was the fixer, builder, arch enemy and sworn adversary when in battle. Adam remembered the day when he didn't come home, it was half past six and his Father was due home from work. He waited by the front door in his pyjamas, his red cape hanging around his neck, as he held two guns, ready to give one to him before launching into the living room for a full blown battle. Whenever the time or place his Father would never hesitate to engage in tomfoolery and get involved in the latest game or role play. But as Adam waited, the clock simply ticked by. In the end it was his mother who picked him up off the cold hallway tiles, fast asleep, and carried him to bed. He woke the next day to a chorus of voices coming from the living room. He stood at the doorway and saw the room filled with people congregating around his mother. They each wore brightly coloured capes and coats in varying colours of green, red and blue. Adam started to realise those people were of the Order of the Quill. What were they doing in his mother's living room? How did they get there? His mind started to trawl through memories of his childhood trying to recall moments where he saw the pin badge, or met his Fathers friends from work. Suddenly he heard Harry's voice and he looked up to see him on an embankment of thick grey cloud. Adam looked around and the cloud had turned from a brilliant white to a dark grey.

"Let's have some lunch. We're near the top and it'll be too windy up there." Harry took off his rucksack, keeping the Sciaths clipped to his body, and removed the sandwiches from the brown paper bag within. He sat up and took a bite from it before tearing off a corner and throwing it onto the grey cloud floor. Adam followed and as he loosened the straps on his rucksack he felt the wind cool the patches of sweat that were hiding underneath. Chester sat at his feet as Adam reached into his rucksack, took out the sandwiches and unravelled them from the foil. Harry looked into the distance, observing the horizon as the sun shone over the distant ocean.

"Are you ok Adam?" Harry took another bite from his sandwich and sat to face Adam, lifting one leg up onto the embankment.

"Yeah of course, should I not be?" Adam felt defensive. Did something have to be wrong?

"You see, clouds are very delicate, they move, grow, and change. Unlike Watchers and Guardians, we must be sure that the clouds move to the right place, block the sun where needed and rain where required. Imagine trying to move a burning candle, now imagine four hundred, each with a fragile flame flickering in the breeze. What would happen if you went to fast? They'd go out, right? And too slow? They'd melt away."

Adam didn't know where this was heading but he grew more and more curious, nodding as Harry asked his questions. Intrigue filled his mind as Harry imparted the pearls of his experience into him.

"Your mind is that tray and this cloud are all those candles. If your mind starts to race, then the cloud will race, withering and drifting in the wind. If you become distressed and allow your mind to chew over something troubling you, then the cloud will react to that as well. See the colour?" Harry placed his hand on the grey cloud as a thin layer of mist wafted over his fingers.

"Yes," Adam answered.

"This shows me that you were dwelling on a moment in your past, unanswered questions that are causing you to worry and become unsettled." He looked up at Adam and gave him a reassuring smile. "Enjoy your time up here and allow the peace and quiet to fill your mind before we head down to the chaos of Benedict and his rubbish jokes." Adam smiled back and felt a flicker of excitement at the prospect of having dinner with Benedict and Harry and the laughs they will have. He watched as the colour under Harry's hand changed and slowly turned from a dull grey to a clear blinding white. They sat and ate their sandwiches, sharing them with Primrose and Chester alike.

"Great! Now we are near the top, get your goggles and gloves out." Adam reached into his rucksack and pulled out the goggles placing them over his head, resting them on his forehead, keeping his long black hair out of his eyes.

"Wow! I didn't know you had eyes under there!" Harry was smiling as Adam bashfully pulled his gloves on. They both buckled up their rucksacks and placed them on their backs.

"Here." Harry grabbed Adam's stick and clipped it to his Rucksack, "Do the honours mate? There is a clip in the centre of the bag." Harry handed Adam his stick and turned around, presenting his bag to him. Once set they headed off towards the top. The wind blew stronger and whistled around his ears as the cloud became narrower and thinner at the top. Adam glanced around and saw the ground below them almost indistinguishable. The sun was now low on the horizon and had turned the sky a vibrant orange and the cloud a deep purple at its base and red at the top. They climbed for a further hour before eventually reaching the top. Adam stood looking all around him as he tried to work out the directions to Yeolight, Reddington and Torringsdour. The sun was setting and the light fading as Adam stood with the sun at his back, and watched the stars starting to twinkle on the night's sky. Adam looked down at the mountain that they had just climbed and gazed in awe at the journey he had made as Harry sat down at the top and looked to him.

"You know each time I climb a cloud I am always completely overwhelmed by the view up here."

Adam wandered over to where Harry was and sat down beside him.

"Do me a favour bud? Grab me my water container from my rucksack?" He shifted round with his back to Adam. He rose to his knees and pulled it from his bag, handing it to Harry.

"Cheers bud." Harry took it, opened the lid and placed it into the mist of the cloud. "This is the freshest water on the planet. Here, turn around and I'll fill yours for you."

Adam turned round and allowed Harry to grab his bottle filling it from the mist. After a few minutes he handed him a full and heavy bottle that was cool to touch.

"Turn around and I'll chuck it back in your rucksack."

"Thank you." After Harry had placed Adams water bottle back in his bag, Adam returned the favour. Both ready Adam looked to Harry.

"So are we heading down? Won't we be doing it in the dark?" Adam looked around as the light was starting to fade and the stars growing in numbers. Harry turned to Adam with a smirk and tapped the brass handle on the chest strap of the black box.

"Remember I said not to touch this? Well follow me and once clear, give it a sharp tug."

"Clear of what?" A sinking feeling filled his stomach. He felt his palms become sweaty from inside his leather gloves. Harry gave a wink, pulled his goggles down over his eyes and gave one last smile before running full speed at the edge of the cloud. Adam's mouth fell open as he saw Harry jump clear of the top and disappear into the mist of the thinning wisps of cloud.

"Take a leap of faith!" came from the mist as Primrose jumped after Harry, spreading her wings before following him into the unknown. Adam was alone and afraid at the top of the mountain. Where had Harry gone? Why did he leave him? Leap of faith? Chester let out a whimper and rubbed his nose on Adam's leg. As he saw his bright blue eyes shining like beacons in the dimming light he took a deep breath.

"Leap of faith, right?" Adam, placed his legs apart, pulled down his goggles, bent his knees and ran as fast as he could towards the ledge. His heart was racing and his stomach turning as he came closer and closer to the edge. Feeling the firm ground underneath his feet he took one last step and jumped. His arms were spread wide and he felt the wind drag through his fingers as he entered the mist surrounding the mountain. He brought his hands in to his chest and reached for the brass pulley pulling it sharply. Two huge wings snapped into place either side of him from the black box on his back and in that moment his fears vanished, the black pit of sadness that had filled him for so long dissolved away and for that single moment he felt free. Free to live, free to decide his fate, and free to fly.

Gliding through the sky, Adam saw Harry up ahead, leaning forward he felt himself speed up and slowing down by leaning back. The wind was pressing up against his face and he looked around admiring the view. Chester was gliding to his right with his legs tucked up underneath him as they flew as a pair into the dusk. He put his head down and sped towards Harry arriving there quicker than he expected to. Primrose was on his right and Adam took his place to the left with Chester behind Harry. They flew straight in this formation for a while before Harry turned to Adam with a huge grin and shouted to him.

"You would have never jumped without a reason!" Adam knew he was right and his face lit up with a grin as he looked at them all gracefully shooting across the deep blue sky.

"We head for Yeolight." Harry pointed off to the distance towards a bright light burning on the horizon. "A beacon to guide us home!"

Adam could feel the adrenaline pulsating through him as they flew through the sky watching the world below.

"You reckon you got the hang of this?" Harry shouted across to Adam.

"I think so." Adam called back.

"Well let's see." Harry placed his head forward and sped off in front of them all before leaning with one shoulder and performing a perfect barrel roll. Nervous, Adam looked to Chester who glanced across, nodded and then dipped his right shoulder to move away from Adam. Following Chester, Adam dropped his right shoulder and moved across in that direction. Chester was now looking at Adam before he dipped his left shoulder and drifted towards him. Adam copied and for each movement his confidence grew. Chester then moved himself below and slightly behind Adam and was looking up at him. He threw his shoulder down and forced his body to turn causing his wings to follow, thus performing a perfect barrel roll. Once he levelled out and regained his balance he looked back up to Adam.

"I can't!" he bellowed to Chester.

"You can, trust him!" Harry shouted. He was next to Adam now and had been watching the whole time.

"He is your protector, Primrose taught me as Chester will teach you." Harry was smiling and Adam was struggling to make him out through the black lenses.

"I can't see! The lenses are too dark" Adam called out.

Harry shouted across to him.

"Turn the wheel on the side of the goggles clockwise, they will change the colour of the lens."

Adam felt the brass frame on the side of the goggles for a wheel and turned it clockwise. The lenses changed to a sharp yellow causing the ground to clear up underneath them and Chester to return to his view. Adam took a deep breath and pushed his right shoulder to the ground causing his body to turn and the wings to follow. The ground became the sky as Adam felt his stomach turning and the sandwich he had earlier almost make a second viewing. As he continued to spin he pushed down with his left shoulder causing the wings to resist against the wind and level out. His stomach turned and he looked around trying to regain some form of balance orientation. He heard Harry laugh from above him before shouting.

"An impressive effort for a first go, now let's get to Yeolight before we're completely in the dark. They flew on towards the flame as it shone bright, illuminating the valleys and ridges around it. They were not far off when Adam saw the spot on the mountain where Harry pushed him onto the cloud. The path that they walked fed down into the valley and vanished into the darkness.

"I shall lead us in, follow my lead and copy as I do. Chester will do his thing so don't worry about him for now." Harry drifted forward and headed directly for the tower and the orange glow of the village. As they circled above, Adam saw three buildings feeding into the Tower. He recognised the hall with its large wooden doors at the gable end. Off behind the tower fed the longest building that Adam worked out to be where his room was. Finally, on the opposite side of the tower to the hall was the third building where Adam had met his grandmother. Designed with intricate gargoyles, statues of birds, and various flying machines, the tower looked as though it was the centre point to three ornately detailed Cathedrals. They spiralled around the tower and down towards the courtyard where they had landed the night before in the Nebula. In the centre of the cobbled courtyard there stood a long wooden ramp with a thin net spread horizontally across the raised end. Harry flew out into the valley and took in a large turn to face the ramp so as to line himself up. He pulled his head and shoulders back on the wings causing him to slow before gliding up the ramp and running on the wooden panels. He came to a complete stop just before the net and immediately looked to the skies for Adam who was now over the valley making approach. As he lowered towards the ground he saw Harry now off the ramp and waiting on the cobble courtyard for him.

"Lean back! Bring your legs down and start running before you hit the ramp!" Adam pushed out his chest forcing the wings to slow and turn vertical but instead of slowing, he felt the wings catch the wind and start to lift him off the ground. He pushed his chest out further, fighting against the wind and his legs dropped to beneath him. He looked down and saw the ramp immediately below him.

"Start running!" Screamed Harry, but it was too late, Adam's feet stumbled as he tried to meet the speed of the ground that was hurtling along underneath him. Tumbling forwards he tripped and fell face first into the netting at the top of the ramp. Harry let out a burst of laughter before running up the ramp, his wings safely tucked away, before fishing him out of the net and to his feet. Chester was now running up the ramp to Adam, his face showing nothing but happiness as he saw that Adam was ok.

"No one ever gets it on the first try!" he said smiling as he hoisted Adam to his feet. "Come; let's get off this ramp before they move it for the next landing"

Adam pulled his now wonky goggles from his face and ran his fingers through his dishevelled hair. He looked at Harry and smiled.

"So it wasn't as per the textbooks?" They laughed as they made their way off the ramp and towards the door where Adam had collected his Sciaths that morning. It was dark now and the lanterns were lit masking the twinkling stars from view. Adams wings were still out and each thin metal feather flapping as he walked.

"Pull the clip again to release the catch and your Sciaths will return." Harry pointed to the brass handle now swinging loose from when he pulled it earlier. Adam took it in his hand and gave it a swift tug. He felt the black box click as the wings shot back into place and the handle recoiled back to the leather pouch. Adam fastened the popper and walked with Harry towards the entrance. His heart was racing and his stomach turning with elation as they entered the hall. There were a few people sat around drinking Hunchers Brew as the fire roared and crackled, filling the hall with a warming glow and fierce heat. Benedict was sat with Ruairi at a table deep in conversation. Harry turned to Adam,

"Chuck all your kit in you room, mate. I'll get the brews." Adam walked off down the corridor with Chester in tow. He had a skip in his walk and his head was filled with the events of the day. How majestic and elegant the cloud was as they scaled its precarious, fluffy ledges and ridges. The grippilos and their thin bodies, and how they bowed when they met him. The wings, the 'leap of faith', and the barrel roll. He couldn't contain his excitement and was desperate to tell Benedict all about the adventures in his day. He opened the door to his room, threw down his kit, and tossed his goggles and gloves onto his bed before locking his door and walking at speed back to the hall. The door to the hall was ajar and Adam slowed himself down to appear cool, calm and collected before re-entering. He saw Harry, Ruairi and Benedict sat at the table. The conversation look serious and Harry's face was filled with shock. Adam felt the joy leave his stomach and fear take its place. As he walked through the door he saw them look over to him before Ruairi stood with Benedict and made their way down to the main corridor for the offices. He wondered why they wouldn't stay to talk with him. Had he done something wrong? Did Harry tell them about the cloud and him being unable to control his thoughts? Would he be sent home? He walked over to the table where Harry was sat. There were four mugs sat on the table, of which two were empty.

"Adam!" Harry stood, almost startled to see him there. "Take a seat, here, I got you a drink."

He slid one of the frothy mugs over to him as Adam sat down.

"Is everything Ok Harry? Have I done something wrong?" Adam struggled to hide the worry in his voice as Harry looked from the table to engage with Adam. Chester let out a shallow whimper as Primrose ventured over to touch noses and sit down next to him.

"No, it's….it's not you." Harry stuttered and then picked up his mug before placing it back down and leaning forward to whisper to Adam. His eyes had turned from the glazed look he had only moments before to being bright with colour and life.

"It's the Trill," Harry spoke softly. "They have attacked Torringsdour!"

Adam's heart stopped for a moment as his head thought of only one thing.

Etty!

Eleven

Adam sat in his chair and tried to allow the news to sink in. Torringsdour? How? He looked to Harry for answers.

"Was anyone hurt? Why did they attack?" Harry was deep in thought as Adam dragged him from it.

"I don't know mate. Ruairi and Benedict just said to be careful and to ask you to go through to see them. They need to speak with you in private. Here, I'll take you there." Harry leapt from his seat and shook himself down before turning to Adam.

"Thank you," answered Adam as he pushed his chair backwards along the flagstone floor, allowing himself enough room to stand. They walked under the tower and towards the corridor which held the office where he met his grandmother. Marching down the corridor they passed several flickering lanterns and aged portraits before arriving at a thick wooden door. Harry placed his hand on Adam's shoulder and looked him in the eye.

"Good luck, see you for dinner?"

"Sure!" Adam was nervous and took a long breath before turning to the door and giving it a loud knock.

"Come in!" Adam recognised Ruairi's voice as he turned the heavy iron handle, pushing the door allowing the heat of the fire to warm his face.

"Thank you Harry," called Ruairi as Harry turned and made his way alone back to the hall. Adam closed the door and looked into the room. Ruairi was sat in one of the winged leather chairs facing the door with Dietrich sat proudly next to him as Benedict stood by the fire with Henrik sleeping at his feet, curled in a ball.

"Sit Adam, I gather that Harry told you about Torringsdour?"

Adam wandered over to the empty winged chair and sat down. Chester took his place on his right and looked up to him with a concerned face before resting his head on Adam's knee. Adam looked towards Benedict who was now watching him intently. He looked different, his face was not filled with the glee that it normally was but was grave and serious.

"The Trill have made a deliberate attack on Torringsdour, the Home of the Watchers. We believe that they were trying to capture The Ophy's daughter, Etty."

Adam's eyes grew wide as the news came to him.

"Is she ok? Did they get to her?" His voice was raised and filled with fear.

"No, unfortunately for them, The Ophy was there. Etty has been moved to a safe location for now. We believe that they are trying to gain momentum to throw the Order in to chaos. There have been rumours that the Commander is back and is looking to destroy the heirs to the Order."

"Destroy the heirs to the Order?" Adam's face was now cast with a frown as he attempted to process what he had been told.

"But Etty isn't an Heir, she is just..."

"She has been selected to replace the Bee when she turns sixteen. That is why she has been moved to Torringsdour ahead of time, prior to her sixteenth day of birth in preparation for the ceremony." Benedict interrupted Adam.

"We are unsure if the Trill are aware of your presence here but we felt the need to make you conscious of the full situation and to warn you." Ruairi continued.

"Warn me of what?" Adam was now starting to worry; he was the next flight! Were the Trill going to come after him too?

Ruairi leaned forward in his chair and spoke softly.

"The Commander is the head of the Trill. He was the Guardian who captured your Father and since that day he hasn't been seen nor heard of. His return signifies a drive within the Trill to seek out the heirs and seize control of the Order."

His Father? Adam felt the adrenaline surge through his body as he learned more about the disappearance of this man that was his hero as a boy.

"You must be honest with us Adam, has there been any strange goings-on since you arrived here. Anything that would signify that the Trill know you are here."

Adam sat back in his chair as he cast his mind back over the past few days.

"Well there was one thing." Benedict and Ruairi exchanged glances before looking to Adam. "On my first night here there was a pin badge on my pillow."

Benedict moved from the fireplace to stand next to Ruairi's chair as Henrik raised his head, watching them all for a moment before scratching his ear and returning to sleep.

"It was of a winged serpent, upright, looking down. The same as what Lafayette wore on the Steam Paddler, and the one you described that day I met you Benedict."

Benedict stood with his hands on his hips as Ruairi maintained his gaze.

"Why didn't you mention anything before?" asked Benedict.

"I just forgot, it's been a lot over the past few days, I'm sorry." Adam felt ashamed that he didn't say anything to Harry or Benedict as he fiddled with Chester's ear nervously.

"It's ok." Ruairi spoke softly and offered Adam a reassuring smile.

"We know now and that's what's important. Adam, I need you to keep this conversation and the pin a secret. Tell no one. Someone knows who you are and we need to find out whom. If they know that we know then they may go into hiding. Promise me you will tell no one."

Adam looked down at Chester as he thought about the burden that had been placed on him.

"Not even Harry, I'm sorry mate but we need to keep it to as few people as possible." Benedict crouched down next to Adam as he placed his hand on Chester's head. Adam knew instantly that Benedict was in his head, reading his thoughts. He smiled before releasing an accepting sigh.

"Ok, I promise." As the words left his mouth a broad smile grew on Benedict's face and Ruairi sat back in his chair.

"Brilliant! Now let's get some dinner. I don't know about you but I am famished!" Benedict sprung to his feet and looked down to Ruairi who was shaking his head in dismay at him.

"Ok, Benedict, let's go, and Adam, I want to hear all about your day." Henrik stood and stretched before ruffling his wings and following Dietrich to the door. They left the room and made their way to the hall where the saw Harry sat with three other men in blue jumpers. Harry saw them arrive into the hall and waved his hand in the air to ensure that they saw him. Ruairi made his way over to the table with Benedict and Adam following behind.

"Good Evening Gentlemen." Ruairi spoke deliberately to the men as they sat and looked up at him.

"Don't get up." Ruairi's voice was now stern as he looked around the table causing Harry and two of the men to leap to their feet apologising. The third man remained seated until eventually he rose to his feet, maintaining eye contact with Adam throughout. Adam noted that with his faded jumper and wrinkling skin, he had to be the eldest of the men at the table.

"My apologies Chief." The man spoke with venom on his tongue as he addressed Ruairi, who was now stood puffed and with a fixed gaze on him. He walked around the table and headed towards Adam. The man was tall and wore his long brown hair in a ponytail with a few wisps floating around his eyes and ears.

"A new Architect, I don't believe we have met." He offered out his hand to Adam.

"Adam this is Bergyl Dinglasar. Bergyl, this is Adam." Ruairi introduced them and Bergyl gave Adam's hand a tight squeeze as he glared into his eyes. Adam felt uncomfortable as Bergyl smirked knowing who he was before introductions were made.

"Harry has told me all about you, Adam. First days climb done? I take it you met the grippilos?"

His voice was cold and rhetorical. As he went to respond Bergyl interjected.

"Yes, I'm sure it's very interesting." He looked up and nonchalantly glanced around the hall, examining those seated around.

"Chief," He nodded to Ruairi and wandered off as the other two Architects followed. Adam felt a rage build up in him. Who was that man and why did he treat him so terribly? He watched him walk away as the two younger men scuttled behind. He felt his fists clench as Chester's hackles began to rise.

The four of them stood in the awkward space left behind before Benedict stepped forward.

"Well, that was awkward!" He smiled before grabbing a seat and looking around the room for an attendant.

"Come Ruairi, sit" Benedict encouraged them all to sit and join him at the table as an attendant arrived to take their order.

"Four Hunchers Brews please."

"Who was that guy?" Adam looked to Benedict as he sat in his chair. Henrik jumped into his lap and wagged his tail before a chuckling Benedict placed him onto the floor. Harry sat down keeping one hand on Primrose as Ruairi took his place and placed his hands across his lap. As they sat there it was Ruairi who spoke first.

"That was Bergyl Dinglasar. He and I joined the Order around the same time. Despite several attempts to become a Chief, he has never passed the selection board or the tests that would qualify him."

Adam grew in curiosity as Ruairi spoke softly to them. There were tests? Who sat on this board? Ruairi continued,

"He remains bitter to this day that he is not of Chief status and as such has created this structure of the ideal Order. He believes that the Architects are above the Watchers and Guardians. He also believes that those new into the Order must earn their place and become subservient until they have completed enough time to warrant a voice that is heard. This is however, not the Flights plan for the Order as she, and we all believe, we serve the balance and in turn, each other."

Adam smiled as he thought of his grandmother. He thought about how she was in charge of such a monumental entity and yet he had memories of her general tomfoolery and creative disasters. He recalled a time of her slipping on the ice rink that they had made by pouring water on the drive from Grandpa's hose the night before a big freeze. She fell so hard that she swore she had broken her hip. Adam would laugh and roll around in the snow unable to contain himself as the moment of her slip played back in his mind. He gave a wide smile as Benedict started to chuckle. Adam looked at him as Benedict met his eyes and gave a wink before tapping his temple.

An attendant arrived and placed four mugs on the table. A second attendant followed carrying a large tray filled with small plates of steaming vegetables and a succulent variety of freshly carved meats.

"Aha! Dinner!" Benedict was excited to see such a spread as he sat forward in his chair.

"Harold, how was today?" Benedict was filled with joy and lifted the mood of everyone sat around the table. Adam sat and watched as the conversation turned to his first day and what he had achieved. Harry spoke of how Adam climbed well and what they would attempt tomorrow. Adam sat there watching the table come alive as the conversation took the path of humour and frivolity, his mind drifted. He thought about his mother and her becoming the next Flight, about Etty and how she escaped from Torringsdour. Where was she? Was she ok? Who was Bergyl, and why did he have such disdain for him? As Ruairi spoke directly to Harry, Benedict seized the opportunity to lean across to Adam and hand him the winged serpent pin that Adam saw him wearing on the very first day they met. Adam frowned and looked up at Benedict as the pin rested in the palm of his hand.

"Keep it moving in your hand. Your brain will focus on the action therefore blocking your mind from revealing itself. It's the basic way to keep your thoughts to yourself." Benedict was smiling and his words were warming. Adam turned the pin in his hand allowing his fingers to caress the detailed metal work. He looked around the table and felt a comfort as he saw himself surrounded by friends, a new family of which his grandmother was the head of. His head dropped back down to his hands as he watched the serpent flicker with the orange light from the fire. It was after they finished the main course when Ruairi stood up and addressed the table looking at each of them in turn.

"I must retire for the evening, Gentlemen, goodnight." As he walked away from the table Adam saw him make his way back towards the tower and the heavy door they left from.

"Does Ruairi live down there?" He asked Benedict and Harry.

Harry looked over to where Ruairi had gone as the door was now drawing to a close.

"No, those are study chambers. Ruairi is the Chief here, the second-in-command to the Flight. He has work to do aside from Cloud Architecture. He has to write to all the other Chiefs in the other Outposts" Harry said as he turned back to the table.

"It's not all cloud clambering, Adam." Benedict smiled and leaned forward to devour the last of the meats that remained on the

105

table. Adam smiled at the three of them sat in the warmth of the fire as two attendants promptly appeared at the table and cleared away all the dishes before leaving nothing but three full brown mugs brimming with Hunchers Brew. Adam pondered over what Harry had said about the outposts. He imagined small villages with a single burning tower, a community of Architects sitting around a small table talking of the day's adventures. He thought about the mountaineers that he imagined as a child, on their way to the summit, chatting about the day's adventure and future obstacles that they may encounter.

"Outposts?" Adam was overwhelmed by curiosity and questioned further causing Harry to smile before picking up his drink and taking a sip.

"Yes, once you've completed your training here, you then get assigned to an outpost. There are many all over for all of those in the Order"

Adam's heart raced with the thrill of the possibility of traveling the world, building the clouds.

"The best go to the most demanding of environments, Ruairi was in the rainforest for five years."

Adam's eyes grew wide with intrigue as Harry continued.

"I heard he did a stint in the Frozen Islands. That's a lonely job and a tough one, turning water to different types of snow and ice!" Benedict's voice was now that of wonder and awe as he spoke of the travels of Ruairi.

The hall was now emptying and the fire was burning low. Harry looked around before finishing his drink and then looking over to Benedict.

"Gentlemen, I shall bid you a good evening." He stood, nodded to both of them and walked towards the corridor that led to the bedroom. Primrose rose from her place at the fire, stretched and followed him through the door.

"Come on mate, I think we should retire as well." Benedict stood and brushed himself down before looking over to Henrik who looked up and over to him. As Adam stood, Chester who had been sleeping at his feet stretched and shook himself off before looking up at

106

Adam. As they walked over to the door leading to their chambers Adam offered the pin badge back to Benedict.

"Thank you for that. Sorry for bothering you with my thoughts." Adam felt peculiar saying those words as he realised that they were his thoughts, exclusive to his head. A feeling of irritation fell over him as he considered that it was Benedict who was intruding on his thoughts. Before he could finish his thought process that would inevitably result in him getting worked up into a rage, Benedict placed his hand on Adam's shoulder.

"Keep it. Here, follow me; I'd like to show you something." Benedict led the way down the corridor towards his room before unlocking the door and entering. Adam followed into the room that was in the same layout as his but instead of walking equipment, he saw cages and nets scattered across the floor. A cane, topped with a silver dragon head, rested against the bed, Adam recognised the cane as the very same that Charlie carried when he met him in London. A black cloak hung over the door of the wardrobe that was steaming at the edges and along the red thread seams.

"Come in, close the door." Benedict was at his bedside table rifling through the drawers as Henrik took his place on the bed. Adam closed the door and Chester sat against it as a wedge to keep it shut. Adam stepped over the thin wire cages and noticed how they were all broken in some way. Some had doors buckled with hinges sheered, others with the wire pulled apart. Adam's mind raced as to what could cause damage to these miniature prisons and why Benedict would have them in his room.

"Here!" Benedict had found what he was searching for and closed the drawer before turning to Adam. He held in his hands a small brown book with embossed gold writing on the front. It was the book that Cella had given him. Why did Benedict have it? Had he been in Adam's room? Was he the one that placed the pin on his bed that night? Was he in the Trill? Adam felt his stomach sink as he thought about how he was trapped, he had nowhere to go. He edged towards the door as Chester now moved from the door to stand in-between him and Benedict.

"Relax Adam; this is the handbook for the Order of the Quill. This is my copy; I haven't been in your room. Come, sit." His voice was reassuring yet tinged with exasperation as he looked across at Adam. He sat down on the bed and patted the spot next to him signalling Adam to join him. As Adam sat on the edge of the bed Benedict looked at him with a fierce look on his face.

"I've brought you here to kill you Adam!" His voice was deep and aggressive as he placed his hand on Adams arm giving it a tight squeeze. Adam looked to the door as he planned his escape route, the room grew darker as the lights began to dim and the oil burners' flames reduced. Adam considered his options as his breathing increased and the adrenaline surged through his veins. The window was closed and he was at an extreme height so he had to make a run for the door if he wanted to have a chance of getting away. Chester was now snarling at Benedict whose grip on Adam's arm was starting to soften. Adam turned to see him smiling before breaking out into a roaring laugh, releasing his arm and slapping him on the back.

"Adam, you need to stop worrying, I am here to protect you, and I am not going to kill you! I am your Guardian." Adam felt the room grow brighter, his pulse and breathing returned to normal as Benedict placed the book in his lap.

"This is the Handbook that tells you all you need know about the Order and the creatures within it. The heir is assigned a Guardian who is there to protect them until they are ready to assume their rightful position in the Order."

Benedict stood and walked over to the window before turning and looking at Adam.

"I am connected to you until you release me back to the Order. Don't ask how but I can hear more of your thoughts than any other Guardian because of the role that I have been given. Don't worry though, as the Royal Guardian, I will remain loyal and discreet. It's why I was chosen."

Adam looked down at the book and felt the soft leather in his hands. The book was more beaten and worn than the copy that he had been given.

"I have a copy of this. I was given it in London." Adam looked up to Benedict who was now distracted and inspecting one of the crates that covered the floor.

108

"Great, well give it a read sometime and some things may become clear…or not." He smiled and placed the crate down before walking over to a bowl on the floor, scooping it up and disappearing into the bathroom. Moments later he returned with it brimming with water as he placed it down next to Chester who immediately started drinking. Adam watched as he lapped up the cool water. He could see the relief it brought him after a hard days climbing and Adam felt a pang of guilt for not bringing him water sooner.

"Don't feel bad mate. There is plenty of water in the hall. He just decided to stay with you. It's my fault for not keeping mine topped up."

As Chester drank the water he froze before raising his head and releasing a snarl.

"What is it?" Adam asked Chester as he started to look around the room. His hackles were raised and he started to sniff around the doorways and skirting boards. Henrik raised his head as his hackles became raised as well. Benedict looked at them both before walking over to the corner of the bed and picking up the cane.

"Adam, go to the bathroom." Benedict had his Cheltiagh in his hand as he placed his thumb on the edge. Adam saw the carvings starting to glow red as he looked at Chester who was now stood next to him. Suddenly there was a tapping noise from the window. Adam looked over and glaring through the small panes of glass were a pair of large green eyes that were stark against the black sky.

Twelve

Adam stood as he knew immediately who it was at the window.

"Benedict! Open the window and let him in."

Benedict looked over to Adam before rushing to the window and heaving it up. As the wooden frame groaned and squeaked, the small body crawled underneath and into the room.

"Mr Crumbleton! How did you get here?" Adam offered out his hands as the shivering pixie floated across the room towards him. As he landed on his hands, Adam saw how his body had turned a shade of blue and that he was carrying a folded piece of paper. Mr Crumbleton stood and took a look around the room before handing over the paper and fluttering his wings to move over to Chester. He landed on him and nestled into the fur on his back in the space between his wings as Chester looked over to Adam with a bemused look on his face.

"Well, this is interesting, an Architect with a Pixie."

Benedict closed the window, returned his cane to the end of the bed and walked over to Henrik who was now curiously sniffing the wisps of hair at the tips of Mr Crumbleton's ears as he nested in the black fur of Chester.

"That's Mr Crumbleton, last time I saw him was at the port in Reddington." Adam looked at the dark yellow paper in his hands. It was delicately made and rough with a dark red wax seal keeping it closed. Adam rubbed his thumb over the embossed wax Bee imprint as he thought of Etty and how she would have written the letter using a candle to seal it.

"Adam," Benedict interrupted his thoughts with a gentle hand on his shoulder.

"I think you should get to bed. We need to conceal Mr Crumbleton, and if he came to this window then others may follow. Go to your room and get to bed." Adam nodded in agreement and stood from the bed. Chester walked delicately so as not to disturb, a now sleeping Mr Crumbleton on his back. When they got to the door

Benedict called out to him. Adam turned to see him holding up his copy of the Order of the Quill.

"Don't forget about this book." Benedict was now waving the leather bound book as the lettering shimmered.

"I won't. Thank you Benedict." Adam turned to the cool corridor and made his way back to his room. He turned the brass key in the lock and cautiously opened the door, being sure to keep Chester and Mr Crumbleton out of view. As Adam poked his head around the door, he saw that the bed was still pristinely made and all of his belongings that he had dumped earlier were still strewn across the floor. The oil burners were at a low flicker and the dark wooden panelled walls made the room look warm and inviting. Adam stepped in and ushered Chester in quickly before closing the door and locking it behind him. Once in the room he scooped Mr Crumbleton off Chester's back and placed him on the bed. As he drew the curtains around the bed to a close Chester jumped onto the bed and curled up into a ball. The cool sheets made Mr Crumbleton sit up and look at Adam blinking and bleary eyed. As he rubbed his eyes with the back of his hand his empty mouth chewed over and he rubbed his tummy.

"Food!" Adam remembered how much Etty fed him and that he had made the journey from Torringsdour. He grabbed his canvas bag and jumped on the bed drawing the curtains behind him. Crossed legged he pulled the rucksack into him, unbuckling it and pulling open the drawstrings to remove a shiny green apple. He handed it to Mr Crumbleton who stumbled back before dropping it on the bed. The apple stood as tall as him as he looked it up and down with disdain before diving head first into the rucksack and pulling out two hands filled with the sweet mint cake that was in the packed lunch. He stuffed both handfuls into his mouth before smiling at Adam with cake smothering his lips and pointy teeth as he clambered back to the bag. Adam smiled back before turning his attention to the letter Mr Crumbleton had given him. He pulled the letter apart as the wax clung to the brown paper causing it to crumple releasing a waft of perfume from the paper as he unfolded it. The writing was intricate and detailed as Adam assumed she must have written it from quill and ink. That seemed to be the only form of writing tools here and

111

Adam imagined her scribbling away in the candle light as she dipped the nib in the ink pot.

My dearest Architect,

I hope you are ok and made it to your destination ok? I'm sorry I am being vague but I think there are people who are trying to source your location and I would feel desperately unhappy if I were to find out it had come from this letter. Durward and I are ok, we made it here but it was a scary journey. I do miss you terribly and I simply had to write to you to make sure that you are well and safe. Father tells me that the Trill Commander is back and is intent on finding you, you can't trust anyone Architect. How is Chester? You must remember to inspect his wings daily; his feathers can break and so will need to be removed so that new ones can grow through. He trusts you so won't put up a fuss, just remember to praise him for reassurance. I hope that we will meet again soon. Keep safe.

Always,

Your Watcher

Adam's stomach fluttered as he reread the letter again and again. She missed him but did she know how much he missed her. He looked down to the bed and saw Mr Crumbleton flat on his back giving out a little snore. His hands were sticky and covered with the cake as he lay with a large protruding belly. Adam looked into the rucksack and saw the remnants of what Mr Crumbleton had devoured and as he removed the brown paper bag, crumbs littered the bed.

"There was a large piece of cake in there!" Adam whispered so as not to wake the resting pixie before sneaking out of the curtained bed and making his way across to the desk leaving the scraps of cake on the bed. When he got to the desk he sat down, placed the letter from Etty flat before grabbing a sheet of yellow paper and plucking the quill from his holder. Adam dipped the nib into the ink and stared at the blank canvas. What would he write? He couldn't confess his

112

feelings, nor reveal his location or indeed what he had been up to, for fear of the letter being intercepted. The nib hovered over the blank page before Adam placed it back onto its holder. He picked up the letter from Etty and sat back in the chair. The oil burners were low and the letter looked inviting and mysterious as he felt the paper between his thumbs and fingers. Sitting upright and looking over to the bed Adam felt the surge of adrenaline in an idea. He stood and walked over to the bed drawing back the curtains to reveal a now loudly snoring pixie and black winged dog who were both flat on their backs. Adam inspected Chester's wings that were now spread wide covering the entire bed. Each feather was precisely aligned and placed with perfection as Adam ran his hand gently across them. Chester stirred, releasing a groan before sneezing and then returning to his dream causing his legs to run frantically. Adam saw that as Chester moved his legs, one feather was not moving in line with the others. He moved his face closer to get a better look in the dim light as the feather looked to be hooked on to the wing by the other feathers and not attached to the wing itself. Pinching at the tip, he pulled sharply at the loose feather as it came free from the wing. Chester remained at a casual running pace in his dream before toppling over and lying on his side bringing his wing in and tucking it alongside his body. Adam stood with the loose feather in his hand and smiled as he thought that this would be the best gift to send Etty, a symbol of his receipt of her letter, a symbol that he had read it, a symbol that he was ok. He clambered onto the bed, moving the bag on to the floor as he lay down, resting his head on the pillow. He lay there in the bed with a fat pixie, a dreaming dog, a letter from Etty and a grey tipped feather.

Adam awoke to a loud knocking at his bedroom door. He sat up on the bed to Chester standing alert with his head through the curtains. Mr Crumbleton was now laid on his side, asleep as Adam climbed off the bed and walked towards the door.

"Adam? You awake mate?" It was Harry. Adam cleared his throat before answering.

"Yes, hold on." He reached into his pockets and fished out the brass key to unlock the door. As the key turned the heavy lock Adam opened the door just a slither, peering out into the corridor.

"Indecent I see? Well breakfast is ready bud, come down when you're dressed. I'll see you in there?"

"Sure, I'll just grab a shower and I'll head down." Adam closed the door and looked around the room. Chester was now drinking from the bowl of water and Mr Crumbleton had poked his head through a gap in the curtain.

"I'm going to shower, Mr Crumbleton. Feel free to finish what is left in the packed lunch. I'll fetch you some water." Adam picked up his rucksack and pulled out the remainder of his lunch from the day before, placing it on the desk. Mr Crumbleton fluttered his wings and drifted over to the desk, picking up the biscuits and taking a large bite. Adam looked around the room for something to put water in before he could take a shower as Mr Crumbleton flew ahead of him to the bathroom. Adam followed observing as he allowed his sticky hands to dangle down beneath him. He watched as the pixie drifted over to the sink landing on the edge and walking over to the golden tap. Knowing not to intervene, Adam stood back as Mr Crumbleton hugged the tap and struggled with all his might to turn on the water, turning his face red in the process. Suddenly water burst out of the tap and into the sink causing Mr Crumbleton to look up to Adam with a look of pride and glee spread across his sticky face. He jumped down into the sink and stood under the water, washing himself. Adam chuckled as the pixie was having a shower all of his own. Feeling awkward watching the pixie shower, Adam headed back into the bedroom to tidy up his belongings and ready himself for the days walking ahead. He drew back the curtains and collected them up around the four posts before lifting the rucksack onto the bed. Pouring out the contents, Adam inspected each item and then placed it back into the rucksack. Doing up the straps he returned to the room and picked up the Sciaths placing them next to the rucksack. Once the bags were packed, Adam pulled some clean clothes from the drawers, placed them on the back of the chair and made his way to the bathroom to be met with Mr Crumbleton stood on the edge of the sink with a white flannel around his waist. Adam smiled and walked over to the towel rail grabbing one of the larger towels and turning to the shower. Mr Crumbleton looked around the room and then fluttered off into the bedroom, leaving Adam to shower. Once finished, Adam got dressed and picked up all his things for the day. As he collected his stick from the door he turned to take one last look at the room to ensure he had everything only to be met by Mr Crumbleton stood, arms folded looking at him with the flannel now folded onto the bed. .

"Ok, climb in." Adam knelt down and removed his rucksack, unbuckling the flap and pulling open the drawstring. Mr Crumbleton's frown turned into a smile as he fluttered across to the bag. Once in, Adam left the drawstring undone, the flap unbuckled and the bag on the floor as he made his way over to the bed. He plucked the feather from the pillow and walked back to the bag. He offered it to the flap of the bag as a small hand reached out, took it from Adam's fingers and returned inside, with the feather. Adam smiled, gently placed the rucksack on, collected his Sciaths, and made his way to the hall, ensuring that he locked his bedroom door behind him. In the hall sat Benedict and Harry at a round table filled with the same delights as the day before. Adam walked over to them as Chester wandered off to the kitchen. When he got to the table he placed his bag down next to him, lifted a pastry from the table and placed it into the rucksack. Harry gave him a confused look before Benedict spoke to Adam.

"Think you need more than the packed lunch they give you here?" Benedict winked at him before stuffing his face with a spoonful of cereal.

"Yeah, I don't blame you, smart thinking mate." Harry smiled and leaned across the table, collecting a variety of pastries before wrapping them in a napkin and placing them into his rucksack.

"Thank you. What's on the agenda for today Harry?" Adam looked at him before sneaking a smile at Benedict.

"Today you'll work with the grippilos, and we'll cover splitting clouds, cloud traversing and hopefully we'll touch on cloud transition."

Adam's eyes grew wide with excitement. There was so much that he was going to learn and this was only the tip of the iceberg. They sat there and finished their breakfast before standing, collecting their kit and making their way towards the exit to start the climb.

"I shall leave you here gentlemen. I need to speak with Ruairi, safe climbing." Benedict waved them off and walked towards the study chambers.

"Come on mate. We have a lot to do today." Harry handed Adam a packed lunch. As he took the brown bag he noticed that Harry was quieter than normal and failed to look him in the eye. Unnerved Adam wondered where Chester had got to as he appeared at the door licking his lips with Primrose shortly behind. They were now in the preparation area where Adam collected his Sciaths the day before. As Harry placed on his rucksack, Adam knelt down and pulled the flap open to place in his packed lunch and to reveal Mr Crumbleton eating the last of the pastry given to him only moments ago. Harry was sorting his kit and preparing himself as Adam spoke softly to Mr Crumbleton.

"Are you coming with me today Mr Crumbleton, or are you departing this morning?" Mr Crumbleton stood up and crawled out of the bag dragging the feather with him. Adam watched as he ran over to the pegs and took refuge under a long cloak hanging off the wall. Buckling up his bag, Adam grabbed his Sciaths and his rucksack before looking at Harry and nodding to signal that he was ready. Adam felt nervous about departing Yeolight that day. Would Mr Crumbleton get away ok? Would Etty get his message? He watched as Harry glanced down to his Cheltiagh and turned to walk up the hill along the path as Primrose spread out her wings to fly off down the valley before soaring up into the clouds.

"Let's do this bud!" Harry called back as Adam looked down to Chester and then back up to Harry who was now a considerable distance away. They ran up the hill and made their way to catch up with him. The day was overcast and there was a chill on the wind as they walked through the snow covered path and up to the top. They walked in silence as Adam and Chester glanced around the murky valley. The fog was now sinking and the air around them was thick and heavy. His mind was filled with thoughts of what would happen that day and what he would learn as he rhythmically placed one foot in front of the other.

116

"We're here now bud." Harry turned to Adam as they reached the top of the mountain. As Adam looked around he saw a figure sat on the floor looking off into the mist. He focused his eyes as Chester came between him and the figure. Adam's stomach sank and he felt his fingers clench the stick in his hand as the mist cleared and he realised that the man sat down was Bergyl Dinglasar. Adam looked to Harry who was now stood with Primrose at the top.

"Good Morning Bergyl. Jumping on the morning cloud?"

Bergyl looked over to Harry and a smile came across his face.

"Good Morning Architect! No, I heard there was a problem with the grippilos. The Chief asked me to come up before sunrise to check on them."

A confused frown was now cast across Adam's face as he looked around the mountain wondering why Ruairi would send him up here, and if he sent him up here at all. Harry nodded to Bergyl and then looked over to Adam, walking over to Adam and placing his hand on his shoulder

"Come on mate, let's get on this one."

They walked to the edge of the mountain, the same way that they had done before. Harry spun the wheel in the Cheltiagh and the cloud started to thicken into a milky white. Adam was nervous and felt unsure, could he trust Harry? Why didn't Ruairi and Benedict want Adam to tell him anything? Harry led the way and stepped off the ledge vanishing into the cloud. Adam stood on the edge and looked down to Chester who was now alert and at his right side.

"See you on the Cloud." Adam spoke softly to Chester who winked before jumping off the edge and spreading his wing wide, disappearing into the mist. Adam took a deep breath, closed his eyes and lifted his leg to step onto the drifting surface. As he leaned his body weight forward, Bergyl spoke.

"Mr Dempsey, Good Luck!" His voice was cold and unwelcoming as Adam turned to look at him before the cloud took him away. The mist covered what Adam could see but he swore he saw a smirk from Bergyl as he rose to his feet. The wind picked up and the cloud moved away from the mountain as Adam realised, he was now alone.

Thirteen

"Harry?" Adam called out into the mist as he looked around for any traces of Harry. The cloud was thick and the only noise that he could hear was the wind as it howled through the cloud. Adam started to climb and see if he could find Harry in the daylight. As he clambered up the cloud he felt the chill of the vapour drift over his fingers. It was colder than normal and he felt dread wash over him as he reached up to heave himself up towards the clearing. As he climbed higher and higher Adam saw the cloud get brighter and whiter as the sun's rays started to pierce through. Eventually he crawled on all fours into the bright light to be met by Chester licking his face and Harry with Primrose looking over him.

"You alright mate? You look freaked?" Harry bent over to help Adam to his feet. Adam thought about the coolness of the cloud and the words Bergyl said to him before disappearing. He wondered if he had made it on to the cloud with them and was it him who made the cloud feel different.

"I'm ok, thank you." As Adam stood, he felt a tugging on his jumper.

"Stand still bud, I am snagged on your jumper." Adam saw that Harry's gloves were hooked on the shoulder threads of his jumper.

"Hold on, I'll get my pliers." Harry reached into his pocket to pull out a multi-tool. Placing both hands on his shoulder he pulled apart the tool to reveal a pair of shiny metal pliers cutting the connection between them, Adam became free of Harry.

"I pulled the threads mate. Sorry." Harry was now patting the spot where he had torn the jumper and gave it a rub before stepping back and placing his multi-tool back into his pocket.

"When we get back we'll get it exchanged. I'll send a request to Cella to get a new one sent out to you."

"Thank you Harry." Adam felt relieved that Harry had it all sorted and figured out. Even though he was a few years older than Adam he was already permitted to be a mentor. He watched as Harry knelt down to stroke Primrose before looking to Adam and standing again.

"This way mate." Harry turned and made his way off up towards a prominent clearing.

As they crested the hill Adam saw a gathering of grippilos stood waiting ahead of him.

"What are they doing?" Adam asked Harry as he stood next to him watching over the plateau of cloud.

"They are waiting for their Architect. Grab your Cheltiagh."

Adam fished into his pocket and pulled out the cross, holding it tight in his hand. Chester took his place at his right side as Harry stood next to him and spoke softly.

"Turn the wheel and think about the cloud growing, billowing, and moving."

Adam took a deep breath and spun the wheel watching as the engravings glowed a brilliant blue. He thought about the fluffy balls he would watch as a child as they sailed across the skies, and the towering beasts of clouds that sat like huge whipped egg whites on the stark blue back ground.

"Look!" Harry's voice was filled with delight as Adam opened his eyes and gasped in wonder. The grippilos were now kneeling with their hands flat on the floor as the mist beneath them rose into a thick white cloud that surrounded them.

"What are they doing?" Adam asked

"They are building the cloud you are thinking of. Using the water beneath them they are drawing it from the earth and turning it in to vapour." Adam watched as the cloud thickened and grew.

"How do I make it stop?" Adam was growing nervous as the cloud became a part of the mother cloud and was multiplying in size.

"By stopping the wheel, just loosen your hand and the connection will be lost." Adam did so and the wheel fell to a rhythmic lull inside the cross as the engravings returned to their original dull colour. The grippilos stood in the fog and looked over to Adam for their next command.

"Come on mate, let's get further up." Harry looked over his shoulder and carried on up the cloud. Adam looked back at the grippilos who were now stood in a circle looking at each other. They looked as though they were having a conversation and discussing his performance. Before Adam turned to follow Harry he saw one of the grippilos turn to look at him and then walk off into the cloud, disappearing as the mist gathered around him. Chester nudged Adam reminding him to catch up with Harry. As Adam approached him he was climbing fast and with a determination to reach the top. They climbed for a few more hours before Harry stopped and sat on the edge of a ledge that jutted out into the open.

"Sit mate. We'll have lunch now." Adam perched next to Harry as Chester sat proudly next to him.

They sat and watched the clouds around them slowly move on the wind with them.

"Harry?"

"Yes mate,"

"Are there Architects on each one of those clouds?"

Harry smiled before releasing a chuckle and taking a large bite of his sandwich.

"That's part of cloud splitting and transition that we are going to cover in a bit mate." Adam thought about how you get from each cloud. Would you fly on the cloud or use the Sciaths?

"You know, we have a game that we play as Architects. You want to try?" Harry interrupted Adam's thoughts.

"Yes!" The excitement burst out of Adam as he looked over to him.

"Cool," Harry was smiling and met Adam's wide-eyed gaze. "Take your Cheltiagh and look at that cloud over there." Adam placed his Cheltiagh in his hand and looked at the cloud Harry pointed to.

"Now spin the wheel and think of anything. I dunno, maybe a crocodile."

Adam spun the wheel and took a deep breath before thinking of the long, abrasive beast. As his mind thought about the nature channels he would watch of the reptiles hiding in the water before lunging out to snap and capture their prey.

"See, Look what you've made."

As Adam looked out onto the horizon he saw the cloud that he was looking at before now changed into the rough shape of the very crocodile that he was thinking of.

120

"That's awesome, but how...?" Adam felt a rush of adrenaline surge through his veins as he slowly saw the crocodile become misshapen and revert back into the round swollen shape it had before.

"You can create whatever you want in your mind; the only issue is that it's forbidden by the Chief."

Adam smiled and thought of the all the creatures that he and his Father would spot in the sky on a warm summers evening. They would keep a list and the one with the most would win. Adam always won at this game. Despite his Father's hard line of teaching the value of an earned win, he would let him have this.

"Why is it forbidden?" Adam's mind was puzzled as to why this would be banned. It was just harmless fun. His thoughts churned over as he tried to determine the worst possible scenario for making a shape from a cloud.

"It's because we keep the balance. This is not a game and we must strive to ensure that life survives and the balance is maintained. Keep this one a secret, ok?" Harry winked at Adam before standing up and looking around at the cloud and then the surrounding valley they were passing over. Adam was nodding at what Harry had just said, and how it made perfect sense to him and a wave of guilt washed over him. He stood and leaned his head back to gawk at the cloud that was now starting to topple over them.

"Right, let's go and split this cloud! Grab your goggles, you may need them." Harry adjusted his rucksack, placed his goggles on his head, before tearing the last of his sandwich in two and throwing it down for Chester and Primrose. They walked for a few more hours up the cloud as the ground beneath them was getting further and further away. The wide valleys turned into small wrinkles and vast lakes into insignificant puddles. As they walked, Adam could feel the wind grow in strength as it tried to pull him from the cloud with long gusts. Ahead, Harry stopped in his tracks standing motionless.

"Is everything ok Harry?" Adam was growing in concern as the wind whistled past his ears. His voice was carried off into the void as he looked around and shouted to Harry.

"Harry!" Adam was now forced to kneel as the wind became more intense and was pushing him off his feet. Harry slowly turned and looked at Adam with wide eyes.

"What are you doing mate? What are you thinking of?" Harry sounded fearful and there was dread in his voice. The wind was now beating down on Adam as the cloud slowly started to turn a deep grey.

"I'm not doing anything!" Chester was now stood by Adam leaning into him as the wind swooped down and punched a gaping hole into the cloud. Suddenly there was a flash of light followed immediately by a rush of noise that cracked through the air knocking Adam off his feet.

"It's a storm cloud! Adam, jump!" Harry pointed off the cloud into the open space now closing between the gathering clouds. Like magnets, the clouds were now joining together to form one huge storm cloud.

"Go, before the gaps close! Head back to Yeolight, I'll handle this!" Adam looked to Chester who was now looking around the cloud for possible launch points. Rather than a timid pup, Adam saw a brave animal seeking out a way to protect his master. Another flash filled the now black cloud as the same roaring crack followed causing Adam's ears to ring. He ran and jumped off the thundering mass that was starting to cover the blue sky above him, trapping them in a cocoon of black cloud. As he pulled the brass handle the Sciaths snapped into place and lifted him up on the rushing winds. Adam pulled down his goggles over his eyes and began his fight against the turbulence as he pushed his shoulders down forcing the wind to push down on the metal feathers of the Sciaths sending him hurtling to the ground like a bullet from a gun. Adam strained his neck up to see if he could capture a glance at Harry before he broke through the canopy and entered the curtain of torrential rain underneath. He saw a tiny figure high up on a steep precipice with a small winged creature next to him, it was Harry and Primrose. Adam saw the bright blue glow of the Cheltiagh emanate from his hand as he stood firm facing the cloud, battling its vicious winds. Chester barked at Adam causing him to refocus as he entered a large clump of black mist causing him to level off and glide with the wind. Adam looked around and saw the silhouette of Chester on his right, gliding in the cloud as it was illuminated from the flashes of lightning as they grew faster and faster. Fear and adrenaline now coursed through his body as he twisted and turned through the mist, trying to find his way out. The sound of the thunder shook Adam to his core and he felt his brain rattle as it echoed around his head. Another flash, then another, and another, then a yelp as Chester fell limp and tumbled out of the cloud and into the rain below.

"Chester!" Adam screamed out to him as he watched the black cloud consume Chester's lifeless silhouette leaving him alone in the cold dark abyss of the storm cloud. In desperation he dipped his right shoulder into space that Chester was once flying and pressed down to follow the path where Chester fell. He was approaching the bottom of the storm cloud now and the rain stabbed at his face like a thousand relentless needles. Adam searched the mist calling out to Chester as the rippling thunder washed away his panicked screams. It was then that beneath Adam he saw an orange glow gliding in the darkness. He wiped away the hair that was now soaked and sticking to his goggles. The warm orange glow grew brighter as Adam saw the beating of wings climbing higher and higher. He stared as a thought crashed into his mind; it was the Trill! He panicked as he pushed on his right shoulder trying to steer away from the creature, his mind panicked with the thoughts of getting to Yeolight as quick as possible to warn the others. The beast emerged from the dark shadows of the cloud and was now in full view of Adam as he witnessed its tremendous wings fight against the driving winds causing them to hiss and sizzle in the rain. Adam struggled to make out the shape of the creature but recognised what appeared to be the head of an eagle and the body of a large four legged animal. Its wings were larger than the length of the body and were dripping large molten globs of a heavy red liquid with each beat of its wings. It was smothered in the smelted liquid as it pursued Adam and continued to gain on him. With fear growing inside of him, Adam raced and searched for Chester dipping and soaring in a vain attempt to lose this glowing beast. Suddenly, there came another flash and Adam lost control of his body as it seized and stretched in blistering agony. His mouth stretched open to shriek, but no sound appeared as a scorching sensation roared through him, boiling his blood. It found its way to his head that was now a bubbling cauldron of agony and fear as his fist clenched and legs locked. His right eye burned fiercely before he lost all vision and fell limp, plummeting to the earth. In the last moments before he passed out, he felt the warmth of the creature approaching him. The rough talons carefully wrapped around his flaccid body before beating its wings and climbing up into the darkness of the storm cloud. Adam's body was screaming in agony as he tried to reach out to release himself from the clutches of the beasts grip. In that moment his head filled with a multitude of thoughts; thoughts of his grandmother and her playful smile, Chester and the moments before he was hit with the lightning, his mother and her loving embrace on days when he felt scared and alone, his Father and his powerful strength, Benedict and his friendship, Harry and his guidance. As the light began to fade from his mind he dwelled on thoughts of Etty; her gentle touch, her sweet perfume, her letter to him. His thoughts grew blurry and weak as he clung onto a final thought; *I do miss you terribly...*

"I miss you more." He mumbled in his head before the darkness finally claimed him.

■■

"Adam?"

The voice echoed around his ears as his head pounded in agony.

"Adam?"

Again the voice came, but this time it sounded familiar to him. Adam opened his mouth to speak but his throat was dry and he croaked before coughing uncontrollably. He felt a straw touch his lips as he sucked, the water trickled down to soothe his throat, quelling his cough. He tried to open his eyes but they were bandaged shut along with his hands. He panicked, and started pulling frantically at the bandages. Why was his face covered up? What had happened? Why couldn't he see? His wrists were restrained as he felt a pair of hands firmly holding them down.

"Calm down mate, relax. It's ok. Relax." The voice was assertive and warming as Adam felt the grip lessen. His breathing was fast and his mind racing as once again he thought of Etty before slipping into the darkness once more.

■■■

The light was beaming through the window as Adam opened his eyes to inspect the room he was resting in. It was his bedroom in his grandmother's house. He lay there watching the dust drifting and floating on the air. He remembered the morning that he left that room, the last look he took before running down the stairs and out the door towards the train station. The thoughts of the journey that he had taken, the people he had met, all these memories brought a smile to Adam's face as he lay there in the comfort of his room. He tried to sit up as a wincing pain shot through his head and right eye. He yelped as he held his hand to his eye, suddenly he heard the murmur of talking coming from downstairs stopped. Adam sat on the edge of the bed as he heard footsteps slowly coming up the stairs. His heart rate started to rise causing his head to pulsate and ache as he looked around the room for something to defend himself with. Picking up his camera tripod he grasped it firmly in his hand before listening out for the footsteps as they grew louder. The pain in his head became more intense as the footsteps reached the top of the stairs and came to a stop. Adam looked up at the door as the adrenaline surged through his body only to be met with a familiar face smiling at him.

"Hello mate." It was Benedict. He smiled as he dropped the tripod onto the floor and rushed over to the door to hug him. Benedict's arms wrapped around him and Adam immediately felt safe knowing that he was there with him. As he stood back his head throbbed, causing him to place his hand over his eye. Adam looked around the room as he searched for Chester but he couldn't be found.

"Benedict, where is Chester?" As the words left his mouth Adam saw a nose poke into the room from around the end of the bed, it was Chester. His heart pumped with excitement and joy as he saw Chester coyly walk from around the end of the bed and into view. Adam felt confused as to why Chester was acting in such a bizarre manner. He crouched down to the floor, feeling his body creak and twinge with each movement as he called Chester over to him.

"What's up with him?" Adam was confused.

"He feels like he has failed you as he was unable to protect you from the storm. He has been told that this is not the case but he won't have it. It has to come from you."

Adam smiled and welcomed Chester in his arms as he nuzzled his nose under Adam's chin. Adam looked back and stared into Chester's eyes before wrapping his arms around him and whispering in his ear.

"It's not your fault, I am sorry I didn't protect you." Chester looked up at Adam and licked his face before wagging his tail and jumping on Adam's bed to rest. Adam saw a large pink scar spread across his back from where his wings were to his tail.

"Was that…"

"From where the lightning struck? Yes." Adam walked over to Chester and ran his fingers gently over the raised skin as Chester winced.

"I am sorry pal. It'll get better in time."

Benedict walked over to Adam and placed his hand on his shoulder.

"He wasn't the only one that had a mark left from the lightning." Adam looked at Benedict with a confused look.

"I don't understand. What…what do you mean?" Adam rubbed his hand across his face as his head began to throb again. Benedict walked him over to the mirror on his desk before picking it up and handing it to him. Looking into the mirror, he saw the reason behind his sore head and eye.

"Someone had tampered with the copper insulation in your jumper, so when the lightning struck it was unable to find a clear path away and so spread to the nearest metal it could find; the metal in your goggles. The heat generated from the lightning caused the yellow dye in the goggles to react with the blue pigmentation in your eye and, well, as you can see, left a mark."

Adam drew closer to the mirror to inspect his now, green eye.

"Come, there are some people downstairs that want to see you." Benedict removed his hand from his shoulder and made his way to the door.

Fourteen

Adam placed down the mirror and found a folded set of clothes placed on his desk chair. Quickly changing, he collected a pair of shoes and followed Benedict out of the room. As he left he looked back to see Chester raise his head.

"You can stay here if you want bud." Adam spoke to Chester who got up from the bed and hopped down to follow Adam.

"I don't think he'll be leaving you anytime soon mate." Benedict was now looking at Chester as he rubbed his head into Adam's limp hand. He crouched down and gently draped his arms around him before drawing back and looking into his blue eyes

"Ok, come on then."

They walked down the stairs together towards the kitchen. With each step Adam took he could feel the pounding in his head growing more intense.

"I'll get you a water mate, that'll help with the pain." As they reached the bottom of the stairs they entered the kitchen where Adam was met with a room of familiar faces.

"Granny!" Adam smiled as he raced across the room to fall into her embrace. She was in less elegant clothing than before and stood in her classic black turtleneck top complete with pearl earrings, jeans and high heels. Her hair was, as always, in pristine condition and her red lips glimmered in the daylight. Her eyes filled with tears as she held her hands on his face and looked into his eyes causing her bottom lip to quiver.

"My dearest Adam, I am so glad you are ok." Adam returned for one final hug before looking around the room.

"Durward, Wilbur, Charlie." They all stood in the tiny kitchen and watched as Adam beamed with elation before shaking hands with each of them.

"How did you all get here?"

"We came when we heard the news. I told Benedict to bring you here after your initial treatment at Yeolight." Charlie spoke softly and deliberately to Adam who was now looking to Benedict as he placed a glass of cool water down on the breakfast bar next to him

"But the Trill...that beast in the sky...it took me...I felt its claws." Adam stumbled as his mind ran wild trying to piece together what happened that day. Benedict lunged forward and caught him before placing his arm around his waist to keep him steady.

"Here, sit down mate." Benedict pulled out the breakfast bar stool and sat Adam down on it before moving the glass of water in front of him. Charlie stepped forward.

"The Beast was an Igneus"

"Derek, I call him Derek." Benedict interrupted and smiled at Charlie who, albeit vexed at the idea of naming the creatures, couldn't help but return the smile due to the ridiculousness of the name of such a majestic beast.

"He lives within the mountains, only appearing when summoned." Adam looked at the glass of water before raising his head and looking to them both.

"So the liquid dripping from its wings...?"

"Lava" said Benedict pouring himself a glass of water. Adam's eyes grew wide as he turned the glass on the table allowing his memory to play over the moment when the Igneus floated beneath him.

"We suspected there would be an attack but we didn't know when or where it would happen." Benedict looked at how Adam was staring at the glass and turning it gently, clearly mulling over his thoughts.

"I see Benedict has taught you well." Adam looked up confused as he glanced over to Durward before gaining eye contact with Benedict who was tapping his temple. Adam smiled before picking up the glass and taking a large mouthful of water. Durward now stepped forward and looked at Adam.

"We need to move you to a location more secure than here and we haven't much time."

"What about Harry? Is he ok?" Adam looked around the room as each one of them avoided his gaze before finally his grandmother stepped forward.

"He wasn't found." Adam felt a lump form in his throat as his grandmother took his hand in hers. Chester was now standing on his hind legs as he rested his head on Adam's arm. His eyes welled and he took another large mouthful of water, forcing it down to wash away the lump, his friend, his mentor, taken by the cloud, by the Trill. He felt immeasurably sad as the prospect of not climbing the clouds with Harry became a stark reality to him. She let go of him and returned to her space in the kitchen.

"How long have I been asleep?" Adam wanted answers. He wanted to know why no one rescued Harry, why wasn't anyone looking for him. He felt a rage simmer in his belly as he looked around the room at the vacant faces that met his.

"A week mate, and we searched for him but we couldn't find him." Benedict spoke with compassion as he stroked Chester's head.

"We don't know who started the storm, or where the lightning came from..."

"But it was made te kill ye!" Wilbur interrupted Charlie as his thick Scottish accent cut through the room. Adam looked over to him and noticed that his hair was still and unkempt as the day he met him. He had a look of determination and focus as he glanced around the room before resettling his gaze back onto Adam.

"Storm clouds can be made and unmade. Architects can decide if a cloud is a Storm Cloud or not. *That* was no accident. All we do know is that the Trill knows you are alive and were in Yeolight. Someone told them." He looked at Adam before turning to his grandmother.

"We need to go now. We've been here too long!" He spoke quieter and directly to her and she reluctantly nodded and turned to Adam.

"We can't all be together for too long. We need to get you to safety. You will travel with Durward as Benedict goes on ahead. I will travel to Reddington with Charlie and Wilbur to send a message to the Order about this attack. We need to consider the ramifications of this and what action we take."

"We could strike back...!" Wilbur pressured her.

"No!" Wilbur recoiled from her snapping and cutting him off as he silently apologised

"We maintain the balance! We are not warriors, soldiers or some militia force; we are the Order of the Quill! Regardless, I said that we will not discuss this here!" Adam saw a different side to his grandmother, a side that he had yet to see. She was firm and strong and was not to be bullied or pressured into making a decision that she wasn't fully content in making.

"Taxi anyone?" Benedict broke the silence first as he smiled at Adam.

"Flight, Ophy, Durward, Wilbur, Adam?" He addressed them all and paused briefly before placing his hand on Adam's shoulder, giving him a wink and offering them all an overzealous bow as he reversed out of the room. Charlie chuckled before shaking his head in dismay and then looking to his grandmother.

"Prat!"

"I'm just around the corner you know!" Shouted the voice in the corridor before the room erupted into laughter.

"Get out of here!" shouted Charlie before he heard the front door close and the room return to silence.

"We need to make a move." Durward spoke again as he moved over to the door.

"Adam, meet me in the basement." He looked at Adam before departing the kitchen leaving Adam with just Charlie, Wilbur and his grandmother. Wilbur turned to his grandmother.

"We should go too. I shall be outside. We need to get the train to the departure site; Arfigerous said he would meet us there."

"I agree with Wilbur. Elizabeth, we should make haste." Charlie spoke with authority and urgency.

Wilbur and Charlie approached Adam; both shook his hand before wishing him a safe journey and leaving the room. Adam was now alone with his grandmother in the kitchen. With his head still pounding he stood and walked over to her. She placed her hands on his face again and reached up to kiss his forehead.

"You be careful now! Trust only those in this room that you saw today and I shall see you soon. I fear that the Trill are growing in strength so we must be prepared for the worst. I will do what I can but please be safe. Remember Adam, sometimes the greatest pain we have is the one we think we can't control."

130

Adam looked at her face that was now awash with fear and concern for him. He smiled before, pointing to his green eye.

"Try all they might, they can't kill me!" Adam spoke with defiance as he felt a swell of courage and hope bubble inside of him. He took comfort in the knowledge that he had survived one attack but next time he would be alert and ready, he would be waiting. He stood straight with his shoulders back and wished her a farewell before walking out of the kitchen and down towards the door that led to the basement. He left his Granny alone surrounded but the quaint mismatched crockery and in that final moment he saw he for what she really was; a scared girl looking for hope. It dawned on Adam what she had done to protect him from the Trill, the decisions she had made. She was a watcher first; she saw the love and beauty in all around her and was now having to make choices that meant others could get hurt. Like a bruised flower she wrapped her arms around her and as she looked around the room a single tear escaped and trickled down her cheek.

The door that led down to the basement was open and the light at the bottom of the stairwell softly cast its yellow glow over the worn wooden floorboards. Adam walked down the stairs and as he reached the bottom, was met by an enormous copper squid resting on its side. He ventured into the dimly lit room as his jaw dropped marvelling at the size and intricate design of the machine. He wandered round and inspected the brown contraption as Durward worked furiously from an open panel at the back. Suddenly the engine started to chug and splutter into life as white steam poured from the tiny chimney at the rear of its cylindrical copper hull. Durward slammed down the panel, wiped his hands on an old rag and climbed into the cab of the machine. A smart line of clumpy rivets forged the brown metal panels together creating a patchwork of copper bending and curving itself around the engine as it simmered into a gentle growl. From the front of the machine spouted multiple arms fixed with wires and cogs that were connected to large cogs and pistons beneath a large window where Durward was now sat working away. Each arm had a shallow digging bucket at its end that were scratched and covered with a thin layer of mud at the blade.

131

"Climb in!" Durward shouted, tapping on the window as Adam looked down to Chester who cautiously sniffed the muddy tracks resting either side of the giant metal squid. The engine churned before releasing a loud bang forcing Chester to jump and bark out in retaliation. Adam chuckled as he walked to the rear of the machine and placed his hand up to the copper, placing it over the cylindrical shape as the heat of the engine warmed his skin. Durward leaned across the seats of the cab to open the heavy door before shouting out.

"Put Chester at your feet, we need to go now!" Adam walked down to the door and stood on the tracks, clambering into the metal squid and taking his place on the cherry red leather seat. Chester jumped in after him and curled into a ball at his feet as Adam secured his seat belt.

"What is this?" Adam asked Durward as the door slammed shut muffling the noise of the engine leaving them in a vibrating cocoon.

"This is the safest way to get you out of here and out of harm's way." Durward smiled revealing his brown teeth before looking down at the panel of levers and lights blinking on a brass dashboard in front of him. He pulled and pushed at the levers as a set of lights flicked on and shone down into a tunnel ahead of them. The pistons and cogs churned slowly getting faster and faster whilst the arms lunged out to claw at the air before recoiling back toward the cab and then lunging again. Suddenly Adam realised that this metallic squid was going to dig its way out. His heart pumped faster as he held his now throbbing eye, looking to Durward who pulled more levers causing the vibrations to increase before placing his hand on one large lever at his feet.

"Onward!" He said with a chuckle before releasing the lever to the floor jolting the machine forward as the tracks kicked into action. As they entered the tunnel, Durward fiddled with the dials and levers before sitting back and watching the monster claw its way through the mud creating a fresh path towards a new destination.

Adam looked around as the darkness of the tunnel consumed the machine they were travelling in. He looked down to Chester but

132

struggled to see him in the darkness as he breathed gently on Adam's feet.

"Are we headed to Yeolight?" Adam asked as Durward stared forward, watching the mechanical arms plough into the dirt ahead.

"No Adam, we are headed to some place very different, safer."

"What about my things in Yeolight? What about my Cheltiagh?" Adam grew worried as he thought of his belongings in his room, his clothes, his rucksack, his letter from Etty.

"They are being moved, Cella saw to that. From what I hear however, Benedict insisted that he pack this for you. He collected it when the Matron in Yeolight was tending to your wounds." Durward leaned behind him and picked up Adam's rucksack. It was the rucksack that he packed when he left his grandmother's to meet Durward for the first time. His heart skipped as he held the bag in his arms. Chester woke and sat upright, placing his paws on Adam's knees. Opening the bag Adam saw his Camera, hooded jumper and a fresh set of clothes carefully folded. He plunged his hand to the bottom and felt a sharp object stab his finger. Recoiling sharply he reinvestigated with care, pulling out a blackened, misshaped pin badge. It was the Quill pin badge he was wearing the day he was struck by lightning. Adam ran his thumb over the buckled metal as he thought of the last moment that he saw Harry. He felt a surge of pride in having known someone so courageous to protect him before sacrificing himself to fight the force creating the cloud. Placing the badge down on the dashboard, he reached back into the bag before quietly praying that Benedict had packed the one item that he was desperately searching for. His searching hand ran over his Cheltiagh causing him to remove it from the bag and place it in his pocket. His hand continued to search the bag as he became more worried and frantic, realising that it wasn't in there. He looked up to Durward who was now holding a yellow folded piece of paper in his hand with a broad smile on his face.

"He asked me to hand deliver this though." Adam breathed a sigh of relief as Durward handed the yellow paper to him. He unfolded it gently to reveal the curved writing of Etty and in that moment he was filled with the hope of maybe seeing her again. Would she know where he was being moved to? Did Mr Crumbleton get his feather?

He held the letter in his hands as he placed the pin in the bag and put it back behind his seat.

"I didn't read it but I am no fool. She spoke about you the entire way to Torringsdour, quite smitten I would say." Durward smiled as he returned to the dials and levers leaving Adam to his thoughts. Smitten? His stomach turned as it filled with butterflies and his head began to spin. He sat there as the copper squid chipped away at the dirt ahead of them and the vibrations rocked him gently. Adam fought the fatigue that washed over him, he was tired and his head was muddled as his eyes grew heavy. Gripping the letter tightly between his fingers, he allowed the sleep to take him as he dreamt of the valour of Harry, the strength of his grandmother, but mostly he dreamt of Etty. Smitten! He smirked before slipping into a deep sleep.

■■

"Wake up Adam, we are here." Adam woke to his shoulder being shaken by Durward as he pulled on a lever causing the machine to incline and dig upwards. He felt himself being pushed back into his seat, Chester whimpered and jumped up onto his lap. With the letter firm in his hand, he held Chester tightly to his chest as the mechanical arms now broke through the final layer of soil allowing the light to break through blinding them both. Large clumps of turf battered the glass screen as Durward pushed and pulled the levers and dials in front of him. Breaking through the final layer the machine hauled itself onto the surface as Adam squinted, trying to look through the muddy window so as to identify where they were. The tracks came to a slow halt and Durward turned to Adam.

"Let's get out of this thing!" Durward switched the engine off before opening the door and jumping out onto the lush green grass.

Adam grabbed his bag from behind his seat before opening the door and jumping out into the crisp breeze. He looked around as Durward made his way over to a figure stood on the edge of the field. Stuffing the letter in his pocket he looked around and stared up at the smoking volcano that was jutting out on the skyline. The surrounding valley was green and lush with a broad range of flowers and wildlife buzzing around. Adam watched as the grass beneath his feet sprung back into place after each footstep he took. Mesmerised, he made his way over to where Durward was now stood chatting. Leaving the shadow of the machine he immediately spotted the huge lake filling the valley as the sun danced on its surface. It looked like he was in some picture book drawing as the clouds drifted across the sky like large balls of cotton.

"Good Afternoon Master Dempsey, I am Fiachra Princepitus, Chief Guardian here at Frackingshulme, home of the Guardians of the Order, and this is Babesne" Adam shook the hand that was offered to him and returned the compliments in kind. Fiachra Princepitus was tall and wore the same coachman's cape that Ruairi was wearing on the day he met him in Yeolight but this was in a brilliant red. Her lips were purse and her face long and stern but as she looked at Adam she met him with a warming smile. Proudly sat next to her was a grey winged hare. Its ears stretching high above its body as they turned from grey to black at the tip. It approached Chester and stretched its wings before bowing. Chester copied and the two then stood to touch noses. Behind her Adam saw a huge castle standing proud in the green valley

"Oh, that's where you'll be staying. Come lets head inside. I take it Benedict is with you?" She asked Durward.

"No Fia, he left before us to secure the route. Has he not arrived?" The warmth drained from her face as she looked at Durward with alarm.

"No, he has not. Quick, let us move inside." Her voice was urgent and she walked with purpose to the large grey building. As they got closer, Adam saw a moat that fed the lake on one side and filling up by a waterfall cascading off a moss covered cliff on the other. He marvelled at the natural engineering that would place an island large enough to build a castle next to a waterfall in such a manner.

"Not natural engineering Master Dempsey, Watchers and Architects decided that this place needed to look friendlier. I am not so sure I approve but any attempts to remove it would cause much distress to the Flight, after all it was her daughter that made it." Fia's voice was calmer and less urgent the closer that they got to the Castle drawbridge. Adam dwelled on her words, the flight's daughter, his mother, she made this? Adam thought about her standing at the

Castle with the Cheltiagh in her hand, commanding the pixies. He thought about how she would go out on adventures with the Order and build fields filled with brightly coloured flowers and slithering rivers.

"We must press on Master Dempsey, to my Office." They crossed over the drawbridge and into the open courtyard that was littered with people draped in green, blue and red outfits. Each one stopped to allow the Chief through or rose to their feet as she passed by. Some called out to Durward welcoming him to Frackingshulme. Adam felt immediately at home and watched as everyone went about their daily business. They exited the courtyard and went through a set of heavy wooden doors at the far end. They walked straight and into a corridor that was lit with oil burning lanterns. Portraits of men and women in red outfits lined the walls, each with a winged creature somewhere in the picture. Fia approached a door at the end of the corridor and walked straight into the room taking off her coat and hanging it on a coat stand that stood in the corner. Adam walked in after her and noticed that the room had a similar layout to the working chambers in Yeolight. Books lined the walls on the left and right of the room and at the end was a stain glass window of the Ophy Amphipteroto, with its wings spread wide. This time it was different, it was still lying down but rather than looking up its head was turned and it was looking into the room as its eyes were filled with fire and its face menacing. Fia placed herself behind the large oak desk that stood between the door and the window. She sat down in the large leather chair and offered Adam to sit in one of the two deep leather sofas that sat opposite the desk as Durward closed the door and took his place in the other.

"Tell me, what time did he leave. What route did he take?" Her voice was authoritative and she demanded their attention. Adam looked to Durward who sat with his legs crossed in a relaxed manner. His fingers were crossed as he sat there working out the timings of the day. He opened his mouth to speak and before the noise left his mouth there was a loud knock at the door.

136

Fifteen

"Yes!" Fia's voice bellowed as the knocking came again but this time it was louder. The handle slowly turned and the door creaked open to reveal a timid looking boy of comparable age to Adam standing in the doorway. Fia let out an exasperated sigh and rubbed her forehead before looking back up at the doorway.

"Yes Hubert?"

Hubert held his hands together and fiddled with a tissue in his fingers as he opened his mouth to speak before a figure jumped in and pushed him out the way. Durward sprung to his feet as Fia picked her Cheltiagh up from her desk and stood with her thumb hovering over the edge. Alert, Babesne stood next to her, teeth bared and ears back. Adam stood and drew his Cheltiagh from his pocket as Chester stood beside him with his hackles raised.

"Slackers!" The voice from the doorway was filled with excitement as a smiling Benedict came into view. Adam relaxed and smiled as Benedict walked into the room with Henrik by his side.

"Where have you been?" demanded Fia.

"They knew we were moving and were waiting Chief." Adam noticed how he was wearing the same black coat that was hanging on the wardrobe the night Mr Crumbleton delivered Etty's letter. It was again steaming at the edges as he held his cane in his hand and his Cheltiagh poked out of his pocket.

"Is there anything else Hubert? If not then close the door thank you" Fia addressed Hubert who was again standing at the door, this time he was dishevelled from the shove that Benedict had given him.

"N...N...No Chief, thank you." He was stuttering as the nerves got the better of him. He closed the door with a gentle click before Durward turned to Fia.

"Still having issues with the lad, Fia?"

"Warden, he is so fearful, I am not sure what to do with him. I would take him on myself but I grow in concern that it may only make it worse." She looked at Durward before sitting back down in her chair. Adam was now confused and looked at Benedict who was sporting a deep scratch across his cheek. His hair was a mess and there was a thin layer of black soot covering his face and hands. Chester stood to greet Henrik as they bowed and touched noses before returning to their respective owners.

"Guardians are the protectors of the Order Adam. We have no time to be afraid because the things we command feed off it. Remember what I said about the darkness?" Benedict spoke to Adam before laying his cane on a nearby reading table as he peeled off his fingerless gloves to reveal the clean hands underneath. Adam nodded and looked to Fia who was staring at Benedict.

"How many? Was it the Commander?"

Benedict nodded at the question and perched on the table as Adam felt his heart race at the thought of the Commander being out there. Benedict was very serious now and the joy and humour had vanished from his face. He was addressing the Chief and as such he was very professional and deliberate when speaking.

"Do they know about Master Dempsey?" Her voice remained authoritative and assertive throughout the questioning, as though she was interrogating Benedict to make an informed decision about what to do next.

"No, it was clear they were after someone else." Adam's eyes opened wide. Who were they after? Etty? Were they trying to kidnap her again? He took refuge in the knowledge that she was hidden somewhere safe and out of danger.

"And they don't know that you came here?" She asked before leaning back in her chair and placing her hands over her lap, interlinking her fingers.

"No Chief, I gave as good as I got and ensured that I was not followed."

"Right then, I need you to show Master Dempsey here to his living quarters." She stood and walked around the table to the same side as Adam and Durward. Addressing Adam she spoke softly looking into his eyes.

"Chief Architect Whisspe will arrive in the morning to continue your training. You need to be well rested. I have things to discuss with the Warden."

Adam thought about going back up into the clouds and felt a twang of fear rush through him. Questions filled his mind as he sat there processing what he had just been told. What if it's another storm cloud, what if he gets hit by lightning again? His palms grew sweaty as he rose from his seat and followed Benedict to the door.

As they walked through the door, Fia called out.

"Benedict? It's good to see you're ok, and Adam? You're in safe hands here. Try not to worry." Her face had softened and as she spoke Adam felt his nerves settle. Benedict offered a shallow bow before looking at Fia.

"Chief." He closed the door as it left them in the dimly lit corridor.

Standing alone in the corridor, Benedict threw his powerful arms around Adam, who was completely unprepared and released a groan as the air escaped from his lungs!

"Adam! I'm glad you made it; I always hated that blooming squid thing! It's the…the…arm things at the front! Such peculiar looking things!" his arms were now clawing at the air in front of him as he bared his teeth, gnashing away before breaking out into a broad smile!

"Come on mate, let's find your room and then grab a brew in the castle hall. I'll show you around later but first, I think you need some Hunchers inside of you!" Benedict slapped him on the shoulder before crouching down and scratching Chester behind the ears causing him to roll straight onto his back, spreading his wings wide filling the corridor. Henrik rubbed his head against Adams legs as he bent down to stroke the fur between his wings. They remained there in the dimly lit corridor outside of Fia's office as Adam watched Benedict now roll around on the floor with both the protectors, laughing as they tried to pin him down to lick his face.

"Enough now come on! Follow me." He rose to his feet and made his way down the corridor towards the courtyard. The light was bright as they entered the large, grey courtyard. Overhead grew a large white cloud as it filled the sky, causing Adam's heart to start beating heavily. He was reminded of the cloud that struck him and

Chester and that consumed Harry. He felt a gentle hand on his shoulder as Benedict looked with him into the sky at the rising cloud.

"That will be Wilbur. He only ever travels by cloud." Benedict chuckled and shook his head before walking off towards a large wooden door on the edge of the courtyard.

"What about the Sciaths?" Adam called out to him as he followed through the door and down a stone, spiral staircase into a long narrow corridor lined with dark wooden doors. They came to the first door before Benedict burst through into the room with a roaring laugh.

"Sciaths! I am not sure that they make a pair big enough for men like him!" he smiled before looking around the room and holding his arms wide with his palms facing up.

"Welcome, to the dungeons." Benedict grinned as he walked over to the window and pulled the curtains wide, allowing the light to shoot into every corner. The room was square and small with the bed pushed up against the wall underneath the window. There was a writing desk on the right with a wardrobe on the left and a square porcelain sink with gold taps in the corner. The sink rested on a metal frame as two maroon towels hung off the rail underneath. Adam turned to Benedict with confusion as Benedict smiled, knowing his question.

"The male showers are four doors down. Unlike Yeolight, things here are not as plush. Some believe that because we are Guardians we need to live in harsh conditions that will prepare us for the severity of our role. Less comfort keeps us focused." He walked over to the sink and looked back at Adam with a menacing grin,

"I believe it's because we need to hone our towel whipping skills to keep you Architects inline."

He spoke as he pulled a towel from the rail holding the corner in one hand before allowing it to hang and rotating his wrist like a merry-go-round. Flicking it out to Adam it made a loud cracking noise causing Adam to skip out of the way.

"Ooh, swish moves Architect. Let's see how quick you are with two." Benedict grabbed the second towel and was now flicking them both at him, one after the other. As Adam moved he felt the thrill of this game race through him. Like a boy he giggled with fear and exhilaration as Benedict made his way over to him, stepping over the cases of clothes and equipment that littered the floor, whipping as he went. Adam jumped on the bed and picked up a pillow before raising it above his head and bashing it into Benedict's smiling face. The force of the pillow struck Benedict hard and he stumbled back dropping one of the towels as he struggled to regain his balance.

"Oh, it's on now Architect!" Benedict lowered his gaze, maintaining eye contact he scooped the second towel off the floor and started flicking the towels faster. As the cracking grew louder, Chester dived in and took one of the towels in his mouth before tugging on it and placing himself between Benedict and Adam. Henrik lunged and grabbed the second towel in his mouth before they both beat their wings causing a gust that sent Benedict tumbling backwards again, this time he hit the wall and fell hard onto his bum. Henrik and Chester stood between them, panting as Benedict heaved himself to his feet.

"I shall let you have that win Architect, but next time you may not have your Cavalry!" He bent down and started to fold the towels before hanging them back over the rail underneath the sink. "And you...Judas!" Benedict pushed Henrik's nose causing his tail to wag and jump up into his arms, licking his face.

"Well I shall be practicing, Guardian!" Adam stood on the bed with his shoulders back and his hair now ruffled. He smiled wide and threw the pillow into the air, catching it with his other hand before looking back at Benedict and winking. Benedict now laughed loudly causing Adam to join in as they looked around the room. The laughter became contagious and louder as Adam realised that it had been years since he had a friend like him that could make him laugh about the most ridiculous of things.

"Let's get a brew, come on!"

They walked out of the room, closing the door behind them as Benedict tapped on the door opposite.

"This is my room, right across the corridor. Knock if you need anything, alright?" Benedict looked at Adam and he could tell that he meant it and that Adam could depend on him. They made their way up the stairs and back into the bright sunshine of the courtyard. As they crossed over, Adam looked to his left to the open gates that led out onto the drawbridge. Walking in was Wilbur with Dolly trotting along beside him. The noise in the courtyard simmered down to a low mumble as he entered the courtyard and approached Adam and Benedict. Dolly bowed to Chester as he returned the compliment before they touched noses. Wilbur offered his hand out to Benedict and then Adam shaking them firmly.

"Were they waiting for yoo?" he asked in his thick Scottish accent. Benedict looked Wilbur clear in the eye and met his scowl with a stern look.

"Yes, they knew. I saw three of them, one being the Commander." Wilbur nodded and rubbed his chin with his hand.

"Mmm, things are ainly going to get wurse before they get better. We must prepare." He nodded to Benedict, patted him on the arm before looking at Adam, winking and smirking. He walked off at a pace towards the corridor that led to Fia's office, not without shouting at a couple of young watchers who blocked his path as they planted flowers in the shallow troughs that lined the courtyard.

"He is a misery but when you get to know him, he's actually...no, he's still miserable." Benedict smiled and carried on walking towards the door across the courtyard. They entered a tall and ornate room that held several iron chandeliers hanging from the ceiling. In the centre of the hall stood a long oak table with benches along the sides and two large thrones at either end. Several groups of people sat around the table as it stretched off into the room. A fireplace crackled at the far end of the room as Adam strained his eyes to make out the two winged serpents carved into the stone mantelpiece.

"Grab a seat mate, I'll get the brews." Benedict pointed to an empty space around the table as he wandered off to get the drinks. As Adam sat down, he marvelled at the intricate carvings on the edge of the table; doves flew over trees and mountains as bees rested on flowers and built large honeycomb structures. Behind each carving of a cloud and in the shadow of every intricate tree there was a serpent, watching. It was hard to make out but Adam could tell that it had been deliberately placed in obscurity for each scene. As he looked down the table, he saw hands wrapped around warm brown mugs, quills writing on light brown paper before being delicately dunked into pots of ink, maps with hands passionately waving over them discussing routes and paths. The hall was a hive of conversation, learning and laughter. Adam watched as new Guardians undertook their training, Architects discussed cloud patterns and future developments with Watchers, and friends met to catch up. It was then that Adam saw it. His face fell clear of all emotion as he rose from his place at the table and walked towards the fireplace. He watched as he saw a pair of white hands resting further down the table holding a single black feather. It was long and turned grey at the tip. Adam felt time slow as he cautiously walked, watching the soft hands caress the vane of the feather, running it through their fingers, toying with it. The figure was wearing a hooded cloak as it sat in the hall carefully clutching the feather. He watched as a wisp of red hair fell down from the hood before being tucked back into the cloak. His stomach started doing cartwheels as he now stood behind the hooded figure watching the hands inspect the feather, almost like it was a memory to be nurtured and cared for. He opened his mouth to speak but the butterflies churned causing him to falter and begin to sweat. His palms became clammy as he wiped them on his jumper.

"Etty?" He whispered.

The figure now sat rigid as it placed the feather down on the table to remove the hood on the cloak. Her bright red hair was loosely plaited and ran over her shoulder tucking into the front of the cloak. She slowly turned to look at Adam as her green eyes met his. Realising who it was she burst from the table and into Adam's arms, holding him tight.

" My Architect!" she looked back at him staring into his eyes as hers filled with tears. She placed one of her warm hands on his face next to his green eye.

"I got your message." He said to her as he placed his arms around her. She smiled and let a tear run down her face before sniffing and wiping her eyes with her other hand.

"And I yours."

They returned to the end of the table where Benedict was now sat nursing three mugs of Hunchers Brew. He stood to greet them back with a beaming smile.

143

"So you found her then?" Adam looked down bashfully as Etty held his hand tightly in hers. They sat down together and looked coyly at each other before grinning and then drinking their Hunchers Brew. Adam felt a flutter in his stomach as he looked at Etty and watched her sip at the brown mug before placing it down on the table, licking her lips and combing the wisps of hair back behind her ear.

"Hello Etty, I am Benedict Baudier, Guardian to the Royal Heir, Guardian to the Flight."

"It is a pleasure to meet you Benedict Baudier, I am Etty Gravelio, daughter to Charlemagne Gravelio, selected to be the successor of the Bee."

They shook hands and smiled before giggling at the bizarreness of their introductions.

"So only a few days off now Etty, how is the training?"

"It's going ok thank you. Chief Watcher Malus Hortius was teaching me every day until I came here. Now I use my Father's copy of the Order to teach me until Cella gives me my own when I turn sixteen. I am not learning as quickly as it's not the same on my own but I hope soon to return to Torringsdour and see the enchanted wood once more. I look forward to watching the flowers bloom with the morning sun, and tease the Tribletts as they try to dance and skate on the smooth surface of the Green Lake." She released a giggle before looking at them both as they met her innocence and joy with confusion and misunderstanding.

"Tribletts?" Benedict shook his head as she questioned them, "Water folk? Well I shall show you both when we go."

She looked sternly at them before a smile returned to her face.

"I would disturb the water with my finger and watch as they would fall and get wet; very stressy little things they are. Chief Hortius would tell me off but I knew that she thought it was funny as well."

Adam looked to Benedict who raised his eyebrows before placing his mug to his lips.

They sat there and chatted for hours. Benedict would regale them in stories of Adam and his first few days in Yeolight, how he crashed on his first landing with his Sciaths, and how he mumbled in his

144

sleep about the grippilos in a boxing match with Adam being the Referee. They laughed and drank as the evening drew to a close.

"How do you know these things?" Adam eventually asked Benedict when there was a natural lull in the conversation.

"I am your Guardian Adam; I see everything that you do. It is my primary role to protect you. I was watching as you made the journey through Reddington to the Nebula, how you collected water from the cloud on your first day climbing with Harry, and how you fell from the sky that day. It was I who commanded Derek to catch you."

Adam felt a surge of joy knowing that there was someone there watching him, always making sure that he was ok. He looked around and realised that they were the only people left in the hall as it was now empty. The fire burned fiercely as it shimmered and illuminated the stone engravings above it. Adam now looked to the door that led to the courtyard and saw Wilbur walking though it and towards them. He was walking with purpose and determination as he arrived at where they were sat.

"Adam, I apologise if I'm ruinin yer Hunchers Brew. The Trill are moving and we need to continue your training. Grab your kit, we leave tonight."

Sixteen

Adam froze in his seat as the news hit him like a speeding bullet causing his brain to explode with thoughts. Tonight? Was he ready? What about Chester, would he be ok? Adam looked around the room as Etty placed her hand on his to steady his mind.

"Tonight?" He looked up to Wilbur who simply nodded as he maintained his gaze at him. Benedict stood from his place at the table and placed his hand on Adam's shoulder before speaking softly.

"I'll help you get your kit mate." Adam stood from his seat and followed Benedict to the door and out into the courtyard as they made their way over to the living quarters. The courtyard was lit with burning torches that rested on twisted iron mantles, bolted to the walls. Adam stopped and looked up as he marvelled at the multitude of stars that littered the black canvas sky. The Milky Way cut into the sky as it glowed majestically amongst the sparkling lights. Adam stood as he watched a single star shoot across the sky before vanishing into the darkness. He thought about the cloud he was about to make and climb and how dark it would be, his breathing rate increased and his heart began to beat faster. As he tried to calm his thoughts and remember that it was him in charge of the cloud, not the other way around and in that moment he felt a hand brush past his hand before connecting with his. Interlinking its fingers with his, he caught the scent of Etty's perfume on the air as she stood next to him staring at the stars.

"Sometimes the greatest pain we have is the one we think we can't control." She whispered to him, he frowned and looked down to her as she gazed at the night sky.

"Chief Watcher Elizabeth King told me those words when the Trill killed my mother."

"Elizabeth King, my grandmother? You met her before?" He held her hand in his, watching her green eyes glimmering in the torch light.

"You'll be great Architect." Adam felt the warmth of her confidence settle his mind as he looked to Benedict who was now stood by him, looking directly into his eyes.

"Don't worry, I'll be watching." They walked together as Wilbur called out to him.

"Adam, meet me on the south battlement." He winked and gave a reassuring smile before walking towards the working chambers, and disappearing into the darkness of the corridor.

Benedict held his arm, gaining his attention, before speaking softly to him.

"I'll take you." Benedict released his arm and walked towards the door that led to the stairwell. They walked together arriving at Adam's door. Etty burst forward and wrapped her arms around Adam before looking up into his eyes and whispering to him.

"Good luck Architect." She walked past him towards the door next to his. Fishing a key from her pocket, she unlocked the door, taking one last look at them both before entering. The door closed behind her as Benedict looked to Adam.

"Grab your stuff mate, I'll wait here." Adam walked into his room and rummaged through the cases that were on the floor. Inside was a new canvas bag with all new clothes and equipment. Adam assumed that the others were destroyed in the strike and so had been replaced. He found a blue Architects jumper with the dove stitched onto the chest, folded in one of the cases and held it up in front of him. Inspecting it, he reviewed the copper thread that was embedded in the fabric, it was intact and ran complete through the seam. Adam quickly grabbed the clothes he needed and got changed before stuffing the things he required into the rucksack. His stick was resting by the door as he looked down to Chester.

"Ready pal?" Chester gave him a wink before Adam walked to the door, picked up his stick and made his way into the corridor. Benedict was stood waiting with Henrik as Adam locked his room door and watched as Benedict reached into his pocket. He handed Adam a small metal object.

"Take this mate. It will replace your last one."

Adam unfurled his hand to reveal Benedict's Quill pin badge. He looked up at him before raising a smile.

This is the second badge that you've given me Benedict. You'll have none left at this rate."

Benedict frowned.

"Well give it back you ungrateful jerk." He lunged forward to swipe it out of his hand as Adam recoiled, closing his fist before bringing it to his chest.

"No, it's mine now!" Adam was now beaming with a smile as Benedict stood off balance.

"Well look after this one." He grabbed Adam and wrestled him into a headlock, ruffling his hair before allowing him to stand, laughing. They walked up the stairs and out into the courtyard before heading up a set of stone steps and onto the castle walls. At the top, Adam looked out at the moonlight as it shimmered off the lakes surface. He watched as the water began to ripple before a scaled head emerged, looked around then returning to the water, vanishing into the darkness. Benedict spoke without turning his head as he continued along the castle walls.

"Don't fear Adam it's an Oarfish. Anguill has lived in these waters since before Chief Princepitus was in training as a Guardian. I like to call him Slippy but the Chief has said that any reference to calling him that is banished and as such, I will be telling the newbies." Adam smiled as Benedict told his story of being in trouble with the Chief. They walked around the castle towards the waterfall and Adam cold feel the water vapour drift and settle on his face, causing drips to form and run into his mouth. Wilbur was stood in the moonlight with Dolly on the castle walls as they drew closer. He wasn't wearing a rucksack and his stick was half the size of Adams, reaching up to his waist.

"Good evening gentlemen." He nodded as they approached.

"Thank you for showing him the way Benedict. I can take it from here." Benedict nodded and turned to walk back down to the castle. Before he left he grabbed Adam by the arm and whispered in his ear.

"Breakfast is at eight, you'd better be up or I am waking you up with a pillow bashing to the face!" He looked Adam in the eyes before raising a smirk and walking off towards the dim orange glow of the courtyard.

"Come Adam, we have much to learn."

Adam removed his Cheltiagh from his pocket and looked to Wilbur.

"Feel this water in the air?" He held his hand out before rubbing his fingers together and looking back at Adam.

"Make a cloud fae it." He picked up his stick and folded his arms before resting against the castle walls looking at Adam. Glancing down to his Cheltiagh, Adam looked up to Wilbur, frowning. He was confused, what about the transfer point, the grippilos. Adam didn't understand what exactly was asked of him as he looked around for help or divine inspiration. With nothing to offer him an idea of what he was required to do, he looked back to Wilbur.

"How? I don't understand."

Wilbur pushed himself off the wall and walked quickly towards Adam.

"Spin the wheel and think of a cloud laddie!" Adam felt fear rising in him as Wilbur marched towards him with conviction. As he got to him he grabbed him by the scruff of his shoulder and dragged him closer to the watery mist.

"There is ney cloud without yoo. Ney grippilos, ney nothing! Now spin that wheel and think of a cloud!" Adam held the Cheltiagh in his hand and spun the wheel watching as the engravings glowed blue. He closed his eyes and thought of a brilliant white cloud drifting through the sky like a majestic whale as it allowed itself to be taken by the wind. Adam opened his eyes and looked to see the water falling from the waterfall as the droplets continued to gather on his face. Bewildered, he again looked to Wilbur for help.

"Tell me what you thought of. Let me guess, a huge cloud in the sky?" Adam nodded as Wilbur shook his head with disappointment.

"Don't think of a cloud up there! Think of a cloud down here!" He pointed to the pool of water churning from the waterfall as his voice became animated and alive. Adam spun the wheel again before closing his eyes and picturing the pool as it frothed and bubbled as the water clapped and crashed onto it. He thought about a white fog forming at the base of the fall and growing into a large blob of mist and water. Opening his eyes, he saw a layer of white cloud settling on top of the water, covering it and hiding the impact of the fall from above. Adam looked to Wilbur who was now smirking as he nodded encouragingly to him. Closing his eyes again, he imagined the cloud now lifting off the surface of the water to form a large blob of thick fog moving towards him.

"Great stuff! Just a wee bit bigger lad." Wilbur spoke with glee and encouragement as he stepped closer to him. Adam opened his eyes and saw the huge mist now filling the space in front of him as Wilbur patted him on the shoulder before climbing up onto the battlements and jumping off onto the marshmallow looking cloud, grunting as he landed. Adam's jaw dropped as Wilbur stood and waved his hand for Adam to follow after him. Adam clambered up onto the edge of the castle, took a deep breath and jumped. His heart dived into his mouth as he looked down to see the gap between the cloud and the Castle walls beneath him. The water of the moat reflected the cloud showing its bumpy bottom as it hovered in the air. Adam landed on the cool surface with his hands and knees before heaving himself to his feet to be met with Wilbur looking up into the stars. He had one leg raised on a mound as he rested his stick across with both hands held together.

"Take us up lad!"

Adam looked around as Chester was now taking flight from the castle wall and soaring high into the skies. He felt confusion and nerves fill his veins looking down at the Cheltiagh as it continued to spin and glow blue in his hand. He thought about Wilbur's words: *There is ney cloud without yoo.* He closed his eyes and thought about the cloud rising up high into the sky as the ground beneath them disappeared and vanished into the darkness. He opened his eyes and looked around to see the castle wall standing firm next to them. The waterfall was still creating its fine layer of water that was now soaking Adam's jumper. He looked to Wilbur who remained staring at the sky with his knee rested on the mound.

"I...I tried...but..." His voice trailed off as he shook his head and tried to form the words to explain to Wilbur that he couldn't do it.

"Listen to me carefully now laddie, cause I'll only say this once..." Wilbur was now turned to Adam as his Cheltiagh rested in his hand. He felt significantly out of his depth and missed the leisurely training of his time with Harry.

150

"Everything that lives in the sky is yours to command. Yoo are the clouds, the wind, the thunder and the lightning, yoo are the shadow, and yoo are the light. If ye can think it then it can be done. If yoo wanna raise this cloud into the skies..."

Wilbur raised his eyebrows at Adam before turning his gaze to the stars and resting his stick back on his leg as he returned to his original position.

"Now, take us up!" Adam looked around as he felt the cool wind of the waterfall gently blowing against his ears. He took a deep breath and as he was about to close his eyes Wilbur interrupted.

"And keep your damned eyes open! Wuid ye drive a car blindfolded?"

Adam now smiled as he stamped his feet into the cloud and looked up to the skies. He thought about how clouds slowly trudge along the blue canvas skies gently being carried on the wind. His eyes grew wide. It was the wind that he needed, not the cloud. Adam looked around as the flags pitched on each tower hung limp and lifeless atop their white poles. He watched as he thought of the wind running and playing with the heavy fabric. Like children playing with a large sheet on a washing line the flag would billow and jump with life before cascading and crashing to the ground dancing with the wind. Adam felt the wind chill his neck as the cloud started to move. At first it moved and strained like an elephant pulling a heavy carriage as Adam willed the wind to blow and gust around them. Adam felt the pressure of the breeze on his back as it displayed its strength to him. His mind came alive with thoughts of the cloud lifting and soaring. Without warning, it shot forward and lifted them high above the castle walls. Adam moved his feet forwards and backwards on the soft misty cloud as he felt his body dance in the wind. There was a fire in his belly as he raised his arms up and pointed to the skies wafting the cloud high to the stars. The ground was fading fast as it flew higher and higher. The burning torches resting in the courtyard melded into one single orange blur as Adam glanced down to view the lives that slept peacefully below him. Looking around he saw a clear dark sky with the moonlight bouncing off the mountains and lakes all around. He could now see the inside of the immense volcano as it sat proud, displaying its fierce and lava

151

filled throat. Steam spat from its bubbling crater like a simmering kettle moments before boiling. In the far distance there was a dull orange glow burning on the horizon, he looked to Wilbur as he slowed the cloud to stand still on the night sky.

"Where is that Wilbur?"

"That there is the sea town of Reddington, Headquarters to the Order of the Quill."

Adam shot his gaze back to the light as it burned gently on the horizon. He thought of his grandmother, working in Reddington, dishing out demands and instructions to those working in the Order. He smiled as the wind gently brushed on the back of his neck, he felt alive as he stood on the edge of the cloud watching the life below him carry on its normal business. Wilbur walked over to Adam and spoke abruptly to him.

"Now build up this cloud, split it in two, and send the other on its way to Reddington." Wilbur sat down on the cloud and pulled a short pipe from his pocket. Packing it with tobacco he struck a match and puffed on the mouthpiece as the space around his head filled with smoke. Adam spun the wheel of the Cheltiagh and looked down to the cloud beneath his feet. As his mind started to race he could see the cloud growing and filling the air around him. It made no noise as it spread out into the stars around them. Suddenly he saw a large mass of red floating on the horizon. He watched as it grew larger and faster as it moved towards them both. Adam felt his heart race as the mass of red split into small balls of burning fury, beating its wings slowly as it drew closer. Wilbur chuckled to himself drawing Adam's gaze before removing his pipe from his smoking lips.

"It's a flock of Igneus, that boy Benedict has sent them!" Adam turned to watch as the giant mass of molten lava swooped over them making Adam duck as the heat of their bodies wafted over their heads. Following them were two smaller creatures chasing in pursuit and Adam recognised them immediately as Dolly and Chester chasing the flock as they shot past. The cloud was now a thick blanket that spread across the sky shielding the beauty of the stars from the land dwellers below. Chester and Dolly broke free of the flock of Igneus and were now approaching the cloud causing the mist to build and swell as the beat their wings in landing. Chester ran to

Adam as he crouched down and opened his arms for him. Dolly curled into a ball next to Wilbur before tucking her wings away and closing her eyes. Adam stood and looked to Wilbur with a sense of pride as to what he had made. Wilbur acknowledged his gaze and spoke before Adam swelled with pride too much.

"Well done lad, now cut it in two. Call the grippilos." Adam looked alarmed, the grippilos?

"But how, we don't have any here."

Wilbur smiled and shook his head.

"They live in the clouds, part of it. Consider a seed, when you put it in the ground, is it complete with leaves, bark, branches and twigs? Or do you let it grow and watch as the parts that are meant to be, grow and blossom. A cloud is the same. Just because it isn't there when you first build it doesn't mean that something wont blossom from it. Call them."

Adam thought about the tall sluggish creatures slowly trudging through the clouds and making their way to the surface. He looked around and watched as the round lifeless faces poked through the vapour. They pulled themselves up on to the surface before rising from their knees to stand tall, towering over Adam as they looked around at the blanket that spread far and wide. He watched as they wandered towards each other forming a large group standing in the wind high above the ground. He remembered how he got them to grow the cloud before and so he allowed his mind to drift like the mass of cloud that he was standing on. He thought about the cloud tearing apart like a large ball of floury dough being torn by a pair of Baker's hands as it gets kneaded and pounded with powdered grainy fingers. Adam saw the grippilos standing in two lines across from each other. They leaned forwards to each other, placing palm on palm before pushing against their partner. They stepped forward and continued to push as Adam saw the mist starting to tear and part at one end. The ground beneath became visible as the grippilos pushed forming an archway of bodies over the void. Finally they let go of each other and watched. The cloud finish pulling itself apart as the two sections now drifted away from each other. Adam watched and his eyes opened wide as he saw Wilbur stand and drift away from him with the other half of the cloud. Alone he stood with a gaggle of grippilos and Chester for company as Wilbur bent down and dragged his stick through the cloud floor around him causing the section that he was standing on to fragment and drift towards him before removing his Cheltiagh from his pocket. The wind picked up as Wilbur spun the wheel and it started to glow blue before pushing him towards Adam. Arriving at Adam's cloud he stepped off the small fluff of cloud and walked over to him slapping him on the shoulder and smiling. Dolly appeared, landing next to him as Wilbur looked around at the two clouds now moving slowly apart as they lingered in the sky.

"Nay bad lad!" Wilbur removed his pipe and allowed the smoke to snake from his mouth as it danced off into the darkness. The bright moonlight illuminated the skies, making the second cloud look haunting as it loitered in the sky, hung there like a spacecraft floating in the abyss of space. Wilbur walked over to the edge of the cloud and looked down to the ground below.

"Alright, noo make that ane go to Reddington and rain and take this ane down. I think you've had enough fae one evening." Wilbur walked away from Adam, finding a spot to sit down and looked over to him, nodding for him to get on with it. Adam looked over at the second cloud as he saw the grippilos return to the mist below. He looked down to his Cheltiagh that was still glowing blue in his hand and looking at the cloud he took a deep breath before thinking about rain. The thought of rain came easy to him. He remembered how he and his dad would go out into the pouring rain to kick and splash in the puddles. His dad would always go out with a thin coat and get drenched whereas Adam would be dressed up with so many layers that he found it tough to wrap his arms around himself, his mother would always worry about him getting a cold or slipping over. He smiled as he remembered kicking the puddles at his dad who would laugh and jump out the way before launching in with both feet making the water splash him in the face. They would be out for hours as the rain ran off their noses and down their necks. After a while they would hear an aggressive tap at the window as his mother would haul them inside to remove the several layers from Adam before wrapping him in a towel. His Father would receive a stern telling off for allowing him to get so wet followed by a warning that '*should there be any early morning calls from an ill Adam then he was getting up in the night'.* His father would smile and look down at him to wink before going into the kitchen and sneaking him chocolate. Adam dwelled on the thoughts of his Father. He wondered where he would be, if they moved him regularly, is he still alive? He remembered the love that he felt from the man who would talk to him at whatever time in the night he would call, his patience, his humour, and his gentleness. His mind wandered towards the darkness of the loneliness of living without his mother and Father, the thought of never seeing them again. The abandonment he felt of his mother dying. The loneliness of the hospital waiting room as his grandmother cradled his head in her lap. The hurt and anguish that smothered him like a thick, black smoke, choking and filling his lungs. Suddenly Adam saw the cloud below him flash with light as a loud clapping noise crashed into his ears. He looked up to Wilbur as his heart rate started to beat fiercely and a single thought repeated through his head, getting louder and louder. It's the Trill, they're back! Panicked, he dropped his Cheltiagh to the ground and reached for the brass toggle of his Sciaths. Realising that he wasn't wearing any he looked around for an escape. It was a trap! He saw Wilbur walking towards him and thought about how it was Wilbur who wanted to go in the night, it was Wilbur who didn't mention not having any Sciaths before bringing him up into the clouds, Wilbur who was on the Paddle Steamer when Lafayette showed up, and Wilbur was the one at his grandmother's house that morning before Benedict was attacked heading to Frackingshulme. Adam walked backwards tripping over as the fear consumed him. He sat stranded on the cloud as Wilbur walked slowly towards him, puffing away on his pipe.

Seventeen

There was another flash and a crack that rippled through the air like a whip splitting it in two. Adam winced at the echo of the sound as it sent waves of fear through him. He looked around as the mist concealed his Cheltiagh from view. Wilbur stopped and scooped it up off the floor before looking at it as it burned blue in his hand. He walked over to Adam and looked down at him with a stern look.

"Stand up!" Adam's breathing was getting faster and faster. Without Sciaths or his Cheltiagh, all Wilbur would need to do is push him off the cloud and Adam would be gone forever. There would be no heir for the Order and the Trill would take over.

"Please, why?" Adam pleaded with Wilbur as a look of confusion spread over his face.

"Whit are yoo talking about lad?" Wilbur offered out Adam's Cheltiagh to him as he bent down and scooped him up from off the floor.

"You're here to kill me! You were there on the Paddle Steamer when it was attacked, and you attacked Benedict when he was on his way to Frackingshulme. I know who you are! You're the Commander! You took my Father!" Adam lashed out at Wilbur as he held him close to him tightly. The cloud lashed out with another bolt of lightning but this time is was brighter and faster. The thunder rolled through the skies and shook the cloud causing Wilbur to fall and let go of Adam. He stood with the cloud beneath him as the fear within him turned to rage. Gripping the Cheltiagh tight he stood over Wilbur as the moon shone down onto them both. The cloud turned black beneath them as thunder and lightning filled the air with the wind picking up and fiercely blowing around them. Chester stood at Adam's side as Wilbur tried to bring himself up from his knees.

"*Stay down!*" Adam shouted above the noise as he placed his foot on Wilbur's back forcing him back to the floor.

"I should kill you where you lay!" His rage now boiled in his blood as he stepped back looking at Wilbur. Surrounded by chaos and noise Adam's rage and revenge consumed him. Dolly jumped on

Wilbur's back and growled at Adam as Chester snarled, his teeth gleaning in the light.

"I was there!" Wilbur shouted up from the floor.

"I was there the night the Commander took your Father!" Suddenly there was silence. The lightning stopped and the wind ceased. Adam stumbled with the information as it struck him hard.

"What? What do you mean?" The cloud now turned white as Adam watched Wilbur roll onto his back looking at Adam.

"I'm not here to kill you; there were three Trill that day on the Paddle Steamer. I stopped two of them."

"Why should I believe you?" Adam roared at Wilbur as a single bolt of lightning shot from the cloud crackling across the sky.

"Because your Father was my friend, I was there that morning, in the living room. The morning your mother was told the news, it was me who told her. That was my cloud. He was my Guardian. I vowed on that day to protect your grandmother as she protected you, until you were ready to take your place as the Flight."

Adam fell backwards landing on the cloud permitting the moisture to seep through the seat of his trousers as Wilbur spoke to him about his Father.

"I have spent my life making sure that you and your grandmother are safe."

"But...but the lightning, and this storm? That was you!" Adam stuttered as he pointed to the cloud around them, his face searching for answers. Wilbur smiled and rose to his knees.

"No Adam that was you. This whole evening has been you. I left my Cheltiagh in Frackingshulme. Your fear brought the lightning but then it changed. You controlled it, with the rage that swelled up inside of you." Wilbur was now stood on his feet as he walked over to Adam before taking a knee next to him. Chester snarled as Wilbur offered out his hand and scratched him behind the ears. Looking into Adam's eyes he breathed a sigh of relief as he held his shoulder gently.

"Yoo have more power at your age then I ever did. Being able to control the thunder and lightning fae sixteen? I couldna do tha' until two weeks 'afore my Chief examinations! Yoo have real talent there lad!"

Wilbur let go of his shoulder before smiling and sitting back on his knees groaning a little.

"I think we've done enough for tonight. Take us home lad!"

Adam stood and watched as the cloud was now returning to its original brilliant white. He looked around him and saw the glow of Reddington burn on the horizon. He smiled at what had happened that night, at how much power he had controlled, the grippilos, the lightning. A feeling of contentment washed over him as he learnt more about his past and the role that others played in the security that was provided to him as a child, and even now. He looked down at the tiny blur of light from the courtyard and thought about those who waited down there for him; Benedict with his strong hands and ability to see the joy in any desperate situation, and Etty, her soft warm hands that immediately moulded to his. He thought about her white teeth that hid behind her bright red lips. The way the colour of her cheeks matched her hair as she laughed placing one hand over her mouth and the other resting on her tummy. Adam watched as the light started to take shape into the rectangle of the courtyard. The moonlight glistened on the water as he traced the path of the river that fed into the waterfall and up into the mountain. The volcano steamed away patiently, pushing its white cloud into the heavens. Frackingshulme was now starting to become clear as the battlements came into view and its rugged edges filled the valley. Adam landed the mist on top of the castle as he felt the cold stone floor beneath his feet. Wilbur was on his feet walking over to Adam, he rested his hand on his shoulder before looking at his eyes.

"Battled more than that cloud up there lad!" He smirked before wrapping his arm around Adams shoulders and chuckling loudly.

"Let's get a Hunchers before bed." They walked off together with Chester and Dolly in tow as Adam felt more in control of his destiny than he had ever done before. Wilbur had brought a rage out of him that he never knew he had, and a power that he didn't know he was capable of summoning. Stopping the wheel on his Cheltiagh, he placed it into his pocket and walked with Wilbur along the castle wall and down to the hall.

Inside, only a few candles were lit around the hall as the fire burned and crackled at the end of the room. Adam looked down the long table to see Etty sat, staring into her mug with the black feather twirling in her fingers. As Adam stood in the hall she looked up before a wide smile spread across her face. She leapt out of her seat before racing down the hall towards Adam, crashing into him and wrapping herself around his body before jumping up and planting her soft lips on his. Adam's eyes filled with wonder as his stomach fluttered with butterflies. He had never been kissed before and his head grew fuzzy as it filled with emotion. She looked at him smiling before frowning and punching him hard on the arm.

"Ouch, what was that for?"

"That thunder and lightning! I was scared for you!" she had a frown on her face as behind her shoulder Mr Crumbleton fluttered into view. Adam smiled upon seeing Mr Crumbleton before he flew forward and gave him a slap on the face with his tiny hand, folding his arms and scowling at him.

"We were both scared." Etty collected Mr Crumbleton from the air with her cupped hands before placing him into her satchel. She returned her gaze to him before smirking.

"I am not sure who was more scared. You've made quite an impression on him you know."

Adam blushed as he looked down at his feet.

"Well you're back now so that's what's most important. I am holding you responsible Mr Whisspe!"

She pointed her finger at him as she threw him a scowl.

"Indeed yoo are right Miss Gravelio, and I shall seek you oot each day until you feel it fit to forgive me." Wilbur smiled before offering her a long bow.

"Oh hush! Adam was in the safest possible hands. Now Wilbur, you must join us for a drink before retiring for what is left of the night."

Looking at them, Wilbur checked his pocket watch before letting out a large sigh.

"I shall decline Miss Gravelio but thank you for the offer." Wilbur smiled before turning to Adam.

"You did well tonight Adam, your maither and faither would be proud."

He gripped Adam tightly on the shoulder before winking and departing the hall, passing Benedict on the way in. They nodded to each other in passing before Benedict entered and walked over to Adam, pulling him into him for a hug.

"Well done lad! We were worried sick! This one here asked me to send up some Igneus to check on you. They ended up getting chased across the blooming stars by this beast here!" Benedict pointed down to Chester who was grinning as he rubbed his head on Benedict's leg.

Adam looked to Etty who blushed before coyly looking around the room, occasionally shooting her gaze at him.

"Well I was worried." She sat down at the table as Adam looked to Benedict who raised his eyebrows and shrugged his shoulders in confusion. Adam smiled and took his place at the table next to Etty as Benedict followed sitting next to Adam.

They sat there at the table in the hall until the sun painted the sky pink as Adam told them of what happened on the cloud, the fear in his heart and the anger in his belly. How he stepped on Wilbur's back and brought lightening to the cloud with his mind. They laughed and gasped as Adam walked them through the entire event, moment by moment.

As student Guardians entered the hall for their breakfast Adam and Benedict decided to retire and sleep before they let the day run away with them completely. As the three of them walked out of the hall Adam could hear the murmurs of conversations about a thunderous storm that loomed over head that night. He smiled as he made his way out in the cool morning breeze of the courtyard. The sun had burned off the majority of Adam's cloud and the remainder now lingered on the surface of the lake. They made their way down the spiral stairs towards the door that held Adam's freshly made bed. As he placed his key in the lock he looked back to Etty and Benedict.

"Thank you."

They looked at each other before looking back at him.

"For what mate?" Benedict asked.

"For being my friends through all of this."

160

"Oh quiet mate, you'll make me blub!" said Benedict as they stood there in the corridor and laughed before entering their rooms. Adam closed his door behind him before dragging his feet over to his bed and collapsing face first on the pristine white sheets. Chester jumped on his bed and curled up into a ball before resting his back against Adam as they both drifted off to sleep.

Adam was woken abruptly by a banging at the door.

"Adam!" the door opened as Etty burst in, taking a seat on the edge of his bed. She was in the same green pyjamas that she wore on the Paddle Steamer. Her hair was wiry and she had done her best to gather it up and hang it over one shoulder. He rolled over and sat up in his bed wiping the drool off his cheek.

"What's up? You ok?" As Adam asked a beaming smile spread across her face as she stroked Chester on the head causing him to stretch out and then roll on to his back showing off his pink tummy.

"The most wonderful thing has happened! You simply must come and see!" She stood and quickly walked to the door before going through it, out of Adam's sight. Chester now rolled onto his front to look around wondering why the scratching had stopped. Adam sat on the edge of his bed, stood up and looked out of the window. It was the afternoon and the sun was falling towards the horizon as the clouds that filled the sky loitered white and proud. Adam thought about the Architects up there building and splitting the clouds as he watched from the ground below. Like Artists, they placed the clouds delicately on to the fading blue canvas as the light danced around them creating large shadows that raced across the fields and rivers. He looked up to see a winged creature swoop down off the edge cloud and down into the valley that held the lake. Adam gasped and brought his hands to the window to inspect further as the creature disappeared into the clouds. He shook his head in disbelief as he tried to convince himself that it couldn't have been. It couldn't have been Primrose. He stared out of the window, watching the clouds as Etty reappeared at the door.

"Come along Architect!" She was insistent Adam picked up his paced towards her. She was stood in her doorway looking into her room and as Adam joined her, her hand fell into his.

161

"I woke up and she was there. Isn't she beautiful?"

Confused, Adam looked into her room and there on the bed, curled up in a ball sleeping, was a pristine white otter. Etty looked at Adam, her eyes alive with excitement as she kissed his cheek. Chester made his way into the room and jumped to place his front paws on the edge of the bed, stretching forward to sniff the sleeping beast. As his nose touched the Otters it stirred and looked around the room. Standing on the bed it stretched out its wings giving them an almighty beat before touching noses with Chester and bowing. Chester immediately jumped from the bed the returned the compliment.

"Her name is Lillia and she has come to be my Protector!" Lillia then jumped from the bed and walked over to them before standing upright and placing her front two legs on Etty's shins reaching up to her. Etty bent down and scooped her up from the floor clutching her tightly as Lillia nestled her head into Etty's neck.

"Good afternoon Lillia. It is lovely to meet you." She removed her head to look to Adam as he stroked her head causing her to close her eyes in contentment. Benedict appeared behind them placing his hands on their shoulders.

"Aha! I see we are approaching the day soon then. She must have come a day early"

"A day early?" Adam looked at Benedict with a confused looked across his face.

"Etty turns sixteen tomorrow and the Flight is on her way here for the ceremony. Do you not remember? Etty is to be the next Bee." Adam's face dropped as he recalled Ruairi and Benedict telling him in Yeolight. He looked back at Etty as she smiled, placing Lillia on the floor as she moved forward to touch noses with Henrik.

"Right, I only came back for my cloak. I need to head into the Volcano, preparations and all that. The Ceremony has never been conducted here and Chief Princepitus is getting quite antsy about it all." Adam smiled as he thought about Benedict launching himself into the heart of a volcano with Henrik at his side, like a film star walking away from an explosion in super slow-motion.

"The Flight? Ceremony?"

162

"Yes, only the Flight can conduct the acceptance ceremony, that and the fact that she is also the Bee. So she is coming in both capacities." Benedict was smiling now as he walked to his door and placed the key in to the lock.

Adam's heart lifted as he thought of everyone coming to Frackingshulme today. Etty walked back into her room and sat on the edge of the bed looking at Adam in the doorway. She smiled and Lillia jumped on the bed, curling up next to her. Benedict grabbed the cloak and locked his door before wishing them both a wonderful afternoon as he made his way up the stairs and out in to the courtyard. Adam turned to Etty who was now grabbing a towel and toothbrush from the sink.

"You need to get showered and dressed. I want to show you something." She walked out of her room with the towel draped over her arm and walked off to the showers. Adam walked back into his room with Chester in tow as he closed the door behind him and fell onto his bed. A smile grew on his face as he looked up at the ceiling; he was to be the Flight and Etty the Bee and his grandmother was to lead the ceremony. He laughed before Chester jumped on the bed and pinned him down with both paws on his chest to lick his face.

"Oh come on mate! She said shower! Not licked clean!" Adam rolled out from the pin of a panting Chester as he stood and looked around the room. He placed some clean clothes on his bed before grabbing a towel and the toiletries from the sink before walking the four doors down to the male showers. He finished his hot shower and wrapped the white fluffy towel around his waist, leaving the shower room to make his way back to his room. The cool air hit him as the open entrance that led out onto the courtyard blew a gust down the stairs and along the corridor towards him. He ran quickly and leaped into his room to see Chester asleep on his back amongst the clothes that he had laid out neatly only moments before.

"Come on mate!" Adam pulled his clothes out from underneath the beast and placed them over his chair as Chester woke and jumped off the bed to lick the water from Adam's legs. Battling with the rapid licking from Chester, he fought to get his trousers on and cover himself from Chester's tongue. Once dressed he looked around to check that he had all that he needed before taking one last glance out

163

of the window to the clouds in a hope to see the beast that he saw before. Adam left his room with Chester and locked it behind him before knocking onto Etty's door.

"One moment." She shouted from inside the room. Adam wandered around in the corridor as Chester lay down, groaning as he went. Suddenly the door flew open as Etty burst out with Lillia in tow. She closed her door and looked at Adam. She was wearing the same leather Wellington boots and outfit that she was wearing the last time he saw her in Reddington. Her satchel still hanging off her shoulder as Adam knew that Mr Crumbleton would be hiding in there.

"Come!" She took him by the hand and walked him up the stairs, into the courtyard and out onto the drawbridge. She ran with her hand in his down the path and towards the green field that he arrived on in the mechanical squid. Adam followed her as she held his hand tight, her perfume being carried on the wind behind her, filling his nostrils with the sweet scent. Once in the open Chester and Lillia took flight, soaring high and vanishing into the clouds. She ran down to the lake and towards a wooden pontoon that ran out into the water. As they reached the shore she stood and looked out into the valley as the sky now started to cascade with reds, oranges, pinks, and purples. The scattered clouds turned a deep red as the sun filled them with colour. She turned to Adam breathless from the run as she took both of his hands in hers.

"Can I share with you a secret?" She asked him looking from their hands to his eyes. She ran the tips of her fingers over his knuckles and down to the end of his fingers before placing her fingers in-between his and holding them tight.

"Of course!" Adam's heart ran wild as he felt the warmth of her hands holding his. Releasing one, she ran up the bank towards the long grass and knelt down pulling him down to kneel next to her. She took off her bag and placed it down next to her, opening it to allow a sleepy eyed Pixie to emerge before fluttering off into the woods that neighboured the lake.

"Come close and watch!" Releasing his hand she cupped both of hers around the head of a dying flower stranded beneath the long grass that choked it from the light. Its red petals were wilted and brown at the edges with the yellow disk in the centre faded. As she brought her face close to the flower blocking it from Adam's view she blew gently, slowly pulling her head back as Adam saw the flower now start to bloom into colour. Etty slowly removed her hands continuing to blow on the flower causing it to grow tall, above the long grass. She paused and looked to Adam as the flower stood proud, burning red with colour. His jaw fell open as he fell off his knees and onto his bum watching the flower now moving with the gentle breeze that filled the valley. From the sky appeared Chester and Lillia, as they landed on the soft mud and ran circles around each other before walking to the lake and standing with their feet in the cool water, lapping at its shimmering surface.

"But how? Where is your Cheltiagh?"

"I know right?" She jumped on her knees and moved forward to hold his hands again, her entire face alive with life and excitement.

"I was in Torringsdour and walking in the wilted meadow when I saw that as I walked the flowers around me came to life and bloomed!" Adam watched as her face became animated the more she spoke.

"So I went to the library and found a copy of the Order of the Quill as Cella hasn't given me my copy yet." Her speech was getting faster and faster the more she spoke.

"I read about how the original three of the order never had a need for a Cheltiagh as the power was divine. But as the Order grew and the power passed down to heirs and worthy members, the Flight, Bee and Ophy decided to restrict the power to those within the Order. They placed the power to maintain the balance into the Cheltiagh. This made it easier for them to keep an eye on those within the Order and ensure that the balance was protected. Without a Cheltiagh, no one can summon the energy required to command all those that serve the balance." Adam watched as she now stood and walked to the water

"Do you see what I am saying Adam?" she turned and rushed over to him, kneeling in front of him looking into his eyes.

"Divine power of the Order! I don't know how or why but I have it!"

Suddenly there was a crack and boom as the valley filled with noise. They looked up to the volcano as its gentle white steam turned to a dark black smoke. Lightning flashed through the vapour as the valley filled with the deep clap of thunder again.

"Let's go!" Adam looked at Etty as she stared at the sky. Her eyes were now filled with fear as she clutched at Adams hand.

"It's ok; let's just get back to the castle." He stood quickly and picked up her bag, handing it to her. She stood for a moment as a frightened Mr Crumbleton, fluttered from the woods towards her, taking his place in her satchel. He tried to calm her down before taking her by the hand and running back up the hill towards the castle, the pink sky now filling with clouds and turning grey. They crossed the field as Adam held Etty's hand tightly pulling her along. Her breathing was becoming erratic as she filled with fear, running behind him. They crossed the drawbridge and into the courtyard, Adam stopped running and looked at Etty, her gaze was vacant as she looked towards the skies. Adam pulled her into his embrace looking to the black smoke towering overhead. He watched as the volcano started to spit red balls of fire into the sky. He watched as he thought of Benedict and the volcano!

Eighteen

"Inside! Get inside!" Adam heard shouting from across the courtyard as a voice bellowed from the entrance of the hall. They ran towards the hall as a Guardian ushered them in. Adam took one last look at the black cloud as it burned and grew with thick black smoke that consumed the sky like a huge mushroom top. Lightning flashed through the ash, illuminating silhouettes of people fighting within it. Suddenly there came an almighty crash as the sun pierced through the ash, firing light into the valley and shaking the ground that they stood on. Adam held Etty's arms in his hands as he looked her in the eyes.

"Stay here! I need to find Benedict!" Etty nodded and threw herself forward kissing him on the lips before wrapping her arms around him and pushing him out the door into the courtyard. Adam ran to the stairs that he walked up the night before, climbing two at a time before reaching the top of the castle wall. He looked around at the volcano as the black cloud started to fragment and break apart. He felt rain sprinkle on his face as the volcano resumed spouting white smoke and the sky filled with a colossal blanket of cloud. He fished his hand into his pocket to find his Cheltiagh. Standing firm on the stone wall he looked to the sky as he saw people in red and blue jumpers, flying out into the open air on Sciaths as they shot out in all different directions. Adam looked down to his Cheltiagh and spun the wheel. He thought about Benedict and how he would travel up to him to find him in the Volcano. That was the only plan that he had and he knew that he would make the rest up as he got up there. In that moment Chester looked behind him and started to snarl. Adam turned to see a snarling lynx sneaking up on him, its wings spread wide as it hissed at Chester. Chester now moved forward as he came between the lynx and Adam. Watching as they stared at each other, the lynx lunged forward swiping its sharp claws at Chester's nose missing by a whisker. Lowering his stance, Chester darted forward, snapping and growling which startled the lynx causing it to turn and run up the castle wall before beating its wings and taking flight. Adam watched as Chester returned to him placing his head in his hands, his snarl gone and the calm look in his eyes returned, but this time it was different, Adam saw fear and concern. Nodding to Chester Adam looked to the skies as it darkened with the mass of cloud blocking the sunlight. Pockets of ash now dissolved as the rain came faster, lashing onto the stone battlements causing the torches in the courtyard to flicker and fight to remain bright. As the volcano settled in the rain he watched as a red furred beast swooped down towards him before circling up high, catching its wings on the thermals. Adam's heart soared with Henrik as he saw Benedict drifting down towards him on a mound of ash. His face and hands were black and his eyes fought to remain white as red wrapped around his pupils like dye in a pool of water. In his hands was his Cheltiagh glowing red as he removed his thumb and placed it in his pocket before landing on the castle walls next to Adam. With the ash now washing away with the water, Benedict walked over to Adam and placed his arm around his shoulder.

"Come, let's get off this wall!" his voice was calm and steady as he pulled Adam in roughly before releasing him to walk next to him.

"What was that Benedict?"

"The Trill attacked the convoy that was making its way here for the Ceremony." Adam watched as Benedict walked down the stairs, his trouser leg wet with blood.

"Benedict! Your leg!" Adam's voice was alarmed and filled with concern as Benedict placed his hand on his leg and found a hole in his trousers where he had been struck. He looked at his hand as it was now dabbed with blood.

"Dam it! Now I need to get new trousers!" He wiped his red hand on a dry patch of his trousers as he reached the bottom of the stairs and looked up, watching the skies move with the rain.

"Let's get a Hunchers." He looked down at Adam before taking one last look at the sky as he walked over to the hall. Inside, the hall was filled with the buzz of people as they rushed around gathering blankets and provisions.

"Why all the fuss Benedict?" Adam looked around as the room filled with a blur of movement, people wearing colours of red, blue and green turned the hall from a dining room into an operations cell.

168

"Benedict!" A voice came from the mass of people, it was Etty. She ran over to him and hugged him before standing back and looking him up and down.

"You look a state! What happened to you? Oh! Your leg!" She recoiled as she noticed the wet patch on his thigh.

"Don't worry about that, let's get a brew. Sit here, I'll be right back." He pointed to an empty spot at the table as Adam and Etty took their places. Adam noticed that Benedict was distracted and subdued as he walked off to order the drinks.

"Something's not right with Benedict. He's…not himself" He whispered to Etty as she sat next to him placing her hand on his. Her breathing was shallow and she kept her gaze fixed on the table.

"You think so?" She spoke quietly as her eyes filled with tears.

"Hey, you ok? What's the matter?" Adam turned on the bench, taking both of her hands in his. She looked at him as her cheeks turned a deep shade of pink and her eyes welled with water.

"Well, it's just that the convoy was coming here for this silly ceremony. All this fighting and fuss over me being the Bee. And the worst part is that my Dad would have been up there but I've not seen him here." Adams heart sunk as the words from Etty struck him; his grandmother would have been in the Convoy.

"Relax, they are fine. They took a different route. We used the volcano as a distraction to allow the Flight and the Ophy's safe passage through, we didn't expect them to attack with so many though." Benedict sat down as an attendant brought over three steaming mugs brimming with Hunchers Brew.

"You knew they would attack?"

"We had a suspicion that the Trill would mount an attack but we had no idea the size of devastation they would be prepared to cause to stop the convoy."

"When will the real convoy get here?" Adam spoke quietly to avoid any unwanted attention. The room was filled with people and he didn't trust any of them.

"Soon." Benedict picked up his mug and winked at them both before bringing it to his lips and taking a long sip. Suddenly the room went quiet as they all looked to the doorway. Stood in the light was a tall female figure looking around the room, it was Fia. She entered

169

the hall walking straight up to the three of them placing her hand on Benedict's shoulder.

"Are you ok?" she stared around the hall looking at each person that her gaze fell on as she spoke softly. Benedict nodded and she released her hand from his shoulder, nodded to Adam and Etty and walked off to the end of the table where maps and sketches of the surrounding terrain covered it like a patchwork tablecloth. A group of Guardians swarmed around her as the murmuring grew louder and returned to the orchestra of noise that there was before. Adam watched as she hunched over the maps and looked at each of the drawings as one of the Guardians talked her through the attack strategy of the Trill. He could hear them discussing the defensive plan that they should take should the Trill choose to launch a second attack. He listened as they measured and weighed up what actions they should take to reduce collateral damage to both the students in Frackingshulme and the Balance. A Guardian walked up to Fia and leaned over to whisper in her ear. Her body stiffened as the news registered and she looked at Adam before marching out of the room causing a gust to form behind her.

"What were you doing on the castle walls anyway Adam?" Benedict regained Adam's attention as he watched him look around the room.

"He was coming to save you." Etty spoke as a smile returned to her face. Benedict looked confused and watched Adam blush as he fiddled with the handle of his mug.

"Well I am grateful for the thought of help Adam, thank you." Benedict finished his Hunchers Brew and placed the mug down onto the table before standing up and looking at them both.

"Come on, let's get out of here." He turned to walk out of the hall and into the courtyard as the light of the Sun consumed him out of sight. Adam turned to Etty as they picked up their drinks and finished them before standing and following Benedict into the courtyard. As soon as they stood, two attendants cleared their cups away and the space was filled with maps and plans of the castle as two Guardians started exchanging fierce words over the best course of action to defeat the Trill. Adam reached for Etty's hand as they walked towards the amber light that shone in through the door, spilling out onto its stone floor. The rain had stopped now and the sky was awash with bright, vibrant colours. Their eyes adjusted to the light as Adam saw Benedict stood in the centre of the courtyard fixed in conversation with a tall man in a Guardians uniform. The figure spoke to Benedict as a look of fear and dread filled his face. He looked over and met Adam's gaze, Adam could see the sadness fill his eyes. Etty released Adam's hand and ran forward to the man as Lillia gave chase after her.

"Daddy!" he turned as he heard her voice and a relieved smile spread across his face. She ran into his arms and squeezed him tight.

Adam watched as Charlie looked up from holding Etty, kissing her on the forehead before starting to walk forward towards him. If Charlie was here, then where was his grandmother? Adam took a step backwards as he noticed the sombre look painted across Charlie's face. His body felt weak and his knees buckled as he adjusted his feet on the cobbled courtyard. The pink sky now turned grey and it filled with clouds for the second time in that day.

"Where is my grandmother?" He searched around at the sea of faces, struggling to see the bouncy white hair and red lips of his grandmother amongst them.

"Come here Adam." Charlie spoke softly as he stepped towards Adam, maintaining his gaze on him.

"Where is she!" Adam's mind began to chase ideas around his head as adrenaline injected life into his heart, fuelling his body with blood. A heavy lump appeared in his throat as a list of poisonous questions started to run in his head. Where was she? Why do they look sad? Is she with the Quill? Have they hurt her? Benedict was now speaking with Etty as she gasped with the news looking to Adam.

"Adam, relax. Come to me." Charlie was now standing still with his arm stretched out to him. From his side appeared Etty, she passed her Father and strode straight up to Adam taking his hands in hers. His eyes were now filled with tears as he looked into hers, his voice felt fragile as he let her touch his skin in an attempt to soothe him. Rain now gently sprinkled onto their hands as they stood in the courtyard.

"Where is she Etty? Where is my Granny?" He struggled to push the words from his mouth as she looked down to his hands and then back up to his eyes.

"They knew which way they were coming. The Commander was waiting. She's hurt Adam there was nothing they could do."

"Where is she Etty?" he pleaded at her with desperation in his voice looking into her eyes. He was scared; scared of being alone; scared of losing the one person who could protect him; scared of losing her. The rain was now falling heavily onto the stone floor creating a deafening noise as it crashed against the worn cobbles.

"She is in Chief Princepitus' office."

Adam looked up at them before darting across the courtyard towards the entrance to the corridor. His breath was frantic and his legs struggled to keep up with his pace causing him to stumble forward, reaching to the wall for support. He looked up and saw the door looming at the end of the corridor, his eyes now streaming with the tears he had tried so hard to hold back. He was running in quicksand, his head felt fuzzy, and his eyes stung as he pushed his body towards the door arriving before it in a heap on the carpet. He heaved himself to his feet and placed his quivering hand on the cool brass doorknob. The door creaked open and inside he was met with the serpent glaring at him. Fia was stood behind her desk with a watcher standing next to her in a bright green jumper. Wilbur was looking out of the window as he turned to look at Adam, a large rip crossing the front of his jacket, revealing the fabric and blood underneath.

"Adam." It was Fia who spoke first. "She is here."

Adam looked to the dark brown leather sofa that she was pointing to as he ran over to see his grandmother laying there, motionless. He dropped to his knees as the fear of losing her overwhelmed and consumed him. He buried his face into her bright blue coachman's cape that was littered with ash and dirt. He lifted his head to look into her grey, lifeless eyes before placing his shaking hand on her eyelids, pulling them shut. His stomach turned over as he looked around the room at Etty and Benedict who were now standing in the doorway. Rising to his feet he swallowed down the pain that was solidifying in his throat and looked at each one of them. He felt

172

anger, someone was to blame and Adam would be sure to make sure that they understood the rage that burned inside of him. He clenched his fists as the rain from outside grew stronger, lashing against the stain glass window. Suddenly he felt a rough tongue lap against his white knuckled fist. He looked down to see Chester sat by his side looking up at him. There was fear in his eyes as he raised one paw to gently touch Adam's leg before licking his fist again. Adam saw his own emotions trapped in Chester and in that moment he understood what his grandmother meant the last time he saw her; *Sometimes the greatest pain we have is the one we think we can't control.* Was finding someone responsible, someone to blame the right way to seize control, or would he simply lose it? What could be gained from killing those that had done him wrong? He knelt down next to Chester and wrapped his arms around him allowing his heart to melt and the rage to calm, releasing his tears into his fur as Chester sat firm, resting his head against Adam's.

"Adam we need to move you son. The Trill could attack at any moment, and we need to make sure that you and Etty are safe." Wilbur was now stood next to Adam as he looked up, wiping his eyes and looking around the room. It was filled with familiar faces that were all looking to Adam.

"Me? Move Etty, she is the one that they want. I will stay here with Benedict. Make sure she is safe."

"It's not as easy as that now mate." Benedict walked forward looking at Adam as confusion spread across his face.

"You're the Flight now. You are wanted by them as much as I am. If they find out that you are here ..."

Etty's voice drifted off as Lillia wandered around the sofa to stand next to Chester. Staggering on his feet, Adam felt the weight of responsibility hit him square in the chest as the room darkened around him. The clouds thickened in the sky as it started to grumble with a low thunderous roar. Wilbur walked over to the window and looked to the skies as the clouds turned black, building on themselves becoming thicker and increasing in volume.

"Adam, we need to move you now." Wilbur looked back at him with urgency to his voice. Adam thought about them moving him and Etty. Where would they go and for how long? When would this end? He looked to Charlie who had now entered the room and was stood next to Etty. At his feet stood a beast unlike any that Adam had seen before; it had the head of a monkey, the body of a long haired brown dog, the legs of a tiger and the tail of a green snake. It turned to Adam looking him up and down before walking over to Chester, spreading its wings wide and bowing as he touched noses with him and returned to Charlie's side. Etty knelt down and stroked the beast as it closed its eyes in delight to the scratching behind its ears

"When I was on the Castle walls, I saw a Lynx, it came up to me and tried to attack Chester and I. They know I am here."

Charlie's eyes grew wide as he looked at Adam before glancing over to Fia. They both looked to Adam as Fia walked towards him.

"A lynx, you are sure it was a lynx?" Adam watched their minds tick as they processed the information they had just received.

"Yes, it attacked me but Chester gave it what for!" Adam looked down at Chester who was now sat proud knowing that Adam was remarking on his courage and bravery.

"There has only ever been one member of the Order to have a Lynx, surely it can't be?" Charlie spoke quietly to himself, walking from where he was stood with Etty and perching himself on the edge of a nearby table.

"I don't understand. Who had a Lynx?" Adam was confused and felt angry that they were talking in code and withholding information from him. The room fell silent as Charlie walked over to Fia and whispered to her. Wilbur joined the conversation and they became more animated as they spoke.

"*Who had a lynx?*" His voice was raised and he could feel the rage boiling inside of him. Who had a Lynx and why was it a big deal?

"It was your Dad mate. Your Dad had a Lynx called Romulus but he was suspected dead the day the Commander captured your Father." Benedict cut the silence with a measured tone. Adam looked down at his grandmother as this revelation made him think of his Father. How could they turn his protector in to an evil beast that would attack people? Was his Father here? Suddenly a noise bellowed down the corridor, knocking paintings of the walls and shaking the floor. Etty shrieked and fell to her knees as Benedict

174

stood in the doorway with Henrik by his side, Cheltiagh in hand. Chester and Lillia ran over to her standing in front of the door as Adam watched Fia and Charlie, their eyes darting towards where Benedict was stood. Benedict stepped out of the doorway and squinted to look down the corridor into the courtyard.

"It's the Trill, they are here!"

Nineteen

With Benedict blocking the doorway to the corridor, Charlie headed over to stand next to him placing himself slightly in front. As he stared down the corridor, Adam watched his eyes grow at the sight of the battle that ensued amongst the Trill and the Guardians. He pulled Benedict back into the room and closed the door behind them before turning to address the room and deliver his orders.

"Benedict, you take Adam and Etty through the ancient passageways behind the bookcase. Fia, with Wilbur, do you think you can hold them off until Benedict has them clear?"

Benedict turned around and nodded to Charlie before making his way to the fireplace with Henrik following closely behind.

"I shall remain behind with Bartholomew and protect Chief King. I'll make sure she is moved to safety." In a flash the room came alive with movement as Fia and Wilbur nodded to Charlie and left the room with both Dolly and Babesne following closely behind. Etty stood next to Adam as Chester and Lillia took their place next to Henrik, their feathers twitching with the prospect of moving quickly and evading the Trill. Benedict moved past Adam as he inspected the leather-bound books that filled the dark wooden bookcase. Running his fingers over them he pulled at three random books that were placed separately across the shelves. Adam watched before hearing a loud click as a portion of the bookcase popped out of the wall, creaking open to reveal a dark passageway.

Benedict ushered them into the darkness of the corridor with Chester and Henrik leading, Lillia and Etty behind and Adam at the rear with Benedict. Once they were all inside, Benedict pulled at the handle on the inside of the bookcase as the door came to a close. Moments before it clicked to a close, Charlie called out to Benedict.

"Don't forget Benedict, get to the rendezvous point and wait for my Order. You have the hope of the Order now, keep them safe!" Benedict smiled and looked round to see Adam and Etty's worried faces staring at him before replying to Charlie.

"Race ya!" He winked before allowing the heavy bookcase to cut off the last of the light, clicking shut and encasing them in the cold darkness.

"Henrik get ready to lead us out mate." The corridor was dark and a cool breeze drifted by them. Benedict took his Cheltiagh in his hand and placed his thumb on the edge causing it to glow red. Adam looked down into the black abyss of the tunnel as the glow of Benedict's Cheltiagh illuminated the stone walls around them. He reached out his hand to the wall and recoiled as its freezing touch sent shivers down his spine and the hairs on his arm stood up on their ends. They waited in the tunnel and watched as a red light shone bright at the end of the tunnel. Chester and Lillia stood in between Etty and Adam as the light grew brighter and stronger.

"It's ok; I have summoned a fire Salamander to come and light the way for us." Etty held his hand tight in the darkness as the red light grew brighter.

"What's a Salamander Benedict?" Adam asked as the light was now nearly upon them. Before Benedict had time to answer, the small creature was now hovering in front of them as flames licked the air around it. Its skin was made up of intricate scales that covered its entire body as orange flames flickered and burned brightly. It smiled and bowed to them before looking to Benedict.

"Light the way." Benedict spoke directly to the creature as it smiled and turned increasing in colour as the tunnel came into view around them. The tunnel was made up of large stone blocks stacked high that fed into an intricately sculpted ceiling. Adam looked and marvelled at the thick white spider's webs that clung to the curves and curls of the stone. Henrik started to make his way down the tunnel following the Salamander as it shone fiercely in the dank stone corridor. They were running now as Henrik picked up the pace, trotting after the burning figure as it sped down the tunnel. Etty was still clenching Adam's hand as the tunnel abruptly ended and opened out into a large square room. They stood in the opening as the Salamander rose to the ceiling and lit the candles on an iron chandelier that hung from the centre of the room. Henrik made his way forward across the room to a corridor that twisted and turned off into the darkness. The chandelier was now fully lit as Adam looked around, taking in the magnitude of the room. The flickering candles fought to paint the floor in light as a gentle breeze flowed from the multiple corridors that fed into the chamber. The corners of the room remained in darkness as Adam looked down to Chester who had his nose raised in the air, sniffing the breeze.

"We need to keep moving. Down this corridor and we'll be outside."

Etty turned to Adam, leaning in close she whispered in his ear.

"I'm scared Architect. What's going on?" her voice quivered as she spoke and Adam could feel the fear radiating off her. He held her tight and placed her head into his chest, he was scared as well.

"You will die, that is what will happen to you." A voice came from the corner of the room. It was deep and Adam recognised it immediately.

"Adam! Take Etty and get out of here! Follow the breeze down that tunnel and wait for me there." Benedict spoke with urgency as he pointed to a corridor across the hall, the figure still loitering in the shadows.

"That's right Adam, run!" the voice was patronising and sarcastic as the figure made its way into the light, Etty gasped as she recognised who it was. Lafayette smirked as he looked around the room staring at each of them one. Adam took Etty's hand and darted towards the tunnel only to be met by a snarling winged hyena that blocked his path.

"You got away last time, this time however; I don't think you will be so lucky." Lafayette stood firm as he pulled his Cheltiagh from his pocket placing his thumb on the edge. As it started to glow red, Adam felt a surge of anger and hate fill his veins. They took his grandmother and Father away from him; they were not going to take his friends as well. He looked around him and picked up a rock from off the floor, throwing it at Lafayette. It was a perfect throw and cracked him on the head, sending him to the floor with a heavy thud. Benedict looked at him and smiled before his gaze was taken by the hyena that was now sneaking up on Etty.

"Etty!" Benedict shouted causing Adam to turn to watch as the hyena lunged at her exposing its dagger like claws. In that moment a white flash shot across the room and sent the hyena flying with a

178

yelp, it was Lillia. She placed herself between the hyena and Etty as the beast lay on its side whimpering. Etty looked to Lillia as she now had her wings spread wide and was baring her teeth at the fallen beast. Lafayette shook his head and held it in his hand before looking around the chamber to see the hyena now returning to its feet. It wobbled before looking around sheepishly then making its way to Lafayette who was now on his knees.

"What have you done? Vanya? Are you ok?" He looked at the hyena who exposed a large cut along her side that was now dripping blood from where Lillia had scratched her.

"You will pay for that!" Lafayette's eyes were wide open as he took hold of his Cheltiagh once more and placed his thumb on the side.

"Adam! Go now!" Benedict spoke with aggression in his voice as he stood in between them and Lafayette with Henrik now by his side. Etty pulled on Adam's arm as Lillia was now stood in the corridor looking up at the Salamander that was now hovering in front of them lighting the way out. Adam looked at Benedict and he felt a want to stay and fight with him. To run felt cowardly and Adam was tired of running from the Trill. He knew that he would be running for the rest of his life and that he would never be free from the tyranny of them unless he stood up to them.

"You will get your moment Adam, but for now, I need you to get Etty to safety."

Benedict was staring down Lafayette who was now getting to his feet. Adam knew that Benedict could feel the thoughts and emotions that were rushing through him. As he turned to leave he saw that the gaps between the heavy stone bricks were now starting to glow with a deep red and the room was starting to feel warm. He looked to Etty who was now standing with Mr Crumbleton on the palms of her hands. He had a fixed frown on his face as he watched Lafayette and Vanya stand to face Benedict.

Etty looked to Adam as she pulled her hands apart returning them to her sides allowing Mr Crumbleton to hover in the air, his unwavering frown fixed on Lafayette.

"He wants to stay, to protect us."

Adam watched as the pixie floated towards Benedict before taking his place by his side.

"Ok, let's go then." Adam grabbed Etty by the hand and nodded to her, they ran down the corridor towards the burning Salamander that was proceeding without them. Adam followed behind as Chester made sure that he left the room last. They ran as fast as their legs could carry them and Adam thought that his lungs would explode from his chest. Suddenly the Salamander slowed before coming to a stop as it approached a large wooden door. Adam looked to Etty as she stared at the fat iron bars that ran across the worn wood, the large bolts jutting out like brass buttons on a soldier's tunic. Etty placed her hand on the door laying her palm flat against the wood.

"Do you think Benedict will be ok?" She spoke softly before looking to him. Adam nodded as he wrapped his fingers around the cool iron door handle. The Salamander had now taken its place behind them and as Adam pushed down on the handle it vanished into the ancient stone bricks of the tunnel. The door was stiff and Adam placed his entire body behind it to force it open. It groaned and the light from outside was now dimming as the damp air filled their lungs. Overhead loomed dark storm clouds that hung over the land like a thick dark blanket. Adam ventured out first into the open field as the long wet grass brushed along his trousers soaking through the fabric. He looked around and saw that the door was embedded within a steep bank that ran along the edge of a meadow. Etty was now in the field with Adam as she looked around at the sky. She shivered, wrapping her arms around her chest before kneeling down to stroke Lillia.

"Thank you. That was very brave of you." Lillia smiled as she ran her head into her hand, closing her eyes with pride and contentment. Adam looked down to Chester, who was alert and looking around the field, his eyes wide and bright in the failing light. Adam pushed the door closed before walking over to Etty and crouching down next to her collecting her hands in his. The smell of the wet grass filled his nostrils as the noise of crickets and insects filled the air.

"Etty, we don't know who will follow us out of that tunnel. It could be Benedict or Lafayette. We should seek out a hiding place for now. Just to shelter us until I can come up with a plan."

Etty looked into his eyes and Adam could see the sadness wash over her. He knew that she felt the same way that he did. When would they stop running? When would they be able to enjoy the stars in the sky and the flowers in the meadow? She nodded and lowered her gaze as Adam placed his hand onto her cheek raising her eyes back to his.

"The Trill has taken everything from me, my friends, my mother, my Father, and my grandmother. I will not allow them to take any more. With the Trill here, there will never be order and balance."

He looked into her green eyes and without him knowing, she had measured his heart and it was brimming with purpose, with her name sounding the beat.

"This will end and I will make sure of that."

He spoke softly to her as her eyes filled with tears and she pulled him in close and gently touched her lips on his. In that brief moment he felt the fear lift from his heart and a childlike joy bounce in his stomach. Etty fell into his arms as he pulled her in tightly, placing her head under his neck. As the quiet fell around them, Adam heard the murmur of tense voices across the bank. He pulled Etty away from his chest and looked at her.

"Quick, come with me." Adam headed towards the voices as he listened to hear if he knew who it was. As they reached the corner of the meadow he lay against the steep bank crawling up towards the tree lined top. Poking his head above the crest of the bank, Adam could make out the lake near the Castle and the pontoon that jutted out into the water. Stood on the pontoon were two men in long cloaks, one taller than the other and speaking with a raised voice. His arms were flailing around in the air as he paced up and down the creaking pontoon sending ripples across the water. Adam looked back to Etty, who was now on her knees at the bottom of the bank with Chester and Lillia. He brought his finger to his lips and signalled for her to be quiet before looking back at the two men on the pontoon. Suddenly a protector strutted past his gaze sniffing the air around it before moving on. He ducked below the bank, pressing his head into the damp grass as his breathing increased and his heart raced. He listened to the voices talk as the conversation grew louder and louder.

"You are a foolish boy! You had one job and you failed!" The voice was deep and vicious as he attacked the other man with his venomous words.

"I should kill you instead!"

"I am sorry Commander, he was too quick, I did try..."

"Stop it with the pathetic excuses. Let's hope that they use the ancient passageways. If I know the old fool, he will tell them to use that way. Then they will run into Lafayette, He knows better than to let me down again!"

Etty's head rose up, looking to Adam as she frowned, knowing that the Commander was talking about her dad. Lillia made her way up to the top of the bank as Adam raised his eyebrows and shook his head, pleading with her to remain where she was.

"I think I hear something, Commander"

Adam froze in his spot, fearing that they had heard him rustling in the mud as he tried to stop Lillia from making her way over the bank.

Adam's eyes grew wide as he recognised the voice that came from the boy on the pontoon. It was Harry! He was alive but how?

Twenty

As Adam lay there on the damp bank he listened to Harry and the Commander talking. He wanted to dive over the bank and embrace him, ask him how he got away, talk again to his friend. But with the Commander there and Benedict in the tunnel with Lafayette, what was he to do? He looked down to Etty who was now shivering in the long grass as Chester and Lillia nestled next to her, trying to keep her warm. She was innocent and his want to help Harry was not as great as his need to get her to safety. As he looked into the blue light that was now failing fast around them, Adam felt a warm breath panting against the back of his neck. He slowly turned to be met by the white teeth of a snarling lynx. His heart jumped into his mouth as he tried to slowly back away down the bank towards Etty. The lynx shook its head and then ran down the bank blocking his path. Like a sheepdog, it started to herd them all up the bank and towards the pontoon. Chester and Lillia snarled as it lowered its stance and looked up at the bank to Primrose, who was now standing with her wings spread wide. They walked slowly towards the pontoon as Harry and the Commander now became aware of their presence. Adam took Etty's hand and gave it a squeeze as he gently pulled her behind him walking towards the water.

"Good work Romulus!" The Commander spoke, his voice was filled with elation at the sight of Adam. The clouds were now breaking apart as the moon pierced through them, reflecting on the water and illuminating the valley in a stark white light. It was night and the moon was now moving amongst the clouds, casting eerie looking shadows across the ground. Adam looked around and saw smoke rising from the castle as it sat amongst the darkness of the valley like a wounded monument to the Guardians. Harry looked sheepish as Adam tried to gain eye contact with him.

"What have we here?"

The Commander taunted them as Romulus pushed them towards the pontoon. He was tall and his broad shoulders filled the tight tunic that wrapped around his body. In the darkness, Adam watched as

Romulus now made his way up to the Commander and rubbed his head against his leg before looking at them both with a scowl.

"This evening is a real treat, the Bee and the Flight!" He chuckled at them as Adam watched him walk up to, and around them, his pace slow and mocking as his shoes tapped on the withered wooden boards. They were now walking backwards towards the end of the pontoon as Adam turned to face the Commander before pulling Etty further behind him. The Commander walked up to him, the darkness shielding his face. Adam felt his stomach turn to stone as the fear that he once had now turned to rage. Who was this man to taunt him and mock him? He had ordered the storm, had him shot with lightning, and taken his grandmother from him. They were now at the end of the pontoon as Chester and Lillia were now either side of him watching the Commanders every move with Etty behind, gripping his hand tightly.

"Don't think like that Adam. I'm not all that bad. We've had some good times." Adam frowned as confusion filled his head. This man was clearly a Guardian as he could hear Adam's thoughts, but how could he talk like he knew Adam, understood his past, the loneliness and isolation he battled for years. The moonlight now drifted across the Commanders face and Adam saw his features come into view. He felt his heart freeze in his chest as the Commander looked at Adam with his bright blue eyes and long black hair that fell across his cheek bones. Falling backwards Adam felt his head become heavy and blurry. He looked at the Commander who was now smirking at him with a knowing smile.

"But, I don't understand." The heavy weight that pressed in his throat now pushed hard as Adam struggled to comprehend the situation.

"Your.."

"Yes,"

"But…the Trill"

"Say it, son."

"Dad, how is it you?"

Adam's Father now gave him a menacing smile as he turned around and walked from the pontoon towards the woods. He passed Harry and paused speaking softly to him.

184

"Kill them both. Report to me when it is done"

Adam felt a rage surge through him. The man who was his hero when he was growing up, who was taken from him leaving his mum to raise him alone. This man was alive the entire time and Adam wanted to know why he left them, why he abandoned him. His fists clenched as he stepped forward making his way off the pontoon towards his Father. Harry came between them as Primrose snarled and beat her wings, sending a gust that threw Adam backwards. Chester growled as Primrose beat her wings again.

"Why?" Adam shouted out to him.

"We needed you and you left us. My mother died and you did nothing!" Tears came into Adam's eyes as he gritted his teeth to shout at the man that had his back to him. His Father slowly turned around to face him. As he took a step forward he looked down to Romulus who stretched out his wings slowly, demonstrating his dominance to them.

"My boy, you just don't get it do you. You believe this innocent idea of your perfect mother. She wasn't all that perfect. Before you arrived on the scene your mother and I had great plans for the Order. We were twenty when we met, and your mother struggled with the prospect of being the Bee. It was something she wasn't ready for. Her mother, your glorious grandmother, thought otherwise and wasn't prepared to listen. Together we were going to create the Trill and remould the balance, the way it should be, and then you arrived. Your mother loved you so much and from the first moment she saw you I knew that she was never going to want to carry on with our plan. She was going to take her place as the Bee and you would be the Flight. I thought that by loving you I could show her that we still had a cause worth fighting for, but she wouldn't listen. So I vanished, disappeared, left your lives and created the new Order myself, taking my place as the Commander. Your mother however, was the one person that stood in my way so I did the only thing that would stop her from ruining all that we had worked for. I ordered to have her removed so that our vision could be accomplished."

Adam's face dropped and his heart broke into a million pieces as he heard the words that came from his Father. What did he mean that he had her removed? How? His breathing grew deeper and faster as

185

he came to accept the knowledge that it was his Father who killed his mother. A tear rolled down his cheek before being wiped away with the back of his hand, he sniffed and leaned to question his Father.

"You're lying! The Trill was named after a man called Trillian and my mum died from Cancer!" Adam shouted as his Father laughed, looking at the stars before speaking.

"I'm Blake Trillian Dempsey. The Trill is mine! Think about it Adam, what do Watchers do? Grow natural organisms. All it would take is for a Watcher to accelerate the growth of her cells"

Adam's knees buckled as his stomach jumped. He thought of the time Etty commanded Mr Crumbleton on the Paddle Steamer and the speed at which the plants grew, how fast, how aggressive. He was now filled with anger as he watched his murderous Father standing there on the shore of the lake. Running forward Adam wanted to attack him, he wanted to destroy this man that had taken everything from him that he held dear and showed no remorse, but Primrose beat her wings, sending a gust towards them. His Father now looked to Harry before turning back towards the woods.

"Don't fail me again."

He looked down to Romulus and walked off into the darkness leaving Adam at the edge of the pontoon with Etty and a head filled with questions as his stomach churned with the hurt and betrayal of his Father, the man that was his hero.

Harry now walked from where he was stood and made his way onto the pontoon, it groaned under his weight as he stood staring at them both. Adam watched as Harry took his Cheltiagh from his pocket and wrapped his hand tightly around its handle.

"Harry? Why?"

"Don't you get it? We run around all day and night, keeping the balance, for what, for them? Those people, who just crush the land we make, build on the flowers we grow, and take the skies for their own. The Trill will convert the Order to what it should be. They will rule and ensure that the land is used for better things than disgusting buildings and hideous concrete structures."

"But we are friends. You told me to jump that day." Adam watched as Harry looked down at his Cheltiagh and rolled the wheel in his fingers. His face shielded by the darkness that surrounded him.

186

"I needed you away from me! How could I shoot you with the lightning if you were stood right next to me?" Harry spun the wheel and the engravings started to glow blue.

"Enough of this, I have to kill you now! You have nowhere to go. Now die gracefully, not like your grandmother!" Harry looked to the skies as the stars glimmered through the patches of cloud that floated past. Adam's heart raced and his mouth ran dry as he looked around him for some way to get free from Harry. Etty was now behind him and he could feel the fear radiating off her once more. He couldn't help but think about the last time he saw her smile and the joy in her eyes, she was the last good thing to happen to him and he was going to do his upmost to protect that. Adam gently tapped his pocket in hope to feel his Cheltiagh, but it was empty. He tried to recall when he had it last and could only think that it must have fallen from his pocket when he was lying on the bank. The mist started to build around them as Harry commanded the water to build a cloud.

"What are you going to do Harry?"

Harry looked and smiled as the cloud grew thicker and whiter around them. It was then that Adam closed his eyes and let go of Etty's hand as he held his palms down towards the water. He thought about Etty and her smile, how she was giddy and excitable on the bank of the lake, her tears when she saw him for the first time since the storm. Adam then looked to Harry as he imagined the water reaching up and twisting around his ankles. He watched the water as it started to bubble and ripple, Adam's mind raced with thoughts of cufflinks and ropes made entirely from the cool liquid. Suddenly, from the lake emerged two thin tentacles of water that twisted and danced either side of the pontoon. Harry was now looking to the stars as the mist covered the valley from view. Adam thought about the shower in his grandmother's house with the blanket of water over his shoulders and the bath with the spinning globe that spun and turned in his hands. He watched as the water grew up into the air and onto the pontoon. Etty was now looking over his shoulder, she gasped at the water as it moved silently up to Harry. He raised his palms to the sky watching the water flattened out into two great walls of liquid that stood proud, either side of the pontoon, either side of Harry. Harry looked down from the stars suddenly noticing the water either side of him. His jaw fell open as he looked to Adam, his eyes showing the fear that sprung into his heart.

"What is going on?" His voice wobbled as he looked to Primrose for help. She looked to Chester and Adam lowering her stance and snarling. Adam stared at Harry, his eyes fierce and bright in the darkness. He turned his palms slowly inwards towards each other as he smirked taking the hurt and anger that surged through his veins up into his arms.

"Balance!"

In one movement, Adam knelt down on the pontoon and slammed his hands together clapping loudly as it echoed through the valley. The walls of water flew together, slamming into Harry before collapsing into their liquid form, washing Harry's limp body into the water with it as it rushed off the pontoon sending large ripples across the lake. Adam looked up as the lifeless body vanished into the murky depths, with Primrose lying beside him, fully submerged under the dark water.

Rising to his feet, he looked down at his hands that were now red and sore. In the quiet that was now filling the valley, Adam felt completely alone. In that short time he had learnt so much about his past and how his Father was responsible for the devastation that the Trill had caused to innocent people. He watched his hands as he bent his fingers to make fists and wondered if he would follow the path of his mother or his Father. How much like him was he? Did he have the strength in him to do the right thing when it mattered? He had just taken a life, removed the choice from someone and taken the balance into his own charge. As he felt his mind slip into the solitary abyss of his thoughts, he felt something pull him abruptly from it. Etty had her hands on his arms as she spun him around and wrapped herself around him in jubilation. Pulling back she took his hands and rested them in hers as looked at his palms that were red and warm. She let them fall by his side as she looked up at his face, placing her hands on his cheeks and wiping away the tears that were forming from under his eyes.

"There are those in the world that will seek to do harm towards each other. Courage isn't stopping them or standing in their way, courage is protecting those who cannot protect themselves. That is

188

what you did here Adam. You protected the Balance, the Order, you protected those who cannot. That is the mark of the Flight." She smiled at him as Chester rubbed his head against his hand before licking it gently to soothe the pain.

Suddenly they heard a voice from across the shore.

"What on Earth was that?!" It was Benedict. His mouth was wide open as steam drifted from his body into the cool night air. Adam felt a crash of relief as he saw the cheeky smile grow on his face in the moonlight. Resting on his shoulder was Mr Crumbleton, his face was black and he stood like a warrior who had returned victoriously from a great battle,

"It was divine power of the Order!" Etty's whispering was barely contained as she ran off the pontoon towards Benedict, a skip clearly visible in her step. Adam looked around knowing that his Father could be nearby, he walked over to Benedict who was now walking off the bank towards them. He hugged Etty before she collected Mr Crumbleton from off his shoulder and gave him a kiss on his balding head. Adam offered out his hand to Benedict but had it bashed away as he was pulled in, squeezed tight before being pulled back and inspected. Benedict was looking at him as if he was beaming with pride and admiration.

"Well if that's the case, then you need to teach me mate!" Benedict smile as he squeezed Adam again before releasing him and looking at them both.

"What about Lafayette?" Adam's smile vanished as he asked about the man whose aim it was to do the job Harry failed to.

"He won't be bothering us anytime soon." Benedict looked to Henrik who was sporting a large cut across the top of his ear.

Etty let go of Mr Crumbleton as he took flight and immediately went over to Chester. He landed on the bridge of his nose laying up Chester's head, wrapping his arms around his ears. Chester looked cross eyed as he tried to focus on the tiny pixie but instead he looked to Lillia and smiled. Etty took a hand in each of hers as she looked at both of them.

"Look at us!" she smiled and sniffed as the tears fell from her eyes.

"Where do we go now?" She asked as she looked to Adam.

"Yes mate; you're the Flight now, what's the plan?" Adam looked at them both as Etty rubbed her thumb on the back of his hand.

"I need to reset the balance. My Father is the Commander of the Trill and so it is my job to stop him. I am going to go after him; I don't expect you to come with me, head on to the rendezvous point. Get to safety." Etty marvelled at the change in his voice. He was different, determined.

"Then I shall come with you! We are the Order, well what's left, and I shall stick with my Architect" Etty looked to Adam as she bashfully stared at his hand. Nodding, he looked to Benedict as he looked at his hand that was resting in Etty's. Smiling, he spoke softly.

"I am your Guardian, where you go I go."

Adam looked to them both and smiled.

"Last we knew the Trill had made a stronghold in Reemingham. We go there!"

14107583R00108

Printed in Great Britain
by Amazon.co.uk, Ltd.,
Marston Gate.